I0692014

CROSSOVER SPY

First Edition

Published by The Nazca Plains Corporation
Las Vegas, Nevada
2011

ISBN: 978-1-61098-175-0
Ebook: 978-1-61098-013-5

Published by

The Nazca Plains Corporation ®
4640 Paradise Rd, Suite 141
Las Vegas NV 89109-8000

© 2011 by The Nazca Plains Corporation. All rights reserved.
No part of this work may be reproduced or utilized in any form or by any means, electronic or mechanical, including photocopying, microfilm, and recording, or by any information storage and retrieval system, without permission in writing from the publisher. Printed in the United States of America.

PUBLISHER'S NOTE
Crossover Spy is a work of fiction created wholly by *Buck Roberts'* imagination. All characters are fictional and any resemblance to any persons living or deceased is purely by accident. No portion of this book reflects any real person or events.

Washington, DC Photo, Songquan Deng
Male Photo, Konrad Bak

Art Director, Blake Stephens

Dedication

For Steve

The one who makes it all worthwhile

CROSSOVER SPY

First Edition

Buck Roberts

Contents

Prologue   1

Chapter 1   9

Chapter 2   23

Chapter 3   37

Chapter 4   61

Chapter 5   85

Chapter 6   107

Chapter 7   131

Chapter 8   157

Chapter 9   179

Chapter 10   195

About the Author   203

Prologue

Jason stands to receive Captain Ames, shown in by Stone's matronly and efficient secretary, Myra.

"Good to meet you Captain Ames, I've heard so many glowing reports about you and we're pleased that you are willing to discuss a special assignment which, of course, you would do on a voluntary basis." Myra asks if anyone would like coffee, tea, or a diet soda.

Both men declining, she exits the room.

"Certainly, Mr. Stone, I am always available to serve in any way my country needs," said Ames enthusiastically.

Ames was a war hero and had previously served in many covert operations abroad in fighting the spread of Islamic terrorism.

Now, in his early forties, he became a bit old for the rigors of the job.

Brad was brought home before he was completely burned out.

In his new capacity as SEAL instructor, Brad trains the finest brave men America has to offer.

Brad is extremely physically fit, 6'-3" tall, with a cool military bearing.

He has a confident and authoritative persona, which has intimidated no few green recruits.

Blue eyed, black haired with a buzz cut, he cuts a striking figure of manhood.

"Well, Captain Ames, this assignment you'll find particularly challenging," said Stone, mysteriously.

"We have a serious problem in the Middle East with weaponry from the former Soviet Union finding their way into the hands of Islamic terrorists. It is imperative that we stop this flow of arms smuggled out of Russia."

"In what way can I be of service, sir," asks Ames.

"It seems like you need to send one of our Special Forces operatives over there to get to the bottom of the problem." It begins to dawn on Brad that there is more here than is being said.

"Of course you are right, Captain, and that is why we need your help in — ah — training the right individual."

Stone adopts a game face, not revealing much.

"Sir, have you chosen who you think is capable of carrying out your objectives?"

"Well that depends, Capt. Ames, may I call you Brad and please call me Jason. The operative we have in mind lacks some particular skills that he must have if he is to succeed. We believe you will be able to train him to acquire what he is missing." It occurs to Brad that Jason, in wanting to get more familiar, has something up his sleeve.

"Tell me, Jason, about the qualifications that he has that caused you to choose him for this assignment while still having reservations about what he will need to learn." Brad realizes that the plot is thickening.

"As you very well know, Brad, we have an extremely small pool of men that we can call upon to send on these missions. This assignment requires our guy to have extensive background in black operations but he must also speak fluent Russian and — well — be very attractive." What, pray tell, is that supposed to mean, Brad muses.

"Then I am a bit confused as to why this guy needs to have quite so many specific requirements to qualify for this duty and what exactly is it that you feel he lacks."

"Maybe it will help if I explain what this operation entails. You see there is a certain Russian scientist who we have had under surveillance who we strongly suspect is trafficking in these arms sales to capitalize on the enormous profits to be realized. Despite numerous attempts by our team of agents in Moscow, we've been unsuccessful in finding out how and where he conducts these transactions. We have reason to believe he manages his role in the network out of his apartment but our agents haven't been able to determine exactly how he's able to do this. One agent got access by bribing the superintendent in his building but discovered nothing. We need to have our guy work his way into the company of this scientist and be trusted enough that he will then be able to gain access to his apartment where we are certain there is concealed the information about the whole network required to spirit these weapons out of the country. You see, Igor Petrov, the scientist, lives a necessarily secret gay lifestyle in a very homophobic Russia and belongs to a private gay club that we have managed to infiltrate." The dawn is breaking, reflects Brad.

"If I am catching your drift, Jason, you are saying our guy has to develop what — a gay — relationship with this scientist?" Surely, they must be grabbing at straws, Brad thinks.

"Yes, Brad, that is exactly what I am suggesting, as fantastic as that may sound."

"Should I also conclude that our candidate for this job is supremely qualified except that he happens to be a heterosexual?" This can't be happening, what can they be thinking, reflects Brad.

"You have hit the nail on the head, Brad," says Jason, smiling and squirming a bit his chair. "In our estimation, with the proper preparation, out man could pull this off. He would need just the right instructor to take on the job." Oh god, Brad begins to panic.

"Why have you chosen me to take on the rather remarkable, if not foolhardy challenge, of getting a straight man to manage a — homosexual relationship?"

"Clearly you understand, Brad, that being openly gay is really no longer a big deal in America's Armed Forces. We, of course, are fully aware that you are widowed, have no significant other, but live a bi-sexual lifestyle. We were aware that your relationship with Navy pilot, Thomas Brandon, has since dissolved. Being gay or bi-sexual simply is no longer an issue that most people in our Armed Services worries about. It is purely a personal matter."

Yea, right, Brad imagines, it's ok until it isn't.

"While I am glad to hear you say that, Jason, I am not sure why you think this would necessarily qualify me to take on the rather extraordinary job of converting a straight man into one who functions as a — bi-sexual. It just can't work!" Brad wondering what they take him for, some kind of sexual predator.

"We beg to differ with you, Brad. You happen to be a very fine specimen of a man and very charismatic as well as being a natural leader. Your men in the SEALS revere you. We think you are uniquely qualified and capable of managing this for us." I wonder where I got this undeserved reputation, Brad ponders.

"Whew! You must realize, Jason, that as between a man and a woman, the chemistry that allows two men to get together is just as mysterious a thing. It is rather unpredictable. Often couples who have chosen to be together baffle their friends and family. It is such a dice roll," said Brad incredulously.

"Given all that and I do understand what you are saying, I would like you to meet Cliff Bradshaw who was trained as a SEAL, was with the United States Secret Service and is now with us in Homeland Security, Special International Branch," Jason says hopefully.

Brad tries not to be seen rolling his eyes in disbelief. The following day in the same conference room, Jason Stone finds himself in a meeting with Cliff Bradshaw. Cliff, like Brad, is very patriotic and has always shown a willingness to stand up and be counted whenever he is presented with a challenge to overcome.

"Good seeing you again, Cliff! Glad you have recovered from the injuries you sustained in your last assignment in Yemen and are ready for duty again."

"Thank you, sir; it is good to be back after such a long hiatus. The physical therapy worked wonders and I am as fit as I ever was," says Cliff with spirit. Cliff, 6'-1" tall, blonde, green eyed and ruggedly handsome in his early thirties, carries not an ounce of fat from his broad shoulders, slim waist, down to his bulging calves.

"We have an unusual assignment that we would like to float by you to see if we can interest you in it. In this case, it would be at your discretion to accept it or not. It requires all of the many skills you have acquired over the years. However, it also requires that you learn some new — ah — skills," says Jason, somewhat embarrassed.

"It surprises me that you haven't chosen someone more qualified if I am not fully measuring up to what's required," said Cliff, wondering what the hell is up. "That's the thing, Cliff, we think you're uniquely qualified except in this one area."

"And, Jason, that would be — ?" Oh well, here it comes, thinks Cliff.

"Well, Cliff, your sexual orientation is the only hitch."

"I can assure you, sir, that, while I am divorced, I am a heterosexual. My girlfriend Laurie and I split our time between my place in Bethesda and hers in Washington. We've been together since — ," replies Cliff, rather perplexed as to what Stone is getting at.

"Yes, Cliff, we are well aware of your present domestic arrangements. The problem lies with the need to expand your — net." Stone allows cryptically.

"What do you mean, Jason, by expand my net. I've had my fair share of relationships with women but — ," answers Cliff, wondering where this is going.

"Frankly, Cliff, the issue is that we need you to acquaint yourself with being good in bed with a man," said Jason finally, putting it bluntly.

"Ha, ha, Jason, surely you're kidding. How in the world can you expect me to pass myself off as a gay — ha, ha, ha? I'd be found out in a minute. While I do have a couple of gay friends and I have had a couple of gay — 'experiments' — in the Navy while aboard ship, I am an avowed straight guy, damn it," said Cliff with some heat.

"All we can ask you to do is to meet with our SEAL instructor, who is bi-sexual, and talk it over. I think you will come around to seeing that this can work given your willingness to try." On the way out, Cliff stops by the office of his best friend, Debbie Berger, who is manager of their cyber security Section.

She's a 5'-10" tall, stunning brunette, a former model in newspaper ads for local department stores.

Her career is made possible by a stay-at-home husband, Marc Berger, who was a police detective and now is a mystery writer of police procedurals.

He has the time to run the house and take care of their two preteen kids.

Cliff falls in the chair opposite her desk with his chin on his chest.

"What's your problem, big guy, you look like you have the weight of the world on your shoulders!" said Debbie.

"You won't believe what our leader in the corner office has up his sleeve as my next foreign assignment," now gazing up at the ceiling, open mouthed.

"So, shoot, what's making you crazy. You've nailed every assignment that was ever thrown your way. What's different this time?"

"I have to pass as a faggot, complete with up front training in how to successfully spread my legs to please my man," said Cliff dejectedly.

"Aaahhhaaa, don't be pulling my leg, I'm not a rookie around here! Since when did we become clearing house for pimps and whores." she said laughing nervously.

"Since now when I've been given my marching orders to get in the pants of a corrupt Russian scientist who's involved in selling Soviet era arms to Middle East kingdoms."

"What are they on some kind of mind altering drugs to suppose you could pull something like that off?! When I thought I've heard everything — "

"Got no choice, babe, duty calls." A few days later, back in the same conference room for the previous meetings, Jason meets with both Brad Ames and Cliff Bradshaw.

"Cliff Bradshaw, I'd like you to meet Brad Ames," said Jason making the introductions, cheerily.

"Glad to meet you, Brad," said Cliff, trying not to look obvious in taking Brad's measure but being pleasantly surprised.

"Same here, Cliff," said Brad, shaking his hand and also taking stock of his charge and liking what he sees.

"Well, guys, you've heard enough from me about what our agenda is, so I will leave you alone to map out your strategies and get past any — ah — hurdles that you can foresee." Jason is given to understatement.

Jason leaves the two men alone, relieved to leave the rest in their hands.

"Brad, I don't know about you but this idea seems a little insane to me," said Cliff, exasperated.

"Cliff, that was my first reaction to it too but I decided to wait until we met before passing judgment. May I ask you some very personal questions?" Brad is beginning to enjoy this.

"Well, sure, I hope I have the answers you're looking for," said Cliff querulously.

Brad swiveling in his chair to look through the window wall out to the sprawling lawn, surrounded by clumps of well-placed trees, "Cliff, do you consider yourself a — sexual — being. What I mean is — are you open to erotic stimulation, experimentation, — well — uninhibited behavior?"

"I think those attributes fairly well describe me in my experiences with women but I've had very little like experience with men, if that's what you're getting at." What the fuck am I going to do, thinks Cliff frantically.

Swiveling back around to face Cliff, Brad asks: "Do you find the idea of having sex with a man — actually with me — to be an abhorrent or impossible idea to even contemplate?" This is the crux of the problem as Brad sees it.

"No, I don't think so, Brad, I just — really — don't know," said Cliff, puzzled and unsure.

Thinking to himself: How the hell could I know something like that?

"Well then, Cliff, I think we owe it to our country to at least try to make this whole project work, regardless of our serious doubts and obvious hesitation. Here is the plan I am tentatively proposing. You and I will go up to my mountain cabin in West Virginia for a two month stay. During that time, I will indoctrinate you in the many aspects of gay life, to the extent that I'm familiar with them. Having been married myself, before getting in touch with my gay alter-ego, I can well understand the difficulties you are bound to face in making the transition. Sharing a bed and being able to manage an active sex life while we are together may prove to be an insurmountable problem. I've asked for and received Jason's assurance that if one or both of us becomes uncomfortable or unable to complete this — training, then we will pack up and return to Washington."

They end their meeting still conflicted, but with this understanding. Reflecting on these circumstances, Cliff decides to take the opportunity of breaking up with Laurie Taylor, his girlfriend, which he had been contemplating doing anyway.

She is pretty and has a good heart but has become clinging and also unhappy about his work taking him away so much of the time.

This development would surely have put her over the edge.

Cliff and Brad, amongst many lingering doubts, make arrangements to close up their respective residences in preparation for the trip to the mountain cabin.

At least superficially, they could appreciate that the other was a major hunk.

But the prospect of sucking and fucking each other was entirely another matter.

Chapter 1

Brad swings by Cliff's condo apartment in Bethesda, MD and Cliff deposits his bags in the rear of Brad's Jeep Grand Cherokee and clambers aboard with some of his traveling gear.

"How ya doing, Cliff, hope you're not having second thoughts about our adventure," said Brad sheepishly.

"Nah, says Cliff, we've both been through enough harrowing experiences on our classified capers to so many trouble spots that I don't see why this should phase me," Cliff throws this out more to convince himself than Brad.

"I sincerely hope you won't find two months in the country with me to rise to the level of 'harrowing'," protests Brad with a winning grin.

"No, not really, Brad, it's just hard to anticipate what to expect. I am usually comfortable starting something new when I feel fully prepared. Obviously, there's no real way I could have prepared for this." I suppose I could have spent last weekend at the gay baths, Cliff imagines.

Weaving his way through the heavy morning traffic, Brad said, "We're looking at a five hour drive to get to my hide-away. So this is probably as good a time as any to do an informal history relative to your sexual experiences with men," Brad suggests with a touch of anticipation.

He hopes his question doesn't suggest prurient interest.

"Is that really necessary, Brad, I hardly know you and we'd be getting into very personal territory." Wow, already it starts, worries Cliff.

"Well, yes, Cliff, I think it is so I have some idea what I've got to work with. Obviously, if the experiences you've admitted to having with men don't amount to much then I have to understand how to proceed to bring you up to speed." Brad is hoping that Cliff is starting to get the picture.

"I guess I can see what you mean, it's just a little embarrassing. But I guess if we'll soon be getting into each other's pants, it's silly to get all virginal about recounting past experiences," said Cliff, laughingly.

"Just so you know I'm going to expect you to be equally as forthcoming about your previous liaisons." Tit for tat, brother, that's the way it's going to be, Cliff tells himself.

"Fair enough, Cliff, neither one of us appears to have all that much to tell anyway. So why don't you go first. It will be very diverting during the long ride ahead."

"Well, it was during my junior year at Syracuse University that my frat house had a beer party just before the break for the Christmas Holidays. There were only six of us guys left. We'd loaded up the fridge with enough beer to float the Titanic and one night proceeded to get blindingly drunk. All our girl friends had already gone home for the holidays and we were feeling major league horny. Of course, there was a lot of the usual horsing around, dowsing each other with beer, grab assing. One thing led to another and we all wound up buck naked and hard as rocks despite being shit faced. Well, jerking each other off led to some cock-sucking to some guys giving up their cherries. A rousing good time was had by all but all was conveniently forgotten the next day. Everyone, anxious to put the whole episode behind them, went home soon after and that was the end of it, never to be repeated."

Now cruising along country roads at a comfortable speed, Brad asks, "What, Cliff, was your participation in this orgy. Did you give and get satisfaction?"

"Well I'm as horny as the next guy and gave as good as I got." How the fuck much detail does he expect me to go into, for Christ's sake!

"Let's hear it, Cliff, fill in a little detail for me," said Brad, his curiosity tweaked.

Looking out his window at the passing landscape, Cliff reflects: "Well, it was a long time ago but as I remember it, I blew both my buds Steve and Dale and they eagerly returned the favor. Also, Bart, the captain of the football team, digitally fucked me but that was as far as I let him go. He was ready to force me down on one of the couches and pound my young asshole. Jared, the head of the debating society, vigorously jerked me off while he French kissed me. Lastly, Mikey ate my ass while he jerked himself off, spraying both of us with streams of white cum. That was not the full extent of the fun and games but it describes my role in it, such as I can recall. It almost cost me my cherry but I managed to wiggle my butt free."

"How did you feel about letting Steve and Dale fuck your face?" I think he's getting off on this, speculates Cliff.

"At the time, it felt so right," said Cliff with raised eyebrows, now considering why it should be so.

"But how did you like slurping their cocks and swallowing their loads?"

"I actually got off on it, surprisingly enough. It gave me a sense of possession and connection to them I hadn't experienced until then." Except for a couple of sorority sluts, Cliff remembers.

"When they sucked you off, how did that make you feel?" Do I need to draw you a picture, fuck head, Cliff wonders.

"Strangely enough, I liked the feeling of being taken and drained dry."

Firmly gripping the steering wheel with eyes riveted on the road, Brad answers: "Well, Cliff, that was a telling experience in terms of your being able to function sexually with men. As I recall, you also mentioned having some man to man episodes on board a submarine. What was that all about?" Now Cliff knows the fucker is getting off on this.

He's probably ready to come in his pants.

"You know what it's like aboard a sub, Brad, there's a long period of time cruising underwater with no ports-of-call and you're packed in with a lot of young, horny, hunky men who have no outlet for their raging hard-ons. I don't think there are too many sailors who wouldn't drop their pants in a minute to have their dick sucked by another horny guy who's dropped to his knees. If they wanted to get serviced, they knew they'd have to be willing to do as much in return. I got blowjobs regularly from three or four guys and managed to service them as well. One of the guys was hot to plug my asshole but I didn't go for it so I'm still a virgin," said Cliff, stealing a glance at Brad and speculating that the time is probably near when he won't be able to say this anymore.

"As a virgin, you are likely to have an asshole tight as a clamp but with me giving you the right finger exercises, we'll have you loosened up and ready for your first joy ride." Brad felt a little warning might help Cliff get better prepared for what's to come.

"You're making me sound like a pushover, Brad. I think I may be more work than you've encountered with your Navy pilot or other boy friends that came to you willing to be had." Cliff is now sure his days are numbered before he has to give it up.

"Within a couple of weeks, I'll have you begging me to take you, Cliff. At least my cabin is isolated, so all that mewling you'll be doing won't horrify my neighbors," said Brad smirking at Cliff.

"In your dreams, buddy, it's more likely we'll be headed back to Washington long before two months are up. This virgin is no cock-hound!" said Cliff, forcefully.

"No point speculating now, I think you may be surprised at my skills as trainer extraordinaire," answers Brad, rapidly raising and lowering his eyebrows.

"Fat chance, baby, but take your best shot, I'm not going to pummel your chest before giving you a chance to get to first base," Cliff said, challenging Brad.

"Relax, Cliff, we're going to take this slow until you can relax and be comfortable in my company."

"Yeah, guy, but we've only got two months.

That's really very little time to pull off something like this, don't you think," said Cliff, skeptically.

"Maybe, it all depends on how quickly we can build trust in each other." Now there's a concept, thinks Cliff.

"Well, now it's your turn, Brad, to let me hear at least one experience you've had, let's say with the Navy pilot you were balling until recently." This ought to be good thinks Brad.

Now I'll get a little of my own back.

Dappled sunshine from the overarching trees passed over the cruising SUV, partially obscuring Brad's frowning face.

"Ok, well there's not a lot to tell. He had split with his wife because he wasn't paying enough attention to her and their young son and she grew so angry that she asked for a temporary separation until they sorted things out. Imagine throwing out someone who looks like Daniel Craig, 5'-10" tall, blonde and blue eyed, dimples, well you get the picture. He wound up taking a short-term rental in a condo next to my townhouse in Washington and we became friends, which led to us hanging out together and finally getting it on in bed when he was in town, which wasn't often. It was clear from the beginning that he was going to return to his wife and our fling was just filler until they worked out their problems. He was remarkably uninhibited in bed but preferred being a bottom, believe it or not. I guess all that responsibility he had in flying that complicated fighter jet led him to want to be passive with me when he was on the ground and we were together, so he could just let it all go. He was insatiable with wanting my prick stuffed up his ass morning noon and night, anytime he had some time off duty. I was more than happy to accommodate him. He was just 28 years old and wore me out but I can't say it was ever really a chore to haul his pretty ass in the air and grind him into the mattress. He's now back with the wife and they've managed to come to an understanding with the demands of his service."

Shortly after sharing each other's stories, they pull into the long winding dirt driveway up to Brad's very private, red pine, hand-peeled log cabin which Hector Rios, the caretaker, has prepared for their visit.

They settle in for their planned two month stay.

Both are very concerned that they can make this plan happen.

Brad is weary of turning Cliff off before turning him on so he proceeds with caution.

A daily routine is established where they get up out of the king-size bed they share, have breakfast, go for a three mile run, work out in the basement gym, shower, massage each other and then have lunch.

Many afternoons they either do food shopping, errands or walk the property, supervising work the hunky, bare-chested Hector Rios was doing.

They prepare dinner together, eat out on the deck on good days and watch television or movies from Brad's vast collection from the 30's, 40's and 50's.

With this routine in place, Cliff and Brad are able to relax in each others company.

Showering after morning exercise becomes an opportunity for them to lather each other up, getting acquainted with each others body and gradually moving to mutual jerk off sessions as well as digital penetration under the shower spray.

Cliff is coming along nicely, showing no signs of getting turned off with these daily intimacies.

"What do you think we should have for dinner tonight, Cliff," inquires Brad.

"It's your turn to be clever, so what's it to be?"

"Well, I had in mind beef bourguignon, an endive salad, and cherry pie for dessert. Think that will do it for you, my man," says Cliff, now speaking in a more intimate tone.

Cliff has taken to wearing tight cut-off jeans around the house that molds to his round firm ass, driving Brad to distraction.

Brad begins to wear the same to see if he can't get Cliff similarly excited.

"You bet, babe, I'll take out a couple of bottles of wine from the wine cooler to let them breathe," responding now in a more gay specific manner.

"You're not going to try to get me drunk and have your way with me, you pushy son-of-a-bitch," said Cliff in mock horror.

"You found me out, but don't get your panties in a tangle, I may be too blitzed to be able to make a pass," said Brad disingenuously.

"Yeah, right, your tongue's hanging out already. You'll be too sated with my culinary skills to feel very amorous, I'm sure."

"Don't count on it, lover, you've been cock-teasing me for a week, I'm ready to blow, pun intended." Brad knows he's about to jump Cliff's bones if he doesn't get some soon.

"You better respond favorably to my beef bourguignon that I've spent hours this afternoon preparing or you'll get shit," Cliff declares.

———————————

"Shit, man, dinner was incredible, how did you learn to cook like that!"

"Laurie showed me but now I'm a better cook than she is, go figure."

"You have obvious potential in becoming a faggot if you can cook like that." Brad knows he's going to exploit that potential before the night is out.

"Good to know I have a leg up, as it were," said Cliff suggestively.

"Yeah, well that's a position I'll look forward to getting you in when you've mastered the more missionary positions" Brad says, heavy with innuendo.

"Ouch! It's starting to hurt already just thinking about it," Cliff intones.

"Let's go up to our bedroom, I have a movie I want us to watch."

"I hope I'm not too much in my cups to enjoy it," said Cliff.

"Well this film should snap you out of your torpor. It's a gay porn flick."

"Get serious; in my condition you're exposing me to this smut." Now I know he's going to make his move, Cliff suspects.

"Definitely, you have already demonstrated what a quick learner you are so relax and enjoy it.

And guess what, I have a joint for each of us to help get us in the mood," said Brad, lecherously.

Upstairs they climb into the big king log bed with a dimmed iron chandelier overhead, hanging from the beamed, cathedral ceiling.

The movie shows what appears to be a Caribbean Island where the captains of two Navy ships anchored off the coast are on shore leave.

They are shown in a cabin they have rented from a couple, native to the island.

The very private house is up on stilts with distant views to the ocean and the Navy ships in the foreground.

The captains are shown frantically groping each other in the upstairs bedroom with the drapes blowing in the ocean breezes and the ships visible below.

They wind up on the bed nude except for their T-shirts and socks.

One captain is shown prone on the bed, bobbing his head up and down with his face buried in his buddy's crotch who is sitting against the headboard with his legs splayed far apart.

The loving blowjob, filmed from multiple angles, goes on for most of the film until they get into a 69 position and show that they are both talented cock-suckers.

The film concludes with them spewing great gobs of spunk all over each others hairy chests.

Then the fade out.

Cliff and Brad, high on grass and booze, are both struggling with keeping their hard-ons in their cut-off jeans.

"Cliff, sweetheart, let me help you out of those shorts so you'll be more — comfortable," whereupon he unbuttons Cliff's jeans and slides both his cut-offs and his jockey shorts off in one smooth movement.

Cliff's stiff dick bounces against his belly.

Brad kneels between Cliff's outstretched legs and takes hold of his ball-sack and licks the purple cock-head with practiced gusto.

Cliff involuntarily moans with pleasure.

Brad proceeds to lav the pulsating shaft.

He tongues the underside of the swollen cock-head, slips his tongue in and out of the piss-slit, while finger fucking him.

Cliff is close to exploding.

In one gulp, Brad takes Cliff down to the root, teasing the white hot member with his tongue.

Kneading Cliff's balls, Brad works his mouth like a suction machine up and down, repeatedly, until Cliff's dick erupts in a shattering orgasm, wave after wave of hot spunk is swallowed in Brad's greedy throat.

Cliff has never received a blowjob rivaling this for sheer erotic pleasure.

Brad is not done with Cliff yet.

He drops his pants, rises up on his knees, and stuffs all of his fat 10", stiff dick between Cliffs eagerly parted lips and jams his hard shaft to the back of Cliff's throat.

Cliff's cock-stuffed mouth stays closed tight around Brad's thrusting prick, keeping up the pressure until with one final thrust, he rams his load down Cliff's throat so he can gorge on every drop.

Slowly withdrawing, Brad flops on the bed next to Cliff, both their chests heaving.

Brad acknowledges to himself that he never wanted it so bad before and maybe it was because of the person lying next to him.

Brad and Cliff progressed into a new, intense phase of their relationship ever since that night of drinking all that wine, smoking joints, and watching a gay porn flick.

They no longer required a catalyst to have satisfying sex every night and mornings after exercising.

Cliff, always a fast learner, became masterful at giving Brad blowjobs that blew his mind as well as his big dick.

Brad swung on Cliff's prick like the pro he is.

Getting off on swallowing each other's cocks, while great, wasn't the full array of skills that Cliff was going to need if he was to fulfill the requirements of his fast approaching trip to Moscow.

Brad has been enjoying watching Cliff's ass bent over the dishwasher or bent over the dining table cleaning up after meals but it was time to experience the pleasures to be had in that deep crack, his skin-tight cut-offs concealed.

On a Saturday night, after they watched a college football game on TV to see their favorite team win the day, they celebrated by eating some frozen pizza and finishing off the six-pack of beer that they'd been working on and started up the steep staircase to their bedroom to take a nap.

Half way up, Brad, right behind Cliff climbing the stairs, grabbed Cliff's thighs to stop him in his tracks.

He moved his hands up to unfasten Cliff's cut-offs and drop them to the stair tread, kicking them away and leaving Cliff's ripe ass exposed.

Brad crouched down and grasped each of Cliff's magnificent butt cheeks and spread them so that he could dive in with his tongue and give Cliff's tight pucker a thorough working over.

Cliff savored Brad's invasive tongue penetrating his tight hole.

"Oh yes," moans Cliff, "Eat my ass out, I've been waiting for you to take your fill." Brad proceeds to lav his crack all the way up and down, repeatedly, stopping by the now opening pucker for further plunder.

Cliff is driven crazy with longing.

"Ok, pretty boy," exclaims Brad, "move your succulent butt up to our bed, get on your stomach, and spread your legs. You're about to have that cherry you've been teasing me with pounded for the first time."

Cliff proceeds upstairs to comply with his orders, going Brad one better by raising his quivering ass up on a pillow in a gesture of raw need.

"Don't make me wait, lover, pleads Cliff, I want you in me now!"

Grabbing some lube, Brad positions his throbbing shaft in line with Cliff's loosened hole and eases in an inch at a time.

Moving all the way in so the base of his pole is flattened against the proffered butt cheeks, Brad pauses.

"Oh, baby, I've wanted to get into your ass for so long, it's too good!"

"Fuck me, lover, fuck me hard, demands Cliff, I don't care how sore my ass is tomorrow, I want you to thoroughly plow me tonight, branding me as yours."

With that charge, Brad begins thrusting steadily, building a rhythm slowly, until not being able to keep it together any longer, he jackhammers his cock into Cliff, not sparing his tender virgin hole.

"Oh yes, yes, yes, screams Cliff, take me, take me, take me!!!" The thwack, thwack, thwack of Brad's body smacking against Cliff's upturned ass culminates in Cliff yelling: "Aaaaggghhh," as he feels his colon, stuffed to capacity, filling up with a gushing sea of cum.

Brad falls on Cliff's back, still impaling him and moving his chin over Cliff's shoulder, their mouths meeting for a powerful kiss.

"I lay my claim on you now, babe, no matter who gets to plug you in the future, you are mine." Brad swivels his hips to increase the sheer ecstasy he's feeling in mounting his lover.

Cliff twists himself so they both land on their sides and clenches his ass muscles to keep Brad firmly in place.

Moving his hips forward and back, he enjoys the incredible new sensations of Brad's cock's continual servicing.

Grabbing his dick, Cliff jerks himself to climax, hurtling jets of semen.

"Oh fuck, man, oh fuck!!" he shouts before the last jets subside.

They remain in this position for many minutes before Cliff allows, "That was awesome. I didn't know it could be like that, I wanted you so much."

"That was just a taste, babe, we're gonna have to make up for your late start. For the next few days, expect me to treat you like a freshly trained whore," says Brad, nibbling on Cliff's ear lobe.

"What about your tender butt hole, lover, asks Cliff, I'm gonna want at that too, buddy!"

"You can have as much of my asshole as you can handle. You have to know how to give as well as receive."

"After the banging you just gave me, I can't wait to find out what it feels like from the other end. If it's only half as good, it will be more than I can handle," said Cliff, grinning like an idiot.

During the following days, they more than live up to their potential, rutting like teenagers.

After dinner one night, Brad blurts out: "You're going to Moscow is just too dangerous, I'm calling Jason Stone in the morning to tell him that you could never pass as gay, the sex is just not your thing," he said ironically.

"You'll do nothing of the kind, Brad, you know as well as I do that this plan, as silly as it seemed at the outset, now seems to have every chance of working. You just have to calm down; you know you're getting too possessive. It must be a guy thing, once you've had your way, you want to start controlling. I'm not some starry eyed slut you're fucking that you can give directives to," Cliff said, a bit red-faced with pique.

Brad storms upstairs to the guest room, slamming the door, angry that Cliff doesn't appear to share his feelings.

Cliff, left simmering downstairs, cools off long enough to acknowledge to himself what the problem really is.

My god, they've actually fallen in love with each other.

He goes upstairs to find that Brad has closed himself up in the guest room.

Stopping by the master bedroom for lube, he pads down the hall to the guest room, quietly opening the door and moving inside to see Brad, undressed and stretched out on his stomach, under a single sheet.

He moves toward him realizing that Brad is faking being asleep.

What the hell — , Cliff thinks.

Cliff yanks off the sheet and settles gently on top of his naked lover.

Brad hardly moves, nursing his hurt feelings and betraying his fakery, infuriating Cliff.

Uncapping the lube impatiently, Cliff takes a generous helping, working one, two and then three fingers into Brad's clenching gateway.

Brad squirms but otherwise doesn't resist.

Cliff pushes inside Brad, no stranger to his lover's hole, with one forceful thrust, revealing his anger, followed by a frantic pumping until he explodes deep into Brad's cock-hungry hole.

Dismounting Brad, Cliff grabs some lube to shove up his own asshole.

Roughly moving Brad onto his back, Cliff slathers lube on Brad's engorged cock.

Straddling his lover, Cliff lowers himself Brad's slickened shaft and drops down to his groin.

"How does this feel, shit-for-brains," as Cliff rides Brad until he feels the white hot load unleashed up his gripping shaftway.

Climaxing in unison with Brad, Cliff unleashes searing ropes of cum to splatter on the underside of Brad's chin and all over his lips.

"Lap it up, bitch," Cliff demands.

Brad dutifully complies.

"What the fuck was that!" asks Brad, looking nonplussed.

"Make-up sex, asshole and I'm the teacher this time." Brad, looking un-persuaded, Cliff raises himself up off of Brad's softening boner and falls on top of him, giving him a lingering kiss.

"I'm still mad as hell!" declares Brad, unconvincingly.

"Give it up, lover, you know you love me." said Cliff with a wicked grin.

Brad grips the hair on the back of Cliff's head, pulling his head back and gives him a fierce, possessing kiss, acknowledging the truth of this.

"I was afraid to even think that you loved me too," admits Brad.

With this they fall on their backs and stare up at the ceiling with far away looks on their faces.

"What do we do now, this was never supposed to happen," Brad wonders aloud.

"We'll figure it out, answers Cliff, but in the meantime, let's get some sleep, I'm fucked out."

The next morning Brad is still down in the dumps in spite of the dynamite fuck the night before.

Opening up to Cliff, he finally admits that he feels responsible for qualifying Cliff to be sent on this dangerous mission.

"If I hadn't done my job so well, they would have been justified in canning the whole project. It's my fault that you're being put in harm's way," laments Brad, verging on tears.

Cliff tries to calm Brad's fears, reasoning: "This mission is no more dangerous, less so in fact, than many others I've been sent out on."

Brad, whispers, "Cliff, you just can't know that."

The time arrives for them to return to Washington.

They pack-up; leaving Hector Rios the job of closing up the house, load up the Grand Cherokee and leave.

Brad is still upset and consumed with guilt.

Halfway back during the bright sunny day, they decide they need a break and stop to pick up sandwiches and a six-pack of beer.

Then they get back on the road until they find an out-of-the-way rest stop, nestled in the woods, with a distant view visible through the gently swaying trees.

After parking the SUV, Brad moves, turning to retrieve their lunch from the back seat.

Cliff leans over, grabs him by the shoulders mid-turn and looking intensely into his eyes, he drops a hand and cups his lover's bulging basket.

"What the hell ya doin'," asks a startled Brad.

"Just shut the fuck up and help me pull your pants down, bone head." Brad complies, his cock popping out straight up and already rock hard.

Cliff plunges down to gulp the whole member to the root, smashing his nose into Brad's musky crotch.

Brad throws back his head and moans loudly while Cliff proceeds to piston down on Brad's raging hard-on, unmercifully.

Brad lasts only seconds before he rockets his hot load down Cliff's welcoming throat, his meaty balls drawn up and drained dry.

Cliff pulls off, smacking his lips and savoring the taste of Brad's salty cum.

Brad moves to return the favor but Cliff pushes him away, gently.

"I know you're still too bummed out to feel like doing me, Brad. Let's just call this going away sex to give you something to remember me by while I'm away." Cliff has become a master at pushing all of Brad's buttons to pleasure him.

Unenthusiastically finishing their lunch, they get back on the road to face the future.

Brad, having the final word says, "I'll expect to fully 'debrief' you on your performance in Moscow and you will leave nothing to my imagination, fucker. And do not let anyone fuck you in the ass without a condom!"

Chapter 2

Igor Petrov is a Russian scientist working for the Russian government in developing new hi-tech weaponry.

He is a distinguished and well-maintained gentleman who looks younger than his 46 years.

Leaving his laboratory, he returns to his apartment located in the center of Moscow in the commercial district.

Feeling the need of companionship, Igor decides to go to his secret club located at the rear of a commercial building nearby.

The club boasts a select membership of gay and bi-sexual professionals.

Under his conservative trench coat, he wears a black leather jacket with black wool slacks and a black turtleneck sweater.

Polished black boots complete the outfit which looks conservative enough on the street but, sans raincoat, the leather and black outfit alerts potential partners that they may be in for an S and M experience.

They would be correct in making that assumption.

Igor meets his friend Uri Kozlov at the bar, who unbeknownst to him is an undercover US Army Intelligence Operative, working in the city posing as an engineer for his cover.

After downing their first vodkas and in the process of downing the next one, Igor confides that he regrets the fact that he can't find a soul-mate.

Although he's had an affair with another club member, Vasily Borodin, who is a former Olympic cross-country skier and now a sports doctor.

"You are in luck my friend, says Uri, it just so happens that a friend of mine, Anatoly Nevesky (aka, Cliff Bradshaw) is relocating from St Petersburg to work on a construction project here in Moscow. He is a fine specimen of a man who I really think you are going to like."

"What makes you say that, Uri, do you think you are that familiar enough with my taste in men? Don't base your judgment on my having a brief fling with Vasily. I could never teach Vasily to know his place and be an obedient bottom. His wonderful skier's physique turned my head for a time but he's too arrogant for me to dominate and too vain to let me abuse his body in the way that I like."

"From what I know about Anatoly, you will have found someone who will suit you to a T. He's blonde, green-eyed, in his early thirties and ruggedly handsome. What's not to like," said Uri with a knowing smile.

"Physically, he sounds perfect but does he like to be dominated, particularly in the bedroom. I'm not ready to take on training someone again who doesn't have demonstrable aptitude in my area of interest."

"Igor, I happen to know someone who belonged to a club in St Petersburg, similar to this one. He told me in no uncertain terms that Anatoly was a member very much in demand there as an experienced bottom. You'd be wise to latch on to him before some other of our horny members beats you to the punch. You know how hard it is to find a stud who likes to bottom. From what I hear, you won't be disappointed." Uri is planning on bringing Anatoly to the club and putting him up for membership.

Uri is satisfied that he has managed to tweak Igor's interest.

In preparation for Anatoly's arrival, Uri was instrumental in arranging for a sublet apartment from a club member, leaving for a six month business assignment in London.

The apartment is ideal because it is just around the corner from Igor's flat.

Arriving at the Moscow Airport, Cliff Bradshaw, now known as Anatoly Nevesky, is greeted by his contact agent, Uri Koslov, who drives him into the city and helps him get settled in his apartment sublet.

While Anatoly unpacks, Uri lays out the groundwork he has put in place to move the plot forward.

Uri feels sure that Igor is psyched to meet Cliff.

"Let's get you over to the club, Anatoly. There's a membership meeting later this evening so everyone will be at the club beforehand so I can introduce you around." Arriving at the club, Cliff was showcased to everyone.

Many undressed him unabashedly with their eyes, shamelessly leering with obvious interest.

Later, during the membership meeting, there were virtually no objections to accepting Anatoly as their newest member.

After several subsequent visits, Cliff contrived to get an affair going with Vasily Borodin, having been told by Uri of the long over affair between Vasily and Igor Petrov.

Vasily and Igor remain on superficially friendly terms.

Moving in on Vasily, Cliff thought it would be a good indirect way to make a run at Igor.

The plan was that once establishing his bona fides with Vasily, Cliff was sure Igor would be filled in on what joys could be expected with Anatoly in your bed.

Vasily is a handsome man in a uniquely Russian way.

He is very fair with white blonde hair and distinctly Slavic, angular features.

The slight cant to his grey-blue eyes gave him an exotic and mysterious look.

He took to Cliff immediately.

Sometime later at the club, Cliff said, "It's been nice getting together for drinks at the club, but I'd like to see you outside the club. How about coming over to my place for a home cooked meal, say this

Friday night at 8:00 PM? I make a mean beef bourguignon," said Cliff, knowing how successfully the meal turned out when he made it for Brad.

"Hardly anyone I know can cook well enough to entertain at home!" answers Vasily, "so I'd be delighted. Shall I bring some red wine?"

"Great, Vasily, a red will be perfect with the beef dish. Hope you like cherry pie."

"It's not a dessert I have often but I very much like it especially if it's home made," said Vasily smiling appreciatively.

Cliff went to a lot of trouble to set the stage for his seduction of Vasily.

The dining table was complete with a linen tablecloth, linen napkins, and fresh flowers.

He played a tape of a Rachmaninoff piano concerto and adjusted the lighting to a candlelight level.

Vasily arrived right on time and Cliff turned on the charm, complimenting him on how well he looked in tones of blue with his coloring.

The tailored Armani silk shirt in light blue complemented the deep blue of the soft wool trousers showcasing Vasily's delectable ass, culminating in black socks with black Gucci loafers.

Vasily's professional skiing provided all the right curves in his toned body for the beautiful clothes to cling to.

Cliff took the two bottles of a lovely French wine to the kitchen to open, allowing them to breathe.

Hmm, thought Cliff, two bottles of wine, maybe Vasily has the same evil agenda that I do.

Cliff returns to the sofa, where he has seated Vasily, with two vodka martinis, knowing Vasily's preference from having drinks with him at the club several times.

They already had a little buzz on before they got to the table.

"Sit down Vasily; it's time for me to wow you with my culinary skills." The wine begins to flow while consuming the superb beef bourguignon.

Vasily becomes a little tipsy.

"Let's take a break before dessert, Vasily, and sit together on the couch to get better acquainted." Cliff moves back Vasily's chair, puts his arm around his waist and moves him to the sofa.

They fall on the sofa together and wind up in each other's arms.

Laying Vasily's head back on the arm of the sofa and raising his legs up to stretch him out full length, Cliff climbs on top of him and begins to explore Vasily's open mouth.

They passionately explore each other's mouths, each getting obviously aroused.

Dessert becomes irrelevant and Cliff carries Vasily to the bedroom and deposits him gently on the bed.

He opens Vasily's trousers and pulls out his cock and balls, putting into practice lessons learned from Brad.

Vasily, having been a little drunk, revives and moves to kick off his shoes and remove his trousers and under shorts.

Cliff does the same.

Lying on top of Vasily, Cliff begins to rub his stiffening 9" cock up against Vasily's more modest 7" prick.

Vasily raises his knees, reaches for Cliff's hardening member and pushes it between his ass cheeks, signaling what would pleasure him the most.

Cliff pulls back, sliding down to suck his quarry's low hanging ball sac.

Vasily spreads his skier's sinewy legs, allowing his seduction to continue unfettered.

The seducer moves his tongue up the skier's ample 7" shaft, sucking all the way up to the cock-head, tightening his lips lovingly around the fat knob.

Vasily was now writhing in ecstasy, moaning and clenching the sheet beneath him.

Suddenly, Vasily flipped himself over on his stomach and in a continuous motion, Cliff raised him up on his knees, leaving Vasily's forearms planted on the mattress.

Cliff knew what his butt boy craved.

Quickly grabbing the lube out of the night table and slipping on a condom, Cliff scooped up a generous gob and began to penetrate the winking pucker.

Vasily's groans grew in intensity until his gaping hole was skewered with a 9" projectile ramming all the way home.

"Eeeooouuu," cried Vasily.

"Give me all you've got, ram it on home. Show me no mercy. Pound me, please!"

Cliff raised himself up to straddle and screw Vasily's ass, raised up high for maximum penetration.

All that cross-country skiing produced beautifully sculpted legs supporting muscled butt cheeks inviting only studs to take a ride.

Cliff did not disappoint the expectant Vasily, screwing and drilling him like a pile driver, filling his fuck cavern with his cock and stretching his condom with gobs of cum.

Vasily, pumping his dick in tune with the brutal fuck he was submitting to, screamed, "Oh yes, Anatoly, I'm coming, I'm coming, — aaagggrrr — !!" sending streams of cum flooding the sheets.

Dismounting Vasily, Cliff gave his butt boy a final squeeze on his delectable buns and they fell together in a heap to fall into a drugged sleep.

The next morning, Cliff got up first to make Vasily coffee and toast before sending his conquest out to face his day.

After a few more heated sessions like this, alternating between their two apartments, Cliff began to ease back, letting Vasily know that the affair was coming to an end and that he had "other interests." Vasily took it in stride, not really wanting to be involved either beyond having casual, good sex.

As expected, Vasily passed on glowing reviews to Igor, who is now anxious to become more acquainted with the new man in the club.

Cliff puts himself in the way of crossing paths with Igor, moving towards their becoming an item.

From Vasily, Cliff leaned that Igor is into S and M and is a top.

Although Cliff had an intense education in the mountains of West Virginia, he wasn't sure he could satisfy Igor's kinky tastes, but he'd give it his best shot.

Chess night at the club brought a select few to the game room at the rear of the club.

A light supper was laid out on a buffet table for the small group of players, paired up at four tables.

Igor and Cliff are paired for play.

As anticipated, Igor is a master at the game while Cliff puts up a fair showing but his king is soon cornered and Igor announces checkmate.

"I knew I would have you when you brought out your queen too early and I was able to entrap her with a few moves with the help of my pawns and knights," gloats a triumphant Igor.

"As you know, Anatoly, we're not allowed to play for money according to club rules. Compensation or punishment is at the discretion of the victor. Shall we repair to my apartment because I do have something special in mind," he said, smiling with a touch of malice.

Igor's building is a sturdy, unprepossessing concrete structure, devoid of any style in the communist tradition.

They ascend the stairs, the elevator being out of service yet again.

Igor's apartment, in stark contrast to the building, has style like that of an English gentleman's club.

There is lots of dark wood, a tufted leather sofa, and comfortable chairs with down cushions.

There is a large living room containing a formal dining room at one end, adjacent to the kitchen with a bedroom and bath off a rear hall.

Igor motions for Cliff to sit on the sofa while he moves to a French armoire set up as a bar.

He pours them each a brandy, not asking Anatoly for his preference in an after dinner drink.

They sit together on the sofa when Igor says, "Anatoly, as you know, you've lost at the game of chess so now you must pay for that failure."

"Yes, Igor, you are right. I expect you to exact reparation for my ineptitude at playing the game."

"I'm glad you understand, Anatoly, you will now address me as sir when I'm speaking to you, do you understand!"

"Yes, Ig — sir, I do," says Cliff with downcast eyes moving into the developing scene.

"Well get into the bedroom and take off all your street clothes and put on the things I laid out for you on the bed," How the hell did he know I'd be here after losing, wonders Cliff.

"If you're curious as to how I knew you'd be coming home with me, the answer is obvious, I always expect to win at chess, especially with someone I know not to be an expert."

"But you might have been paired with any one of the other players who was there tonight."

"Give me some credit, Anatoly, I've been a member for some time and when my wishes are known, I get my way. Now get in there and get out of those clothes, now!!!"

"Right away, sir," says Cliff meekly, rushing into the bedroom to do as he's been commanded.

Returning to the living room, he's now wearing a black leather sleeveless vest, laced up the front with silver stud decorations along the shoulder line.

Paired with the vest is a tight pair of chaps, open at the crotch, displaying his cock and open at the rear, featuring his delectable ass cheeks.

Completing the outfit are black leather boots and a leather military style cap.

"That's better, Anatoly, you're beginning to live up to the reputation your friend Uri gave you. Turn around, yes, you'll do very nicely. You've displeased me in having that ill-considered affair with that dilettante, Vasily Borodin. You must make amends for this travesty as well. Go behind that chair and bend over the back of it. Do it now!"

Cliff does as directed and finds that his vulnerable ass is now raised high for whatever comes next.

"Like this, sir?" asks a compliant Cliff in a tremulous voice.

"You'll shut your mouth until I give you permission to speak. Is that clear!" With that, the black leather paddle comes down on Cliff's unsuspecting cheeks.

Oh shit, now it's going to get heavy, Cliff realizes.

Thwack, thwack, thwack cracks the paddle as Igor puts his full arm into these next swings.

Cliff's cheeks turn a deep shade of pink, trembling with the punishing strokes of the leather paddle.

After repeating the process a few more times, the spanking is concluded and Cliff is yanked to his feet.

Igor whips him around to face him as he grabs his nuts and stretches them while sliding a cock ring down his shaft.

Cliff's traitorous prick starts to rise up.

Finally, Igor snaps on a black leather, silver studded dog collar around Cliff's thick neck.

"Get around and into the chair," orders Igor.

Now slide down and put your hands behind your knees and draw your legs back to your chest." Cliff's pink cheeks, separated by his deep cleft, are now at the edge of the seat cushion, presented for Igor's pleasure.

Igor slowly strips off his clothes while viewing this wonderful creation waiting for him in his lounge chair.

Cliff's eyes are like saucers in his frightened face, thinking here it comes.

Now on his knees, Igor takes great gulps of Cliff's balls, sucking each one with a connoisseur's deliberation.

Cliff's cock is jumping uncontrollably.

Taking lube from a drawer in a side table and slipping on a condom, Igor begins his assault on Cliff's tight pucker, opening up the gateway to the silken shaft beyond.

Soon all of three fingers are stuffed in the fuck chute.

Igor finds the prostate that will soon be targeted when he enters his slave's asshole.

Balancing himself on the arms of the chair, his body stretched out on his toes, Igor aims his veined 8" dick at the winking hole and plunges it in, in one angry thrust.

Cliff's lips are drawn back from his clenched teeth, stifling his crying out in pain.

Holding his position briefly, savoring the exquisite sensations of Cliff's gripping ass muscles, Igor pulls out, leaving only his cock-head implanted in the butt hole.

Ramming himself in again, he continues the torturous in and out building up to a punishing rhythm, fucking Cliff's hole as if he were a street whore.

"I'm about to come, slut, and when I do, you'd better shoot your load at the same time or else you will be disciplined further. Just then, "Aaaggghhh!!" screams Igor, as he fills Cliff's crammed hole with his sheathed cock filled with cum.

"Aaagghh!" screams Cliff, as he spews a cup of cream as commanded.

They stay molded together for many minutes until Igor, his lust slaked, pushes back out of Cliff's cum leaking channel.

Standing, Igor tells Cliff to go to the bathroom to clean himself up before getting changed to leave.

A short time later, Cliff returns to the living room, head bowed in supplication.

Igor, now fully dressed said, "You did all right, Anatoly, with a little firm guidance, you might do quite nicely. Now get out, I'll call you tomorrow as to when I can see you again."

"Yes, sir," answers Cliff who exits the apartment.

God, Cliff thinks, my ass is going to need surgery when this fucker gets through with me, but at least the hook is firmly implanted.

In the end you'll be mine, motherfucker and I hope that you land in prison where they pass your ass around in exchange for cigarettes.

Igor, now totally under Cliff's spell, demands his company three nights a week while slowly Igor lets his guard down, accepting Cliff in his home.

The sex has ratcheted up to where Cliff is routinely whipped, forced to lick Igor's boots and to be made to crawl around like a dog with that collar snapped tightly around his neck.

One evening, concluding their after dinner bout of sex, Igor ordered Cliff into the shower while he took care of a little business.

Igor headed toward the kitchen as Cliff dragged himself to the bathroom.

Turning on the shower, Cliff wanted Igor to think he had begun showering, when in fact, he was stealing along the wall in the dining area leading to the kitchen, to try and catch a glimpse of what Igor was up to.

Sure enough, Igor had opened a locked door that was supposed to access the pantry but was really a tiny office set-up.

Cliff could see the glow from the computer throwing light up on the walls of the tiny room, one which other agents had missed.

Yes! He had discovered Igor's secret cubbyhole.

Armed with the knowledge of where Igor was likely managing his on-line contacts with the illegal arms network, Cliff hatched a plan to gain access.

The next night that Cliff was to stay over, he put his plan into action.

Unfortunately, the plan required that he let Igor get a giant helping of his poor, cock abused, hole.

Now being more aware of how to get Igor's ardor into high gear, Cliff prepared himself for the likelihood of Igor's getting creative.

Right on cue, he was ordered to stand at the ready while Igor climbed into his favorite fuck chair.

Removing the down back cushion, he lay down on the chair on his back with his legs up over the back.

Cliff maneuvered himself, as directed, kneeling and facing the back of the chair, resulting in his ass hovering right above Igor's eagerly expectant mouth.

Igor grasped Cliff around his waist and lowered his pillowed buns down on his face where his tongue could begin the invasion.

Cliff, holding on to the back of the chair, was now bouncing up and down on Igor's extended tongue, lingering on the downward bounce so Igor could take his fill.

This continued until, delirious with lust, Igor ordered Cliff to get up while he too got up and out of the chair.

"Get back on the chair on your knees again, slave boy!" ordered Igor.

"Now hold on to the back of the chair and thrust up that pretty butt so it is properly presented to your master." Cliff drops his trunk so his back makes a gentle curve sweeping up to his sacrificial butt cheeks.

With Igor's expert job at rimming Cliff's hole, no lube is necessary as Igor presses his cock knob, sheathed in a condom, past the unresistant hole to lodge deep in the cavern.

His face contorted with lust, Igor clamps on to Cliff's hips to steady himself as he begins the inexorable pumping, pausing, pumping motion until his groin was slapping into Cliff's ripening bun feast.

Cliff's slickened passage was also clenching down and releasing in a rhythmic dance with the pole ramming deep into the fuck cavern.

"Beg me for it, bitch, let me know how bad you want it!" Igor demands.

"Fuck me, fuck me, fuck me, master!" shouts Cliff.

"Split me open, rape my ass!!!" With this, Cliff reaches back, puts his hands on his butt and spreads his cheeks wide so Igor can drive his cock all the way up to his throat.

Igor, eyes rolling back in his head, unleashes a heart stopping torrent of hot spunk, flooding the almost bursting condom.

Collapsing on Cliff's back, Igor tries to draw breath into his heaving chest.

Dizzy with satiation, he grunts grudging approval.

"Yes, Anatoly, you will do very well." Extricating themselves from their entwined bodies, they stagger to the sofa in a trance.

"Get me a vodka, orders Igor, and take a glass for yourself too, you've earned it, my slut slave." This is the moment Cliff had planned for when he could slip a drug, earlier concealed in the bar cabinet, into Igor's drink.

Having had their night cap, they head off to bed with Igor squeezing Cliff's well fucked buns, staking his master's claim over his slave.

"These are mine, bitch boy, exclusively until I say otherwise!!"

Sometime later when Cliff was sure that Igor was out cold, he slipped out of bed and stole into the kitchen, collecting his backpack on the way.

Removing the lock pics from the backpack, Cliff selects an appropriate pic and gained access to the tiny cubbyhole with the desk set-up.

Ureka! There on the counter is the elusive computer that went undetected in an earlier breach into the apartment by another operative.

Cliff put the CIA class in hacking into computers to good use by getting past Igor's security and getting in.

Scrolling through various files, he finds what he wants and downloads it onto a disc he brought for the purpose.

After successfully accomplishing downloading the pertinent files, he slips the disc into his backpack, closes up the cubbyhole, leaving it in the condition he found it.

Slipping quietly back into bed, Igor is snoring, none the wiser.

The next morning, still enjoying an afterglow, Igor is unusually gracious and offers Cliff an espresso before sending him on his way.

"Last night proved to me that my hopes to develop your potential weren't unwarranted," says Igor with a sly smile.

"Thank you, sir. I only want to please you any and every way that you choose to have me." says Cliff obsequiously.

Damn I'm good, he tells himself.

"Then I'll bid you adieu until the weekend, say Saturday night, when I'll have had a chance to recover myself before a return engagement." Cliff leaves the apartment and hurries to the post office to mail off the disc in an envelope he had already prepared to Brad's business address rather than an official address that might arouse suspicions.

Meanwhile, back in Washington, Tommy Brandon, the fighter pilot, shows back up on Brad's doorstep.

He and the wife have had another fight and he needs a temporary place to stay.

Brad takes him in and proceeds to have rough sex with him, given that he is still angry over Cliff's departure and needs to take it out on someone.

Chapter 3

Around the same time at Military Headquarters in Moscow, Uri Kozlov reports to his superior in his role as a double agent.

Uri's orders were to let Cliff get involved with their scientist, Igor Petrov, so that they could find out what Petrov was up to, letting a foreign agent unwittingly do the job for them.

The plan also had the added potential of ferreting out other American agents who had infiltrated into Russian society.

A two fer.

Suspecting that Cliff may have garnered the information that they sought, they decide to move on him in case he should slip through their fingers.

They know he's a resourceful and dangerous agent who should not be underestimated.

If they did, it would be at their peril because their superiors in the Kremlin would be sure to exact a stiff punishment.

Cliff is tasered and pulled off the sidewalk into an official car and removed to an underground bunker on the outskirts of the city.

He's stripped and thrown into a small, spartan cell with minimal facilities.

It is not long before he is dragged out in handcuffs and brought to an interrogation room where he is brought before his interrogator, Viktor Sidorov, a former KGB officer and a sadistic bastard with a long reputation.

Cliff is pushed into a sturdy, straight backed, wooden chair bolted to the floor in front of a small wooden table behind which is seated the interrogator.

The guards secure Cliff to the chair and leave him alone with Sidorov and his assistant, Eric Holtz, formerly attached to the East German Stasi.

Cliff slumps in his chair and glares defiantly at his interrogators.

"We must warn you, agent Bradshaw, that there will be a lot of pain that we will be forced to subject you to in order to gain your cooperation. We want the names of all the American agents operating here in Moscow and we also want to know what you found out in your investigation of Petrov. You actually surprise me, Cliff, on how far you were willing to go to get past Petrov's defenses to find out what your superiors in Washington want to know. Did you enjoy yourself or did you find it demeaning and repulsive to prostitute yourself for the sake of your national interests?"

"You'd know all about prostituting yourself, Sidorov. Your depraved activities, aided and abetted by your butt boy here, are well known in our intelligence community. You're nothing but a sexual deviant and predator!" Sneers Cliff.

Sidorov jumps up, leans over the table to administer a back handed slap across his captors scowling face.

"Insolent dog, you will be taught proper respect for a former officer in this country for which you have demonstrated such contempt!"

Viktor summons the guards and instructs them to remove the prisoner to Interrogation Room 2.

The guards release Cliff from his chair and hustle him down to the end of the hall to Interrogation Room 2.

Viktor tells Eric that he won't need him for now.

There is a 3' x 7' stainless steel table in the middle of a 15' x 18' room with a shower niche on the rear wall.

The floors are concrete, the walls are concrete block and there is a corrugated metal ceiling from which hangs a single light with a metal shade.

The ceiling is quite high at about 9'.

The temperature is rather cold at 65 degrees F.

Cliff's handcuffs are removed and still naked, he is laid out on the table, flex-tied to rings in all four corners, splaying his arms and legs.

Viktor steps into the room and the guards leave, silently.

"Well, my friend seems like you are in a spot and have limited, very limited options if you wish to get out of our little playground," Viktor announces.

"It is very simple really, you just have to tell us what you found out about Igor Petrov's illegal activities and to supply us with the names of your American co-conspirators who blatantly ignore our laws."

"There wasn't enough time for me to get the information I was sent to get. Your goons picked me up too early in the game before I had a chance to get anywhere. Besides, with your reputation, I'm sure you'd simply take over Igor's network and grab all the enormous profits for yourself. Surely you know Igor is just too shrewd and cautious for me to get past his defenses so soon." Cliff surmised that Uri Koslov had to be the traitor who gave him up.

"As far as other operatives are concerned, the truth is I know only Uri Koslov, as you must already know."

"I didn't suppose you to be stupid, Cliff, I realize you had to have guessed that Uri gave you up and yes, he is one of ours. You are not the only one who can learn your enemy's language and infiltrate into their midst. Your Russian is excellent, by the way, no one would ever guess that you are not a natural born Russian, bravo. But here we are now with our problem. You see my handlers are not going to tolerate my not producing results and very soon."

"It's a problem I can't help you with since I don't know the answers to the questions you want to ask," argues Cliff.

"Very well, let's do this the hard way. Guards!" The two burly guards rush in.

"We need to adjust the prisoner's position. Turn him over on his stomach and adjust the front legs of the table to their lowest level so that he will be positioned on a slanted surface." They reattach Cliff's extremities to the table corners so that he is constrained.

Sidorov goes to a wall rack and selects a whip from a wide assortment.

He chooses a long braided one.

Cliff hears the first lash parting the air with a sharp whirring sound to land squarely across his buttocks.

"Aaahhh!" cries Cliff involuntarily in response to the sharp pain on an area still sore from Igor's ardent attentions.

Again the whir and again until the whirring is a steady noise piercing the air, flaying his back, buttocks and legs, Cliff can barely stand the intense pain.

"Because I know you are an intelligent man, Cliff, I am going to give you a break today and have the guards take you back to your cell where you can reflect on the futility of holding out on me. I think you will conclude that it is quite useless. Guards!" Cliff is freed and returned to his cell.

After a fitful night of sleep on the spare, uncomfortable cot and after being given little to eat, Cliff is dragged back to Interrogation Room 2 to face Viktor again.

This time he is taken to the niche in the rear of the room which is an open shower stall.

His arms are stretched over his head and his wrists are clamped into rings bolted into the wall.

His knees are also harnessed with nylon straps, designed to be threaded through rings bolted to the side walls at a height of 5'.

Viktor instructs the guards to lift Cliff into place with his knees strapped to the wall about 5' off the floor, placing Cliff's privates at a level with Viktor's privates.

They exit.

"Igor's proclivities are well known to us but I think we can go him one better. Since your American handlers were so willing to turn you into a whore to satisfy their agenda, we don't want to leave your education incomplete." Viktor summons his assistant, Eric Holtz, who joins him.

Eric is a 5'-10" tall, blonde, blue-eyed, square jawed German with an aggressive edge.

He unhooks a flexible hose from the sidewall, which Cliff suddenly realizes has a large, black rubber dildo attached to it.

"If you want to be regarded as a professional whore, you'll need to have a clean colon," says Viktor with a smile that didn't reach his eyes.

Eric rips open a packet of lube and works three fingers into Cliff's ass to allow the dildo access.

Before long the dildo is placed at Cliff's upended butt hole and slowly forced in when a warm wetness floods the length of the invaded passage.

Eric, who clearly enjoys his work, expertly slides it in and out along with a douche solution, to thoroughly clean out Cliff's bowels.

Extracting a portable shaver from his pocket, Eric lovingly shaves Cliff's privates so they are perfectly smooth over his entire groin and ass crack.

"Ah that's better," declares Viktor, complimenting Eric's work.

"Now let's get that chest and his abs nice and smooth too." After Eric finished this task, Viktor declares, "Beautiful, Eric, you are an artist. Now I can commence enjoying our American whore's company. Thanks I'll call you if I need you." Eric leaves reluctantly.

Viktor starts to strip, tossing his clothes on the bench against the back wall of the room.

He has an impossibly exaggerated body like that of an action hero from a video game.

The massive, muscled shoulders and arms give way to magnificent, pillowed pecs, transitioning down to washboard abs to an impossibly thin waist giving way to rising muscle mounds forming his hard butt cheeks, framed by shallow hollows, followed by long sinuous thighs to shapely calves to beautifully formed feet.

Super stud would be the only conclusion to draw in looking at him.

There was no question in Cliff's mind as to what Viktor had in mind.

"I have not had the opportunity of sampling some prime American stud meat so I'm am glad you are going to afford me that opportunity, Cliff, before we get down to the business of you telling me what I need to know."

The use of the dildo has seen to it that Cliff's hole could offer no resistance to the punishment it was about to receive.

Slipping on a condom and lubing up his monstrous, erect 10.

5" pole, which appeared to be 3" in diameter, Viktor placed the oversized purple head right against Cliff's pucker and grabbing his ass cheeks, began the relentless slow torture of invading the captured SEAL.

"Your American fuck channel feels every bit as good as I hoped," compliments Viktor.

"Oh yes, I'm going to ride this pony to the horizon."

Cliff had never taken a fucking like this.

Viktor owned his ass with an endless slow, then fast, then slow again motion, plowing and slamming his prostate with each thrust, making him feel like a whore and a traitor to his lover for wanting Viktor never to stop.

Filled with cum, Cliff's big round balls tightened around the base of his cock that was straining with rushing blood.

"Ooohhh, I'm going to come!!" screams Cliff, as Viktor power slammed Cliff's hot, willing hole, unleashing torrents of cum into the sheathed dick, deep inside his conquest.

Simultaneously, Cliff's dick spewed geysers of cum to rain down on them both.

Viktor remains inside Cliff, firmly clasping his butt cheeks in a gesture of complete possession, until the waves of dizzying pleasure subsides.

Extricating himself, Viktor releases and lowers Cliff's legs to the floor, soaps and hoses him off and then himself.

Viktor wraps one hand around Cliff's low hanging balls and the other around his dick and informs Cliff, "We'll see to these tomorrow. Get a good night's sleep," he said with an ambiguous smile.

The guards are summoned and roughly release Cliff to take him away.

Oh, god, Cliff thinks, I must be easy.

How could I give myself to him like that! Slut, slut, slut!

The next day, Interrogation Room 2 is filled with the sounds of whipping and torture, mostly faked so that the guards wouldn't catch on that Viktor was going easy on Cliff to save him for his next instruction in lust.

Viktor hoped to get Cliff to cooperate in giving over some information so he would not catch hell from his superiors.

Cliff takes his beatings but revealed nothing.

While Viktor admires his grit, he was getting desperate and had to conjure up some false information he supposedly extracted from Cliff so as to buy himself some time.

This day finds Cliff back on the table, nude on his back and flex-tied to the four corners.

"You proved that your American pussy was grade A, Cliff, my compliments. But now I want to sample your cock meat and see if it lives up to the standard set by your talented asshole. You need to demonstrate that you can eat ass with the best of them, as well. I don't want to have to paddle your ass for failure to do so."

Also nude, Viktor climbs up on the table in a 69 position with Cliff.

His privates and ass crack are shaved just the same as Cliff's.

He releases Cliff's ankles and forces his knees up to his chest, exposing the wide-open ass crack and hungry hole.

"Pay attention, Cliff, you need to appreciate a master at this art." Viktor dives into Cliff's silky smooth crack and plunders his asshole, assaulting it and the channel behind with a darting, lapping, knowing tongue.

Cliff never experienced such a thorough job of his hole being eaten out by a consummate master who savored every lick.

Cliff's cock was rioting and bouncing up uncontrollably.

Viktor laved his way from the succulent hole up to the fat, ball-nuts and began sucking each one, lovingly, until he filled his mouth with both roiling balls.

What exquisite torture, thinks Cliff.

Expelling the balls from his mouth, Viktor moves up to the prize and licks his way up to the tip where he thoroughly suctions the mushroom shaped head, laving the sensitive point where the underside of the head meets the shaft.

Cliff can't believe the new sensations he's experiencing.

As Viktor gulps down the entire shaft to its root, he begins to finger fuck Cliff's hole, finding the joy spot to further inflame his hostage.

Power sucking Cliff's dick like a powerful vacuum, Viktor feasts on the rock hard prick, using his inner cheeks and tongue to press and prod the defenseless member to reach climax.

"Oh shit, oh shit!!" screams Cliff as his cock succumbs to the relentless assault spewing torrents of cum flooding Viktor's mouth and throat.

Releasing Cliff's dick, held captive in his conquering mouth, Viktor allows that Cliff's prick is a classic example of prime man meat.

"That was a tasty load you gave up, Cliff, good job! Now let's see if you can give me a demonstration of something you've learned."

Lowering his pulsing pussy to Cliff's face, Viktor invites Cliff's tongue to make an exploration of Viktor's virgin asshole.

"Suck it, baby, you'll be the first that I've ever allowed to touch my hole. I've always been a top, no question, but now I want to let you introduce me to the other side."

Wild to have at the inviting hole, Cliff dives in lapping, laving the expert who had rimmed him and now is to be a willing recipient.

Cliff is, indeed, a quick learner and enjoys the rise and fall of Viktor's spectacular, muscled cheeks as Viktor raises himself up and down to allow Cliff access to his wide-open hole, driving himself into paroxysms of ecstasy.

Viktor, never having allowed himself to be open to this form of pleasure, was struck with the possibilities opening to him especially in relation to his stalled relationship with Eric, whom he loves.

They've had problems with satisfying each other in bed given Viktor's rigidity in not ever wanting to bottom for Eric who is a versatile lover and needs the same to be true with Viktor.

Climbing down from the table, Viktor stares down at Cliff and seems to be having an internal struggle.

Finally, after minutes of putting a hand to his brow and sorting through what he wanted to say.

Viktor finally said to Cliff, "I — I have — a proposition to make to you. I will help you to escape from this dungeon if you'll agree to a couple of stipulations. First, I need you to promise to send any information you've been able to gather on Petrov's arms trafficking network to my superiors at our Military Headquarters. Since you don't trust my intentions in wanting to stop the arms flow into the Middle East, you may send what you have directly to them. I will supply you with the information as to where to send your findings."

"Secondly, I need you to take what I did to you at the rear of this room and apply that knowledge to me. To be plain, I need you to fuck me, take my virgin ass so I will be able to be a complete lover to Eric. You are the only one I could ever let touch me before I would feel ready to open myself up fully to a committed relationship with Eric. You see, we plan on helping you escape this place while at the same time escaping ourselves, leaving our military assignments here in Moscow. Eric's father has died and Eric needs to return to Bavaria to run the family auto parts factory. He wants me to manage the plant which makes parts for Mercedes-Benz, BMW and Audi."

"We have two serious problems to overcome in implementing our plans. One, we do not want the Russian authorities to be in hot pursuit of us. If I can guarantee that Petrov's network can be destroyed with information I've arranged to be supplied to them, I think they will be satisfied with that and allow Eric and me to have our freedom. Two, if I can't function with Eric as a fully committed lover, able to satisfy all his needs, physically as well as emotionally, then our relationship is doomed to failure. He desperately needs to enjoy getting into my ass as much as I do getting into his. I'm — blocked. Can you accede to these two conditions, Cliff?"

"It is true that I didn't trust you at first, but I've come to feel differently now. I think you are a patriot for your country just as I am for mine. Your suspicions are correct; I was able to download from Igor's computer all the information necessary to smash this very dangerous arms network. There should be no problem in my arranging for my government to share this information with your government, given that we both want the same thing. Therefore, your first condition could be satisfied. The second condition, while extraordinary, is something I'm willing to do, I hope to your satisfaction."

"Very well, Cliff, I'm going to have to trust you to fulfill your promise on condition 1. As far as condition 2 goes, we can do that now. I'm going to free you of your constraints so that we can move to the shower stall and begin to satisfy that condition. Assuming you'd be willing to gain your freedom by agreeing to my conditions, Eric has already begun to implement our escape plans. He's unaware of condition 2 as he did not require of me that I learn to bottom for him. He loves me in spite of my limitations in that area. With your help, I hope that my inability to please in this one area will disappear. What you did to me on the table, Cliff, made me confident that you are just the man to get me past my hang-up."

Now free of constraints, Cliff gets up and they move to the shower niche at the rear of the room.

"I think the douche would be pushing it, Viktor, given the fact that your first experience will find your hole so tight."

"Cliff, while I love Eric, I have never been as physically attracted to anyone as much as I am to you. Can you — can you — make love to me like you really mean it, as if we were lovers."

Cliff thinks he can manage this if he thinks of Brad while he's initiating Viktor to the pleasures of being screwed.

"Yes, Viktor, I think that's possible. You must now let me take the lead to sensitize you to being dominated. Just accept that I'm going to fuck you and we're both going to enjoy it very much. Know that your asshole is mine and that you want every inch of my 9" dick to fill your hole. All that I'm going to do to you is just by way of my total possession of your willing body. Just respond to my touching you without your usual need to initiate the action. Relax, react, and allow yourself to be overwhelmed with attentions applied to you without your having to do anything more than permit yourself to be taken. Be willing to be led, submitting to my pleasure that will in turn become yours," Viktor nods his acquiescence.

"Step into the stall, Viktor and face the back wall. You know you have the most beautiful body I have ever seen. Tasting your hole buried in the deep cleft of your magnificent ass was a taste treat. I want another helping." Coming up behind him, both being about the same height, Cliff pressed his stiffening cock against Viktors crack, passing his arms under Viktor's arms and reaching around to get at his tight tits in the massive muscled plates of his chest.

Cliff begins a slow torture of these most sensitive of erogenous zones.

Simultaneously, Cliff kisses Viktor's long, beautiful neck, working up to sucking each of his ear lobes.

Raining kisses on the sides of his sensitive neck, Cliff arrives at the wide muscular shoulders and licks and gently bites each side in turn.

Running his hands down Viktor's broad back, Cliff kneads, squeezes and prods the muscles with knowing hands.

Viktor's prick is now jumping and Cliff's rod is prodding Viktor's crack and nudging his nut sac.

Now approaching his prize destination, Cliff runs his hands over Viktor's high, round butt cheeks, which flare out from the small of his back into long sloping curves, which gracefully curve back under to meet the statuesque legs.

His rock hard cheeks are framed with a shallow hollow on each side emphasizing the voluptuous curves of a bubble butt.

This virgin ass has gone too long unappreciated for the pleasure it has to offer in abundance.

Firmly grasping each cheek, Cliff pulls the cheeks apart allowing his dick to begin getting acquainted with the long, deep crack.

Viktor bends forward slightly, signaling his complicity in the start of the invasion.

Fully aroused, Cliff drops down in a crouch, still firmly grasping and pulling the hard cheeks fully apart and begins a tongue assault on the tight pink pucker.

Viktor now is fully bent over, grasping his ankles with his hands.

From the adjacent bench, Cliff accesses the lube jar and scoops out a large gob and begins working his practiced fingers into the loosening hole, one at a time until three fingers were inserted.

In a circular motion, Cliff worked the fingers around preparing the virgin fuck hole for 9'' of stud cock.

Removing his fingers, Cliff pulled Viktor back up to a standing position and turned him around.

Viktor's cock was rioting with approval.

"I need your help, babe, lean up against the back wall, bend your knees and spread your legs so I can lift you up from under your legs. When your knees reach the rings on the sides of the stall, fasten the attached nylon straps around your knees on each side. Yes, like that, the same position you had me in, except I want your arms free."

Viktor now, with his back flat against the back wall with his legs invitingly raised and his arms braced against the back wall with his hands up as if in surrender.

Cliff moved against Viktor, holding and rubbing their rigid pricks together and took his mouth in a searing, deep, tongue probing kiss.

They, in turn, sucked each other's tongues and fully explored the inside of their mouths.

While frenching Viktor's mouth, he returned to torturing his tits, driving Viktor to a fever pitch.

"Oh, yes, you've made me want your dick in me, rasps Viktor. I can't stand to wait any longer. Slip it in, please, make me feel whole!" Backing up and grabbing Viktor's great globes of ass cheeks, Cliff, having slipped on a condom, places his cock-head at the virgin hole and pushes in to take possession.

Agonizingly slowly, Cliff's prick makes the inexorable journey up the pleasure cavern until his pubes caress the tender opening, now wide-open to receive the pending assault.

Holding steady, getting the freshly invaded channel used to being filled to capacity, Cliff returns to laving Viktor's sensitive neck and inserting his tongue into each ear.

Viktor is now all but conquered, quietly whimpering his surrender.

"Now, babe, I'm going to need your help again. Grab hold of my ass cheeks because I'm going to power pump your asshole, with no further restraint, to open your asslips up for your lover, Eric. Pull my buns toward you when I thrust because I want to achieve maximum penetration so you will remember your deflowering forever."

"Screw my ass off, Cliff, show me no mercy, I want my ass to be the most cock-friendly pussy that Eric ever fucked!!" With that, Cliff's cock began relentlessly ramming and pounding the virgin hole, insuring that forever more, Viktor will be a hungry bottom wanting to be filled with his lover's dick.

Viktor felt the shattering orgasm filling the condom deep in his chasm in wave after wave of hot cum.

Viktor's prick erupts in an answering, explosive orgasm raining geysers of cum in every direction as Viktor screams.

"AAAGGGRRR — "

Pulling out of Viktor's still clenching, freshly fucked love channel, Cliff, chest heaving said, "Viktor, honey, you throw your man or any man a fuck like that and he is your slave. You are a choice piece of ass that will be seeing plenty of action from now on." Cliff gives Viktor's delectable buns an appreciative squeeze.

"It is going to be my pleasure, said Viktor. I never thought that taking it up the ass could feel so good. I'm afraid I'm going to be a pushover now. Will Eric respect me if I let him bang me all the time? He likes macho men. He'll think I'm not a stud anymore!"

"Honey, you'll always be prime stud meat. Having the confidence to give your ass to your lover whenever and wherever he wants it, only shows the confidence of a man. He's going to want to lock you up so you'll never get away, fucker. He'd be crazy to let a stud like you get away, so relax. Now let's get you down so we can get ourselves out of this hell hole."

Cliff and Viktor prepare themselves to leave.

Eric joins them and tells them everything has been put in place for them to make their exit.

One of the two guards is dispatched to sit at the front desk while the other is dispatched to courier a message to Viktor's immediate superior at Headquarters.

The message will explain that Viktor was compelled to release his prisoner in exchange for a solemn promise that a certain disc, downloaded from Petrov's hidden computer, will be sent to his attention at Headquarters.

Viktor was confident that once the disc was received, they'd be off the hook.

Through a little known escape hatch, Viktor, Eric and Cliff scramble up an exit ladder and escape outside to an idling Volga sedan, concealed nearby.

The Volga accelerates away to take the escapees to the rural town of Zvenigorod, where a rich industrialist and friend of the US has a dacha.

The caretaker, Alexi Volkov, Viktor's former assistant, has picked up a big Audi sedan that was brought into Russia by a sales rep of Eric's family business, who dropped the car at a prearranged drop-off point and flew back to Regensburg.

Alexi picked up the car and brought it to the dacha so the escapees could have a fresh vehicle that stood less chance of being noticed.

False papers were arranged for as well as a change in license plates.

An associate, who had acted as chauffeur, drove the Volga away.

Alexi puts them up in a suite of rooms over the garages where they will be safe overnight.

Alexi's employer's personal physician stopped by as prearranged to thoroughly check out Cliff's state of health, finding him fit, except for a little bruising around his tits and for some slight swelling around his asshole.

The welts on his back were subsiding.

Exhausted, after a light supper and some vodka, everyone goes to bed.

A quick shower finds Viktor in bed with Eric.

Viktor explains to Eric the second condition of the deal he made with Cliff.

Miffed at first, Eric quickly sees that Viktor took a big risk only to insure their happiness.

He's more in love with Viktor than ever.

Reflecting on the reality of Cliff's actually having topped the beloved Viktor, Eric is inflamed with lust, tinged with jealousy, knowing he must sample what now is available to him.

Lying next to Viktor, Eric turns to nuzzle Viktor, showering his lips, eyes, nose, cheeks and neck with hot kisses and turning Viktor on.

Eric whispers into his lover's ear: "I need to have now what you allowed Cliff to be the first to sample. Did you — could you have — enjoyed it or — was it just — well — a nightmare."

"Please — don't be put off — if I tell you — it was very, very — thrilling," said Viktor with a look of concern.

"Thrilling! I wasn't expecting thrilling! But you know what, thrilling is good, real good. Turn over babe, my patience is at an end. I want you now!" Viktor rolls over onto his stomach.

"Prop yourself up on your forearms and spread your legs." Viktor complies revealing the love mounds that Eric craved to taste.

Eric slides a pillow under Viktor's groin to elevate his buns and to make his hole more accessible.

Crawling around and stretching himself out between Viktor's legs, Eric grasps the great mounds, parting them to reveal the recently breached, almost virgin asshole.

The tight pucker, still in need of training to be cock-friendly, was winking in invitation.

Diving right in, Eric begins a thorough tongue exploration of the entire crack, the hard buns and culminating in an intense assault on the widening hole.

Getting up on his knees, he grabs the lube he'd placed on the night table, supposing his own ass would be the target and begins to finger fuck his lover, whose hole is no longer off limits.

Viktor is responding by shoving his pretty ass higher into the air so as to be penetrated deeper.

"You are going to be my insatiable whore, aren't you my love," said Eric admiringly.

Pulling out his fingers, he now lubes up his stiff dick and wipes off his hands on a hand towel.

Staring down at the impossibly beautiful sight of his lover's eager asshole, Eric gives the love mounds a series of love slaps to get the skin nice and pink and warm.

Raising himself up on his hands on each side of Viktor's chest and stretched out fully between Viktor's legs, Eric aims his dick at the love spot and pops in the head of his dick.

His dick now introduced to the hungry hole, Eric presses forward slowly, filling the man hole to capacity.

"How does that feel, butt boy?"

"Your whore only wants to supply you with the best pussy you ever had. Show me how bad you want it. Show me your anger for being made to wait so long. Treat me like the hungry bottom I am. Fuck me! Fuck me deep and hard, brand my ass with your dick. Show me that you own me!"

Pulling almost out of Viktor's hole, except for the engorged knob of the cock-head, Eric plunges back, crushing his groin against the raised mounds.

Repeating the process with ever more force and velocity, Eric plunders his lover's steaming hole, taking complete possession.

With a final brutal swing of his powerful hips, Eric smashed into the sizzling buns and spews, one, two, three injections of molten cum.

Viktor moans with pleasure, accepting his conqueror, which only draws two more molten streams of cum to fill his cavity to its fullest, leaking cum between his spread legs.

Pausing for a quick breath, Eric turns Viktor over to continue his attack, this time on the enormous dick he's come to love.

Viktor, already close to the edge, takes little servicing before his back arches, shoving his dick deep into Eric's throat and unleashes a choking amount of spunk, which can't be contained in Eric's mouth and drips out of his mouth all over his chin.

Eric wipes his chin and licks his mouth clean, then falls back to Viktor's beloved dick to lap up the cum, still leaking out.

Viktor lies there looking up at the beloved face, adulation showing in his eyes.

He knows he's a satisfactory bottom and can please his man.

He's filled with joy.

"Oh, babe, to think it took us so long to get to this point. Wow, you were awesome," said Eric, smiling with deep satisfaction.

"To think that we can now give each other anything is just so — fucking good!!!" Lights still on, they fall into a deep sleep in each other's arms.

Sometime later, the door to the adjoining bedroom is opened and Alexi, naked, comes in to look at the lovers he heard making love.

While happy for them in their love for each other, Alexi can't help but feel a sense of loss even though he and Viktor enjoyed only a sexual relationship.

Turning to leave, Alexi unintentionally caused Viktor to startle awake.

"Alexi — what — ?!"

"Forgive me, Viktor! I was lonely and didn't want to be alone. I was just leaving," Alexi moving towards the connecting door.

Eric, now fully awake too, said, "Alexi, we owe you a lot and are so happy that we found each other and are starting a new life that we'd like to show our appreciation by inviting you to our bed."

"It was not my intention of exacting payment from two people whom I consider to be friends. You owe me nothing. I'm just glad that you trusted me enough to put yourselves in my hands to insure your escape."

"That isn't what it's about, Alexi. I know Viktor still desires you and I want to watch him please you in the way you like best. I, in turn, will further stake my claim on Viktor's freshly plowed asshole."

Alexi slips into bed next to Viktor and turns with his back to him.

Viktor wastes no time in lubing up and slipping on a condom to enter his former butt boy with a forceful thrust, reestablishing his dominance on a dedicated bottom.

Eric, in turn, enters Viktor's sodden hole, awash in cum from their earlier lovemaking.

Instinctively, they move in unison, achieving a satisfying rhythm, pleasing to everyone.

Viktor was enjoying reacquainting his cock with Alexi's talented pussy while marveling at his new found joy in taking it up the ass with the utmost pleasure.

Viktor, knowing Alexi's body so well, fondles his balls before beginning to work his hands up and down the 7" stiff shaft, jerking him off and setting off a chain reaction.

As Alexi's cock splatters ropes of cum, soaking the sheets in front of him, Eric's prick unleashed another load up his lover's already saturated ass, driving Viktor to pump Alexi's hole and filling his condom with a sea of cum.

After good night kisses, Alexi left to return to his room and they all fall into a sound sleep.

The next morning, Alexi provides a light breakfast before helping Viktor and Eric to load up their car for their trip to Regensburg.

They say their goodbyes to Cliff.

"You've been a loyal friend, Alexi, we won't forget it and will look forward to your spending time with us in our new home," said Viktor.

Viktor and then Eric, give Alexi going away hugs and depart.

Returning to the garage, Alexi finds Cliff in the garage's mudroom, bathed in sunlight, looking out the window for any sign of the plane which was to arrive any time now.

Cliff is now dressed in one of the industrialist's suits with dress shirt and tie, etc., so that to a casual observer, he would pass muster as the rich Muscovite who frequently flies in and out on business trips.

"Well, Cliff, I guess you'll soon be leaving our country," said Alexi.

"Yes, my stay has been most interesting and educational. Many thanks to you for helping Viktor to validate his promise to help me escape."

"You know, Cliff, you needn't have slept alone last night. I would have been happy for you to have shared my bed."

"Well, since I was only across the hall, I couldn't help hearing that the three of you were entertaining each other." answers Cliff.

"They were only taking pity on me since I spend so much time alone in this remote house," explains Alexi.

"Actually, they only managed to give me a taste of what I've been missing. You, Cliff, are in a position to remedy that fact." Saying this, he pushes Cliff up against the paneled wall, unfastens and unzips his pants and pulls them and his under shorts down to his ankles.

Moving down to his knees, Alexi said, "I intend to make up for my lack of hospitality last night. There's no way you're leaving my country without me sampling some of the prime American stud meat you have been brandishing about in Moscow." Encircling one hand around Cliff's stirring member, Alexi lifts it up, permitting him free reign on the low hanging nut sac.

Now, with the other hand, Alexi kneads the sac and begins feverishly feasting on the cum-packed nuts.

Cliff cups the back of Alexi's head with both hands, encouraging him to feel unconstrained.

Moving his starving mouth to the base of Cliff's now rock-hard prick, Alexi licks, sucks and lavs his way up to the piss-slit and presses the point of his tongue inside.

Cliff is reduced to a quivering mass of need, ready to do anything to satisfy his hunger for release.

Staving off the main event until he had Cliff fully under his control, Alexi sucked in Cliff's pulsating cock, vacuuming it down to his pubes.

Now feasting on the American stud meat, Alexi gorged himself on Cliff's succulent boner.

Cliff lasted no time at all before his beefy balls were sucked dry with a blasting orgasm, spewing down the Russian's throat.

Alexi lingered on with his face buried in Cliff's crotch, lapping up the last few drops of cum leaking from the big dick.

"That was choice, Cliff, but there's still something more I want from you. You must give me a little piece of your American pussy that you were generous enough to make available to Viktor." He was more that complimentary.

Step out of those trousers and kneel up on this bench.

Crouch down so that the back of your thighs rest on your calves.

Perfect, that'll line up your hole with my dick.

It's fortuitous that I chose a suit for you from my employer's closet that has a double vent."

Cliff understands when the vent is flipped up, the dress shirt tucked up, exposing his now vulnerable American buns.

Dropping to his knees behind Cliff, Alexi began lubing Cliff's hole using Cliff's own cum that Alexi managed to hold in his mouth from the servicing he just gave to Cliff.

Standing back up, Alexi views the American, kneeling bent over, half dressed, wearing suit jacket, shirt and tie, long socks, no shoes.

The full round globes of Cliff's ass were stuck out, poised for the coming invasion.

Alexi's prick, sheathed now in a condom, was like a heat-seeking missile, finding the hot hole that it was about to be powered into.

With one punishing thrust, Alexi was planted in as far as he could go with a loud smack when his groin met butt cheeks.

Cliff was now skewered and his cavern packed with Russian dick.

"Oh, Cliff, you hot fuck, I now know how good it was for Viktor." Digging his fingers into Cliff's hips, Alexi began to pound Cliff's ass and ramming the kneeling American.

Alexi's cock-head discovered Cliff's joy spot and battered it head-on with every blow.

Cliff was eagerly submitting to this assault, using ass muscles to massage Alexi's jackhammering cock.

The resulting orgasm made Cliff feel like he was split open with the force of the gushing explosion, barely contained in the condom, in wave after wave.

Alexi enjoyed a few more pumps, savoring the slick wetness surrounding his spent prick.

"Oh yeah, Cliff, that was beyond — ! I'd like to think you'll be thinking of me on the flight back, sitting on a well fucked ass."

Just as Cliff was zipping up the dress pants that he'd only just put back on, they could hear the sound of a plane landing nearby.

"You timed that just right, Alexi. Glad there was time for me to oblige you. We Americans aim to please," said Cliff with a satisfied smile.

"Have no doubt about that my American friend. You tossed me a fuck that will sustain me most completely until my employer's son returns from university on spring break. He'll spend most of his vacation with my cock lodged firmly in his young ass. You see this job does have its perks." Cupping Cliff's ass while embracing him, Alexi gives him a passionate kiss on the lips.

"Time to go!"

Alexi backs a small vehicle, similar to a golf cart, out of the garage and swings around to collect Cliff and drive out to the plane.

Nearing the plane, steps can be seen being lowered to receive its passenger.

Hugging Alexi, Cliff thanks him and dashes to the steps and quickly climbs aboard.

The co-pilot greets him and ushers him inside.

Cliff is startled to see that Jason Stone, the Director of Homeland Security, is getting up out of a big leather swivel chair to receive him.

Cliff is taken by surprise that the boss, himself, would risk coming to Russia in a rendezvous with a covert operative that they would never acknowledge was one of their own.

Other than the pilot and co-pilot, Jason was alone on the plane.

After shaking Cliff's hand, Stone motioned for Cliff to sit in the swivel chair facing his own.

"Please sit down and buckle up. We'll be taking off immediately." They were now alone in the cabin, the co-pilot having joined the pilot in the cockpit.

"You've been through quite an ordeal and we're glad that we are able to arrange this extraction of you from this deteriorating situation we've placed you in." The plane begins to taxi in preparation for takeoff.

Stone, who has taken some heat from his critics in Washington for sanctioning such an unorthodox mission, is anxious to vindicate himself by claiming the mission was a success.

For this he needs Cliff to supply the ammunition he needs to neutralize his detractors.

"Cliff, it is of vital importance to national security that you apprize me of what you were able to accomplish on your mission to Moscow. My ass is on the line." Having cleared the short runway, the plane is now in the air and climbing rapidly to cruising altitude.

It is not lost on Cliff that Jason, attuned solely to his own self-interest, is only interested in protecting his ascent to higher places.

Cliff representing unfortunate collateral damage, should the mission be perceived negatively in Washington.

Cliff begins a narrative of what transpired during his stay in Moscow and coming to the part that involved manipulating events to put him in the company of the Russian scientist.

"You see, Jason, getting into Igor Petrov's good graces so as to be allowed access to his apartment, involved a bit more than Brad could have been expected to prepare me for. It is hard to explain; perhaps a simple demonstration would be more effective to give you a truer picture."

With that, Cliff whipped out a pair of handcuffs that once belonged to Viktor Sidorov and clamped one end on to Jason's left wrist, startling Jason into immobility.

Springing up, Cliff moved quickly around the back of Jason's swivel chair and grabbing his right wrist, clamped on the other end of the handcuffs.

Jason's arms were now fully secured behind his swivel chair.

"Wha — what can you be doing here, Cliff. Have you lost your mind? Release me at once!" said Jason, summoning up whatever authority he could muster.

"No can do, Jason. You need to be made to understand what can result from decisions you've made without consideration of how much of a sacrifice you're requiring of a subordinate. In this case, that subordinate is me."

"Cliff, be reasonable, I am sure we can — well — make it up to you considering whatever it was that has aggrieved you. We can arrange for a couple weeks vacation — or — ," said a perplexed Jason.

"Actually I had something else in mind, Jason. You are too removed from action taken in the field to, in any real way, have a sense of what is required by an undercover agent to achieve the goals that you have set out for them. Perhaps with this greater knowledge that I can provide for you. You will be able to do a more effective job in future." The plane, encountering some turbulence, lurches up and down.

Now, crouching in front of Jason, Cliff removes both his shoes and proceeds to remove his suit pants along with his white boxer shorts.

Surprisingly, Jason wears old-fashioned garters to hold up his socks.

"Cliff, what has come over you — don't — don't do this!"

"Too late, Jason, you are going to get a first-hand demonstration of how you developed one of your best operatives into a cock whore." Cliff now lifts each of Jason's legs over the arms of his chair, spreading his legs wide apart.

Jason's cock started to stir, vetoing his protests for Cliff to stop.

Having learned the techniques of slow torture to one's cock and balls from Igor, Cliff proceeds to demonstrate his newly acquired skills.

Starting with his boss's ball sac, Cliff sucks and swallows one testicle and then the other, filling his mouth with the other man's cum laden nuts.

Simultaneously, slipping his middle finger up Jason's untouched hole to find the often ignored prostate.

Jason's cock jumped to full attention as he involuntarily began to moan.

Jason's vacuous southern belle of a wife and now Washington social climber would never sully herself by including anything like this in her wifely duties.

Thus, Jason was ripe fruit to be so easily had.

With Jason up at full mast, Cliff began the caressing torture on his pulsating and engorged 7" cock.

Jason had never received a blowjob like this from any of his dalliances with women.

Cliff built him up slowly to a near climax before squeezing his prick hard to prevent him from coming.

This procedure continued over and over again until Jason couldn't take it anymore.

"Take me Cliff, please — please suck my dick down your throat, don't take your mouth off of me again!"

Cliff responded by gulping down Jason's fat 7" dick and let him finally empty his balls in a torrent of sperm, almost choking Cliff before he could drink it all down.

Knowing he had softened up his boss sufficiently, Cliff was aware that he could now raise his boss's legs in the air and split his asshole open with one brutal poke with his 9" dick.

That act, however, would have to wait until he got home to a certain SEAL instructor who would soon be privy to all of Cliff's now highly developed skills.

Un-cuffing Jason, Cliff helped him get dressed, given his weakened condition.

Jason settled back in his seat, exhausted.

Staring out the small window of the plane out into the high wispy clouds surrounding the plane, Jason said, "I'm — I'm sorry, Cliff, I — really didn't know what I was asking of you in sending you on a mission like this. What could I have been thinking!" sighed Jason.

"Don't worry about it, Jason, thanks to you I've found the love of my life in Brad. We intend to be together. If that's a problem for you in doing my job in Homeland Security, then so be it."

Sometime later, the plane lands at Dulles International Airport where a black Cadillac Escalade SUV awaits them at the curb to whisk them away to the Pentagon where military officers expect to be briefed on this mission.

Towards the end of the ride to the Pentagon, Jason leans towards Cliff and in a very low voice, so as not to be overheard by their driver, he whispers, "Cliff, I — ah — may need you to come to my office — for a — more in depth analysis of your experiences in getting Igor Petrov's — confidence."

"Certainly, Sir, anytime you have need — ," answers Cliff with a knowing smirk on his face.

They arrive and go inside to give a somewhat abbreviated version of the mission.

Chapter 4

Meanwhile, back in the German countryside, Victor and Eric had made it over the border without a hitch and are driving along Autobahn 3 on the way to Regensburg.

While driving, Eric glances over at Viktor, asleep in the front passenger seat.

Viktor had angled his seat so that he was almost in a prone position and he had pushed his seat as far back as it could go in the big Audi sedan.

Viktor is appealingly laid out with an obvious bulge in his crotch.

Must be having a wonderful fantasy as part of his dream, Eric speculates.

"Time for a break," he mutters out loud.

Turning off onto an access road, he pulls into a cut-out large enough for a single car.

As Eric turns off the engine, Viktor startles awake.

Groping Viktor's erection through his pants, Eric asks, "So what's with the dream, are you getting some?" Not waiting for a response, he unbuckles Viktor's belt, unzips his fly and pulls out the now fully erect boner.

"I want a little of this action now, stud muffin." Going down on the massive dick, Eric gulps down as much as he can stuff into his mouth, vacuum sucking his lover's prick as Viktor squirms in obvious arousal.

"Slip out of your shoes, take off your pants and shorts, I'm coming around to your side of the car!" Eric directs.

Getting out of the drivers side of the car, Eric goes around to the passenger side and opens the door.

Shedding his shoes, pants and shorts, he tosses them over onto the driver's seat.

Eric climbs into the car, stretching out on top of Viktor and closing the door behind him.

Now, while grinding their crotches together, Eric takes Viktor's mouth in a crushing kiss.

"I can't wait to have you until we get home to Regensburg," Eric whispers into Viktor's ear.

Eric slips Viktor's undershirt up and flips the front up over his head securing it behind the long neck and revealing the massive chest and small brown tits.

"Raise your knees up to your chest, babe, I need a little pussy now to tide me over." Eric pulls back to a kneeling position while Viktor reaches behind his knees and raises his legs up, knees pressed to his chest and his feet grazing the roof of the car.

"You can have as much pussy as you want, lover, go for it," challenges Viktor, smiling seductively.

Eric reaches over to his pants pocket for a packet of lube he had brought along and began lubing his lover's hole.

Finding the joy spot with his middle finger, he massaged it, driving Viktor into a frenzy.

"Stuff your prick up my ass, I want to be power-slammed into this soft leather seat." Lubing up his throbbing cock, Eric viewed his lover's welcoming hole, nestled in the stretched crack and framed by the powerful thighs, spread wide.

Bumping his engorged cock-head to the pouting pink lips, Eric pushed in deep with one continuous motion.

Now implanted to the root of his cock, Eric paused, savoring the full possession Viktor afforded him.

"Ooohhh — yes — fuck me, Eric, I wanted you in me so badly!"

Viktor's hungry ass clenched down on the invading cock, caressing every inch.

"Uhhhaaa!" cried Viktor, working his ass muscles to jerk off Eric's prick.

Eric slipped his hands up Viktor's legs replacing Viktor's hands with his own behind his knees, freeing Viktor's hands so they could be placed behind his head, surrendering himself completely to Eric's lust.

"That's right, love, lay back and enjoy the plowing you are about to receive." And power slam he did, ruthlessly plowing Viktor's hole and slamming his buns into the soft leather seat.

Supporting himself with the forceful grip he had on the back of Viktor's raised knees, Eric twisted himself side to side as he thrust forward, opening his lover's passage wider to accept the load he was about to receive.

With a powerful final thrust from Eric, Viktor felt his lover's balls filling his crack just before the explosion that tore through his love canal, sending volley after volley of steaming cum deep inside him.

"Aaaggrrr!" screamed Viktor, as he gave up his own load, bathing his chest, mouth and chin with thick cum.

Eric leaned over to lap up the spoils and taste his lover's mouth splattered with dripping cum.

Collapsing into an exhausted heap, Eric said sarcastically, "You have real potential as a bottom, once I get you to enjoy the pleasure you give me."

"If I enjoyed it any more than that, I'd be a candidate for the paramedics. As it is, I may never walk again. I guess I deserve the battering you give me when you fuck me, given how long I made you wait."

"Regardless of how long I waited, it would have been like this. You are just beginning to know how much I've wanted you, all of you. Now that you are mine, you will never be allowed to forget that you belong to me." They enjoyed a lingering kiss.

"You have demonstrated that you have some natural talent to be an inspired bottom but I don't want you to forget the superior skill of your master in the art of pleasing his man." Eric levers himself up and twists around so that his ass is suspended above Viktor's dick. Moistening his hand generously with saliva, he uses his fingers to open and lubricate his hole while reaching around to feel Viktor's cock, which is still rock-hard.

"Pay attention, love, class is in session! You will be required to master the new position I'm about to demonstrate for you."

Placing his lover's massive tool at his winking pucker, Eric lowers himself down to receive Viktor's entire shaft.

Viktor's eyes roll back in his head.

Now, Eric lies back so he too is fully prone, lying on top of Viktor.

Raising his right foot up on the armrest, he then raises the left foot up on the center console, legs splayed wide.

Viktor reaches around to fondle Eric's balls with one hand and to pinch his tit with the other.

Eric can now lever himself up and down with his feet solidly planted on the arm rest and center console while throwing his head back alongside Viktor's head and turning so that they can now explore each other's mouths.

At the same time, Viktor's cock is rediscovering the pleasures of Eric's asshole in agonizing slow motion.

Viktor, starved for Eric's choice pussy, was quickly close to the edge but Eric, a schooled bottom, wanted him to be tortured long enough to enjoy a spectacular orgasm.

Viktor, no stranger in getting his lover off, began an expert hand job on Eric who was then driven to stop the tease and work his ass like the cock-whore he is.

Frenzied with lust, Eric began working his butt up and down in rapid fire clenching muscles in his love channel, taking Viktor to the heights.

Screaming in unison, Viktor injected a massive load inside his whimpering lover.

Eric's own eruption couldn't be contained in Viktor's hand as the spewing load decorated the roof of the car with splatters of dripping, white cum.

"I'm glad you haven't lost your taste for having your pretty ass serviced. That was truly worth waiting for but I won't be put off for so long in the future," said Viktor nibbling on Eric's ear lobe.

"Did it show that I missed your big boner stuffed up my butt? You've reduced me to a cock slut again. As much as I like fucking your bubble butt and training you to love my cock jammed up your ass, I'll never lose my desire to be filled by your big dick and plowed hard and fast." Viktor's class ends and they collect their clothes and get dressed.

Back on the road, they are reinvigorated to enjoy the rest of the ride.

They arrive in Regensburg at Holtzhaus, a great lodge-like structure in the traditional fashion, home to Eric's family for generations.

The white stucco mansion has many, multi-paned windows, featuring pretty green shutters. Above, the massive tile roof is interrupted with many charming dormers.

The widow, Frau Holtz, greets them warmly in the great, two story entrance hall containing the grand stair accessing the bedrooms above.

Embracing and kissing Eric, she hugs Viktor and said, "Welcome to your new home, Viktor, I am so very pleased to meet you at long last. Leave your things here. I'll have them taken upstairs to your room. The master bedroom has been put in readiness for your arrival. But first, come into the kitchen for some refreshment after your long journey." They follow her, cutting a stunning figure in flowing indigo silk and pearls, into the vast kitchen to the breakfast room, located in a bay windowed niche with a view of the Alps.

Eric and Viktor enjoy coffee with apple strudel and black forest tortes, prepared by Greta, the housekeeper, while Anna Holtz describes her new condo she's moved into in the town of Regensburg.

She relates that the old caretaker, Otto Jahn, has retired and has moved to Frankfurt to be near his daughter and his two grandchildren.

His son, Bruno Jahn, has taken over running the house with the use of a staff that live off premises.

He also is their accountant for both the business and for their personal affairs.

He has moved into his father's rooms over the six car garage, attached to the house.

"I've asked him to join us so you can meet him. He's been invaluable to me since Fritz died, seeing to everything that needed to be done."

Just as they were finishing up their snack, Bruno Jahn came into the kitchen.

He is 5'-11" tall with sandy colored hair, brown eyes, possessing a great body with erect posture.

Anna enthusiastically introduces him to the new masters of Holtzhaus.

"It is good to meet you Bruno," says Eric, "I'm indebted to you for seeing mother through a trying time." Eric said, clearly taken with this striking male with athletic grace.

"My father, being caretaker here for so many years, Holtzhaus feels like home to me. Seeing to your mother during those difficult days seemed only natural," said Bruno.

Eric can only think of the unnatural things he would like to do to Bruno.

"We are so very fortunate to have Bruno, says Anna. After he graduated from Frankfurt University, I was sure he would prefer a bigger city to further his career in business."

Anna introduces Viktor and they shake hands.

"I think you will like life here in the country, Viktor," said Bruno. "We have a lot to offer in the way of recreation. I hope you like riding horses for we have a fine stable here."

It's you I'd like to get in the saddle, Viktor is thinking.

"Yes, I very much like riding and would like to ride out with you, when the opportunity arises, to become familiar with this lovely property." Not to mention checking out whether you have a good seat in the saddle, muses Viktor.

"We won't keep you Bruno, I know you have a date with Gretchen Voss this evening to see a film," says a smiling Anna.

"Enjoy the film! I'll expect to hear your review before I will go to see it myself. Goodnight, dear." He bids everyone good night and shows himself out.

Anna stays overnight in one of the guest rooms, planning on returning to her new home in the center of Regensburg in the morning.

They have breakfast together, served by the housekeeper who arrives every morning promptly at 8:00 AM from her home nearby.

"Are you sure that giving so much responsibility to Bruno is something he is capable of handling, mother?" asks Eric.

"Certainly, darling, he may look young but he is 28 years old and extremely loyal as well as responsible. He was among the top of his class at university and had many job offers that would have been more lucrative than working for our family. I think you will soon come to realize how fortunate we are to have him."

"You see, mother, Viktor and I have plans for expanding the business, requiring one or both of us to travel, staying away for periods of time. This will put an added burden on Bruno that I hope he will be ready for. We will be relying on him a great deal to be our surrogates when we are away."

"You will need to convince yourselves that he can be trusted to run things when you are unable to be in attendance. Give him a chance, I have no doubt you'll be as impressed with him as I am. Well, I must be off, I have a luncheon to attend today and must get home so I can make myself presentable." Anna leaves.

"Well, Viktor, Bruno might be exactly the person we need to take charge of the business and oversee the staff for this house when we're away. I guess I'm a little uneasy, given that I don't really know him very well. He was just a child when I left to go into military service 15 years ago, before I wound up in Moscow on loan from the German government. He's certainly a magnificent specimen. Mother mentioned that he got a soccer scholarship to Frankfurt University and was the star of the team. His academic credentials are excellent as well, a very fine package indeed."

"While you go to the factory to reacquaint yourself with how everything is running, I will remain here to get familiar with the house and the staff. As part of my effort in doing that, I plan to ride out with Bruno to inspect the property and get to know what he is about."

The next day, Viktor and Bruno arrange to meet to tour the 35 acre property.

The well-worn riding paths are a pleasure to use, cantering along through leafy glades and pastures.

Viktor and Bruno sit together on some large boulders that look out onto a distant view to the snowcapped Alps beyond.

They become more acquainted and begin to feel like friends.

Viktor relates to Eric his growing ease that Bruno is going to be invaluable when left in charge while they are away.

Eric invites Bruno to join Viktor and himself for dinner in the family's formal dining room.

Greta, the housekeeper, serves them a wonderful meal full of traditional German cooking.

While she cleans up before leaving for the night, they move down the hall to the book lined study for an after dinner drink.

They sit in front of a large stone fireplace in a comfortable seating group consisting of a large tufted leather sofa facing the fireplace, flanked by oversized leather lounge chairs.

"So, Bruno, you and Viktor have become better acquainted. We're delighted that you have such a keen sense of responsibility for all the various tasks that your employment with us requires of you. That's indeed a great comfort to us, particularly with some plans we have which we'd like to discuss with you." Viktor pours another round of drinks, everyone is buzzed.

"You see, Bruno, my father was content to run his business and keep it small and uncomplicated. While this approach worked for him, times have changed. To remain competitive in today's business climate, one has to constantly expand and keep up with the latest developments in one's industry. Thus, Viktor and I are planning on opening a new plant in the American south to be near German car manufacturers with whom we do business. This will necessitate our being away a lot, leaving behind the running of the business here to others while we are traveling."

"That leads us to the subject of who can perform this function for us. We had in mind that perhaps you would be an ideal candidate. Does this sound like something that might interest you? It would, of course, mean a substantial increase in your compensation package."

"It sounds like an opportunity for me to grow with the company in a way that I'd very much like!" Bruno says animatedly.

"Viktor and I don't really know you very well nor do you know us well. This evening was supposed to get us to relax, let our hair down and explore the possibilities. We know you've been dating Gretchen Voss who is here in our area on a temporary teaching assignment. We were concerned that you may find yourself married and moving away with your bride to a larger city where there are more opportunities for employment for both of you."

"Actually — Eric — I have a — confession — to make. Gretchen and I met at the University and are just friends. I'm afraid I let your mother draw the conclusion that we were dating because it made her — more comfortable with me. I didn't mean to deceive her but I didn't correct her mistaken impression. I did have a relationship in college with my —

roommate — which turned out to be only a — dalliance — for him but a heartbreak for me. He married a girl from our class and moved to Berlin."

Eric poured another round of drinks.

"Thank you for your candor, Bruno. So, having been hurt with an early relationship, you've remained unattached?" asks a puzzled Eric.

"Well I do take some trips into Frankfurt some weekends to seek — a little company but often return home — disappointed. I guess I'm hard to match up."

"It seems to me that you would be a nice catch for someone. Is it that you are too inexperienced to know what you want?" asks Viktor.

"Admittedly, I am a bit shy when it comes to initiating anything of that nature, while I am aggressive when it comes to business and getting things done."

"It's past time that something was done about that," said Viktor, as he moves around to the back of Bruno's chair.

Resting his hands on Bruno's shoulders, he leans over to place a series of soft kisses along his neck.

Bruno displays a tent in his pants.

"Does the possibility of getting it on with Eric and me sound at all appealing?"

"Uh — well — I hope I haven't been too obvious in the way I've looked at you but yes — you both turn me on so it's embarrassing. I was afraid it was showing — in front — that I was aroused." says Bruno, flushing.

Coming around to the front of the chair, Viktor unzips his fly to allow his cock to rise up to its full size.

Bruno with a look of awe said, "I don't think — that is — it's too big," he says tremulously.

"Oh I think you can, Bruno, I have every confidence in you." Viktor presses the big head of his dick against Bruno's full lips, just parting in obvious willingness to meet Viktor's challenge.

Bruno, who has done without for too long, starts to make love to the massive cock-head.

Wrapping his lips around the engorged head, he laps the sensitive underside, inciting Viktor to press in deeper and to begin fucking Bruno's face.

Mouth stretched wide-open, Bruno has the entire shaft in his mouth and pressing the back of his throat.

"Yes, Bruno, show us what a hungry little whore you are." Bruno does not disappoint, feeding lustily on Viktor's raging prick.

"Ugggaaa!" screams Viktor, as Bruno sucks in every drop of the spunk bath.

"You really haven't been getting any lately, my poor starved lamb."

"Come, get up, Bruno, and join Eric and me on the sofa. It's time we saw what chemistry there is between us that we can all enjoy." Bruno, with tented trousers, moves over to stand in front of the large sofa where Eric is seated.

Eric unfastens Bruno's pants and drops them to the floor along with his undershorts.

From behind, Viktor is removing Bruno's dress shirt and slipping up his undershirt so he could begin working over his small brown tits.

Eric said, "I wondered what was making such a large tent in your pants, Bruno, and I can only be impressed by what I can now see." Eric begins feeding on Bruno's stiff 8" prick.

Stripping off his clothes and dropping to his knees behind Bruno, Viktor parts the choice soccer buns and darts his tongue into the tender asshole, sadly fallen into disuse.

"Ooohhhaaa!!" groans Bruno, as he is plundered front and back.

Kneading Bruno's balls, Eric rapidly sucks the hungry dick to climax for there is more to come in exploring Bruno's range.

"Ooohhhaaa!!" screams Bruno as Eric milks his dick of his first bursting load.

Eric gets up to embrace Bruno and to plunge his tongue into Bruno's mouth so that they can both taste Bruno's salty spunk.

Viktor also gets up only to sit down on the sofa right behind Eric.

Eric moves Bruno around so that his back is now facing Viktor, whose massive dick, sheathed in a condom, is pointing straight up.

"Come, my sweet boy, sit on daddy's dick," invites Viktor.

Turning to glance at the towering prick, Bruno looks panicked.

"I managed to take you down my throat, Viktor, but now this, It's — just — too — big!"

Viktor, prepared with a tube of lube, begins lubing Bruno's hole, nestled in the deep crack, separating his high, muscular ass.

Applying a liberal amount of lube on his dick, Viktor asks Eric to help Bruno to slowly lower himself on to the feared dick-head.

"Chill, babe, you're going to do just fine. Now relax so you can open up." Viktor's prick slides past Bruno's loosening hole to begin impaling the great globes of man flesh.

"It'll only hurt for a minute," said Viktor in an intimate whisper.

Bruno, high on the many after dinner drinks he downed, was relaxed enough to sink down to sit on Viktor's groin, ass cheeks spreading to cover Viktor's entire groin area.

"Oh, man, you feel good, Bruno, your butt feels so good against me. Now lie back so I can enjoy you pretty mouth." Viktor is now enjoying the pleasures of Bruno's ass and mouth, French kissing him with an active tongue

Climbing up on the sofa, facing and straddling Bruno, Eric moves his well-lubed ass over Bruno's stiff dick, slips a condom on it and gently lovers himself so that he too is dick impaled.

"As employers, Bruno, we believe in giving as much as we get." Eric, getting into it, begins to ride Bruno's young, unexploited dick, demonstrating the talent of an experienced bottom.

Eric's fuck channel massages Bruno's prick unrelentingly, driving him quickly to the crest.

"AAAGGGRRR!!" shouts Bruno as he releases a shattering orgasm deep into Eric's bowels.

"That was a very respectable load, Bruno, for someone who just got a first-rate blowjob," says Eric immodestly.

"Ooohhh!" moans Bruno, delirious with satiation.

Eric lifts himself off to stand in front of the sofa.

Viktor moves to reposition himself along with Bruno so that they are now lying on their sides, Viktor's prick still lodged deep into Bruno's young butt.

Reaching under Bruno's uppermost leg, Viktor lifts the leg to open the soccer cheeks wide.

"Ummm," groans Viktor as he begins to slowly work his hips to slide his dick in and out of the tight young ass, building up to a rhythm.

Viktor is thoroughly enjoying plowing Bruno's expanding love tract, in no hurry to complete the journey.

Now Eric leans down, resting his hands on the arm and back of the sofa, so as to position his cock to penetrate Bruno's lips, swollen from Viktor's crushing kisses.

Bruno, a quick study after experiencing Viktor's whopping prick, goes for Eric's advancing cock-head and begins to feast.

Being taken front and rear is entirely new for Bruno but will become routine from now on.

Now craving to climax in his new butt boy, Viktor mounts a savage assault and pounds Bruno's tender young pussy with abandon.

With one last powerful swing of his hips, Viktor plunges in deep to inject a searing stream of cum into his new butt boy.

Seeing his lover climax drives Eric over the edge as he stuffs his dick deep into Bruno's throat to release a choking squirt of cum.

They separate and sit on the sofa next to each other panting for breath.

Bruno squirms in his seat, his ass pulsating pleasantly with being stretched to the limit.

"That calls for a nightcap," says Eric, as he gets up to fix their drinks.

"Well, Bruno, let's see how much stamina an ex-soccer star can muster to meet a challenge," says Viktor.

Getting up and grabbing some lube, he reaches around to insert a finger in his hole between the bubble butt cheeks and to lubricate his fuck channel.

"Get up, Bruno!" commands Viktor, as he slips a condom on to Bruno's dick and lubes the rock-hard shaft.

Moving around Bruno, Viktor kneels on the sofa cushion and rests his forearms on the sofa back.

"Stand up on the sofa, Bruno, straddle me and crouch down so you can take your fill." Viktor's magnificent ass, now presented for the taking, drove Bruno into a frenzy.

He did, as directed, and straddled and mounted his big, butch employer.

Feverish with a rising hunger, he plunged into Viktor, not hesitating to possess what he craved.

Viktor, now an experienced and well-plowed bottom, enjoyed being taken hard.

"Go for it, boy. Show me how bad you want it!"

The overexcited Bruno lasted only moments when he pounded a hot blast of cum up Viktor's ass filling the condom wedged in the chasm.

"Viktor, your butt is incredible!!" says Bruno, reeling with pleasure.

As Bruno withdrew to stand back up, Eric joined them with their drinks.

Sitting on the sofa next to each other again, they turn back to the topic for which they came together tonight.

Eric said, "I think it's safe to say that we are feeling more comfortable with you, Bruno. In fact, we'd like you to move into the house so we can all have full access to each other. Would that be agreeable to you?"

"More than agreeable, it would make life here in Regensburg come alive for me, knowing that my two gorgeous, humpy employers will want to bed me on a daily basis." gushes Bruno.

"What bedroom would you put me in?"

"As you know, there is a his and hers master suite in this house, although my parents used only one of them. We'd like you to have the unused suite adjoining ours. I hope this won't make you feel too accessible to us."

"On the contrary, I want you to feel free to come to me as often as you like. In the past, I've often felt lonely here. This arrangement will put an end to that."

"You realize, of course, that with expanding the business, we'll be away a lot. When one of us remains behind, you will be expected to move into our master suite so neither you nor either of us need ever be solitary," said Eric.

"We've come to respect your genuine ability in managing our affairs since father died and hope that the added responsibilities won't prove overwhelming during the periods of our absence. Apropos that, we wondered about the possibility of your acquiring a sometime boyfriend to keep you entertained while we are away. And, yes, we do have someone in mind."

"Since I haven't been able to find someone on my own, I'm surprised that you know anyone who'd be interested," answers Bruno.

"Never doubt our resourcefulness, Bruno, in achieving our objectives. In this case, our objective is to keep you deliriously happy so you won't be tempted to leave us. The young man we have in mind is the Mercedes-Benz representative who is responsible for interfacing with their outside parts suppliers like us. He calls on us twice a month, coming from their Stuttgart factory and staying at the Ring Hotel St. Georg in Regensburg. Since you're vacating the suite over the garages, we thought we'd make it available to him when he is here in our area. His name is Denis Girard."

"What leads you to believe he'd have any interest in — being with — me? I don't believe I've ever even met him," says Bruno, confused.

"Well actually you have, Bruno. Don't you remember after father died when you called a meeting in our conference room to meet with suppliers to announce father's death and to present yourself as the interim manager until I was able to return home? Denis was there and expressed his condolences to you."

"Why yes, now that you've recalled that meeting to my mind, I do remember him — very well! He was a stunning Frenchman, about 5'-8" tall, dark shaggy hair, brilliant blue eyes and a stacked body that clothes couldn't conceal. I assumed he was a happily married man."

"We do have our sources, Bruno, and I can assure you he is quite available. He was very smitten when he met you and would very much like to see you again. We have invited him to dinner Saturday night since he's, at this moment, in town for meetings. We thought that, after dinner, you could take him to see your rooms over the garage to see if he'd like to make it his home away from home." Eric says, smiling suggestively.

"He grew up in Lyon, was educated in Paris but moved to Germany because he likes to ski here and subsequently went to work for Mercedes-Benz."

Saturday night arrived and the four men sat down to a meal that Greta made.

She served her signature Schweinbraten with lots of Pilsner beer, followed up by a German chocolate cheesecake.

"Thank you Eric and Viktor for your invitation to this wonderful dinner. Being on the road so much, I rarely get to share a home cooked meal," Denis said, obviously pleased.

"We hope, in future, that you'll be able to join us often," answers Eric.

Amply fed, they all adjourned to the library for after dinner drinks before Eric suggests, "Bruno, why don't you take Denis on a tour of your rooms over the garage to see if they would suit his needs while visiting in Regensburg instead of staying at an impersonal hotel."

"Yes, Denis, please accompany me next door so that I may give you the grand tour." Getting up, Bruno and Denis go down the hall to the door connecting to a mudroom, which has a stair leading up to the suite over the garage.

Bruno has Denis proceed him up the stair so he would have an ideal view of Denis's edible buns, made hard and round from frequent skiing.

Bruno's prick starts to rise in his pants.

At the top of the stairs, they pass through a small vestibule, entering the three bedroom apartment.

The first room they encounter is a combination living room, dining area and kitchen.

The room is large with clusters of windows at either end, a beamed cathedral ceiling and a parquet wood floor.

A Persian area carpet defines the living room area, appointed with comfortable upholstered seating.

They pass down a central hall with a bedroom and bath on one side and on the other a bedroom/study.

At the end of the hall is the master bedroom.

Entering the room, the large four post antique bed is opposite.

To one side is a large dressing area surrounded with closets, off of which is the large master bath.

To the other side of the entry is a small sitting area with large windows, fitted with a window seat.

Like the living room area, the room has a beamed cathedral ceiling, a wood floor and Persian carpets.

"Why this apartment is nicer than many homes, Bruno. It's really just perfect!" Denis opines.

"We thought you'd like it," said Bruno, relieved that the apartment passed muster.

"You know, Denis, it's late and there's no need for you to drive all the way back to your hotel. Why don't you stay here overnight? It will help you to feel like this can be your own place," Bruno says, hopefully.

"Well, I really didn't bring anything to change into nor do I have any toilet articles," said Denis with regret.

"Not a problem, I have everything you'll need. It seems I always have two of everything, so please, stay," Bruno says looking intensely into Denis's eyes.

"Yes, thank you, I'd very much like to," Denis said warmly.

"Let's sit in here and have us a glass of cognac before turning in," Bruno suggests.

"Sit down and feast your eyes on the beautiful view of the Alps we have since we're fortunate enough to have a full moon tonight." Denis sat in one of the two lounge chairs facing towards the big windows.

The snowcapped mountains were bathed in moonlight and looked awesome in the distance.

Bruno returned with two snifters of cognac, handing one to Denis and sinking into the chair next to him.

Sipping their cognacs, they were quite content in each others company, savoring the moment, enjoying the moonlit landscape.

Bruno reached out to hold Denis's hand.

"I am so glad that you decided to stay. I've been looking forward to your visit all week," Bruno admits.

"There's no place I'd rather be," Denis responds, squeezing Bruno's hand.

"I — hope — you won't be — disappointed — in me."

"Have no fear of that, Denis, I've wanted to be alone with you all evening, to have you all to myself."

Getting up to stare out the window, Denis said, "I could think of nothing else all through dinner, hoping that we'd find ourselves alone together. Now that we are, I'm nervous that my — lack of experience — will put you off."

Coming up behind Denis, Bruno pushes himself against Denis, reaching around to cup his crotch and to feel up a tit through his shirt.

Denis could feel Bruno's rising dick, insinuating itself between his buns.

"Time to get you undressed, my dear, I've wanted to rip your clothes off all during dinner. I'll lay something out on the bed for you to change into while I use the bathroom. I won't be long."

Returning to the bedroom, Bruno finds Denis staring out the window above the window seat, wearing the tight black T-shirt he left out for him with the matching skin tight, cotton shorts.

Between the moonlight filtering through the window and the low lighting in the room, Denis looks like a vision against the magnificent moon-lit scene outside.

Moving towards him, Bruno begins to appreciate the way the tight black shorts are molded over the sensuous contours of Denis's sculpted butt cheeks.

Cross-country skiing has gifted Denis with killer buns, only hinted at in his dress pants.

Now, standing behind Denis wearing nothing but a tight red T-shirt, Bruno places his hands possessively on the high round mounds.

"You look like you've been sewn into these shorts. The fit is so — well — ass hugging. I really like what I'm seeing, my sweet."

"Why don't you take them off so you can see if you like what's inside." Needing no further encouragement, Bruno unsnapped the fasteners and slid the shorts down to reveal the killer buns.

Now on his knees, Bruno's heart began racing as he slapped his hands on the great globes, spreading them as he pushed his face into the deep crack to attack the pink pucker within.

Slurping like a hungry dog, he took his fill, eating out the Frenchman as if he were a starving man.

Coming up for air, Bruno sucks in breath trying to bring himself under control.

"God, Denis, you're packing a secret weapon. Men would kill to mount a butt like yours. I've got to get inside you before I collapse from wanting you."

Stepping out of his lowered shorts, Denis kicks them away, turns and sits on the window seat, revealing a raging hard-on.

"Well, lover, first you must show some attention to this," grabbing his cock and spreading his muscled legs.

"Suck on this, Bruno, get down on your knees and show my dick some respect!" Falling to his knees, Bruno first fondled the ball-sac, licking each ball before sucking the pair into his mouth where his tongue could lap the imprisoned gonads.

"Ooaahh!" moaned Denis.

When he tortured the balls enough, Bruno proceeded to lap the jumping dick, capturing the head in his mouth where it too was imprisoned and lapped, making Denis crazy with need.

"Does that feel good, Denis, because you'd better enjoy being sucked dry because soon, very soon, your ass will be mine. I intend to take you hard and deep."

"Anything, just don't stop. I can't take any more, you're torturing me." Knowing he's driven Denis to the edge, Bruno begins finishing him off, knowing that Denis will welcome a punishing fuck in return.

Bruno's face is now smashed against Denis's groin, having taken in the whole shaft, down to its root.

Slowly withdrawing while sucking, Bruno then swallows Denis's dick down his throat in a steady rhythm.

Moistening his middle finger, Bruno inserts it into Denis's tight little hole to find the joy spot.

Now machine sucking his cock while finger fucking his ass, Bruno sends Denis over the crest as he sucks one, two, and three fierce loads of cum from the conquered Frenchman.

"Oh my god, Bruno, you've — you've killed me, I can't still be alive!"

"You survived that blow-job alright, my love, but the jury is out on whether having your ass plowed will prove terminal. Ok, stretch back, resting on your forearms and lift your pretty legs so I can return to eating you succulent hole." Dropping to his knees again, Bruno pushes on the backs of Denis's knees, raising up the pillowed buns higher to expose the target of his lust.

Diving right in, Bruno launches his tongue in a darting, laving attack, opening up the tight knot.

Foreseeing this moment, Bruno had brought a condom and a tube of lubricant in from the bathroom.

Releasing Denis's legs temporarily, he rolled on the condom and squeezed lubricant from the tube onto his fingers to lubricate his captive.

Standing, Bruno grabbed one of Denis's ankles and held it aloft and with the other hand he lubricated the Frenchman's tight asshole.

Denis was as prepared as he was going to be.

Bruno seized the other ankle, lifting the bun mounds and placed his dick-head at the loosened hole.

With one sharp thrust, he slipped in just the head of his prick.

Denis flinched at the initial pain but did not protest.

Slowly, Bruno worked his boner into the love channel until he was buried to the hilt.

"Oh, oh, yes, Bruno, yes, I want it. You know I want it. Show me how much you want it. Fuuuccckkk me!"

Grasping Denis's ankles in a bruising grip and lifting the muscled globes high, Bruno begins to take possession of the softly moaning Frenchman.

Bruno's groin slapped Denis's raised ass with loud thwacks in a punishing rhythm, stuffing Denis's hole with a rioting cock.

Despite Denis's inexperience, he is a very choice piece of ass that is enslaving Bruno by tossing him an unforgettable fuck.

"Uugggrrr!!" shouts Bruno, as he expends a massive load into Denis that is only just contained in the condom.

"Oh, fuck — Denis — oh fuck! I think I'm having — a — heart attack." Sliding out of the hot hole, Bruno sets Denis's legs down and pulls him back up to a sitting position.

Cupping his face in his hands, Bruno kisses him tenderly.

"I — hope — I wasn't too rough. I just wanted you so — badly."

Wrapping his arms around Bruno, Denis said, "You know I wanted it as bad as you did, you're a tender lover. Pleasing you pleased me even more." They share a long passionate kiss.

"You must be tired, Denis, after a long day, time to get you into bed. I've laid out everything you'll need on the bathroom counter. We'll wait to shower in the morning, ok? Go ahead and use the bathroom first. Don't — be long — babe." Denis pads over to the bathroom while Bruno slips into the big four poster.

Returning from the bathroom, Denis finds Bruno in the middle of the bed, lying on his side with one leg bent forward at the knee, dressed still in the red t-shirt with his impressive buns, molded by soccer, exposed.

Denis's cock jumps to instant alert.

"Am I to suppose that you want my cock up your pretty butt, my friend? Because, want it or not, you are about to receive a well-deserved plowing." You've demonstrated your ability to own my ass, now it's only fair that I get to mount your beautiful butt. Do you want it, babe, or must I slake my lust against your will." Denis said facetiously.

"My hole is already lubed, roll on the condom I've laid out for you on the night table and then slip it to me. I want your dick up my ass now!" Doing as directed, Denis then gets into bed behind Bruno and worked his dick up and down the crack, teasing the winking pucker before making the move to enter.

Reaching around to wrap his hand around Bruno's stiff cock, Denis began to jerk him off.

"Stick it to me, lover, I need to feel your prick filling my hole." Denis slipped his slickened dick into Bruno's butt hole, pushing until his pubes crushed against the great mounds.

Denis held fast, savoring the moment of their union.

"Don't be gentle, Denis, I want it rough, plow my ass, drive your dick into me, and brand me as yours." Denis moved his butt back, pulling his cock out of Bruno's hole except for the knob at the end of his prick.

Holding steady, briefly, he then moved back in, slowly building momentum.

Denis arrived at a steady pace that began to pound Buno's hole open, rising to a brutal assault that climaxed with Denis's dick jammed in deep, pumping everything he had into Bruno, whose cock succumbed to Denis's fierce hand job.

"Aaagggrrr!!" screamed Denis, as Bruno's ass sucked him to a mind numbing climax.

"Oh, Denis, I'm never going to get my fill of your dick exploding up my ass, you've conquered me!"

The next morning, after showering and dressing, they prepared to go downstairs to join Eric and Viktor for breakfast.

"It was kind of Eric to phone here to invite us to share breakfast with them. Usually, I prepare something for myself up here," Bruno explains.

"This will be a good opportunity to tell them that you'll want to take this apartment for your home-away-from-home."

"Yes, this apartment is located perfectly so that I can stay here when I'm visiting your factory or when I'm visiting other suppliers in the area. You'll be seeing a lot of me," Denis said, smiling expectantly at Bruno.

"After seeing a lot of you last night, I can't wait for my next opportunity," Bruno whispers in Denis's ear, while holding him close and splaying his hands, possessively, over his buns.

Entering the kitchen, they find Eric and Viktor already seated at the big breakfast table, sipping their first cups of coffee.

"Ah, gentlemen, come in, join us for some of Greta's wonderful banana pancakes!" Bruno and Denis sit at the table.

"So, Denis, did the old caretaker's apartment meet with your approval?"

"It truly exceeded my expectations," Denis says, with a smirk and sidelong glance at Bruno who was blushing.

"I hope you will find me to be an acceptable tenant."

"We're more than happy that you'll be joining our household," Eric said graciously.

"After breakfast, I must subject you to the formality of signing a lease, which must be done for tax purposes. While we attend to this tedious business in my study, Viktor can explain to Bruno our plans for an upcoming trip, taking us out of the country for a few weeks or so." Finishing up breakfast, Eric gets up to take Denis to the study, leaving Bruno and Viktor at the breakfast table.

Entering the study, Eric sits behind his desk and motions Denis to a chair facing the desk.

"Seeing your bright and shining faces this morning, I couldn't help conclude that you and Bruno enjoyed each others company last night to the fullest." Eric said with a perceptible leer to his expression.

"It was kind of him to invite me to stay over, saving me driving back to my hotel last night when I had had too much to drink."

"I daresay kindness had nothing to do with it. You are a very attractive man, Denis, bedding you has obviously pleased our Bruno very much. You're going to make a nice addition around here that I think all of us can enjoy, don't you think?"

"Well — yes — I'd like to think you and Viktor could take pleasure in my — company — too. Being on the road so much makes me want the comfort of being amongst — friends — as often as possible."

"Certainly, I quite agree, Denis, we'd like to have you here often," Eric says, his meaning unmistakable.

"Why don't you come around to my side of the desk so you can read over this simple lease form?" Denis gets up to join Eric on his side of the desk.

Eric pushes his chair back to allow Denis to stand in front of him.

The lease is held in place on the desk with a large paperweight.

Resting his palms on the desk, Denis leans over to begin reading the document.

Suddenly, he feels Eric's hands on his hips and pressure on his crack from Eric's tented crotch.

"It is an old custom in my country, Denis, for the master of the house to have certain privileges with those housed under his roof. You need to be made aware of that before affixing your name to that lease." Eric says while unbuckling Eric's trousers, unzipping his fly and reaching in to pull out his cock, already rising.

"You feel very good in my hand, Denis, what other delights are you hiding in those slacks?" Denis's pants are now pooled around his ankles, as Eric slips his underwear shorts down to his knees, exposing the bubble butt, still sore from the pounding Bruno gave it this morning in the shower.

"Bend over and rest your head on your forearms, Denis, while I become acquainted with what you undoubtedly made available to Bruno." Denis was now bent over with his ass raised higher than his head.

Sitting back down in his chair and moving up to the waiting bun feast, Eric grabbed handfuls of Denis's butt cheeks and drew them apart to plunder the swollen asslips.

Despite the battering he'd taken at Bruno's hands, Denis moaned with renewed pleasure at the worship his hole was receiving.

Coming up for air, Eric said, "You are indeed a lusty little piece, Denis. You'll keep us all busy stuffing your mouth and pussy full with our stiff dicks. Think you can handle us both alone and in combination because we have great expectations for your willingness to be passed around at our pleasure."

"You'll find me quite willing, Eric, so do your worst to test me, I'm up for serving your needs without reservation. I need to be found desirable by studs like you, who know what they want and take it at will. I'll be your willing plaything. Teach me how to please you and I'll rise to the occasion."

"Well to start with, Denis, I really want to acquaint my cock with your asshole. Step out of your trousers while I slip off your undershorts. Good, now spread your legs apart so I can lube up that battered little hole." Having lubed up Denis's sore hole, Eric slips on a condom and lubricates his rock-hard prick before pushing it into the gaping hole, open for the next attack.

Eric's cock is now filling Denis's ravaged hole and Eric is enjoying the velvety smoothness of the Frenchman's pussy.

"Bruno was a lucky man last night to be the first among our household to enjoy your favors, Denis." Bending over to rest his palms next to Eric's forearms on the desk surface, Eric now was positioned on his toes, enabling him to swing himself forwards and backwards so as to slam against Eric's ass, pressing his groin and thighs into the bent over body.

Denis thought he'd never been penetrated so deeply, enjoying the exquisite pain.

Eric kept up the bruising battering of Denis's upturned butt cheeks, while working Denis's engorged prick.

Whispering into Denis's ear, Eric said: "Are you going to spread your legs anytime we want some? Are you going to get down on your knees and service your masters, slut?"

"Yes to anything you want, just keep on fucking me. Your dick feels so good inside of me; I never loved it so much, taking it so hard!"

With renewed vigor, Eric slammed and pounded into the sex-starved slave, turning his muscled cheeks deep pink.

Roaring with ecstasy, Eric released gobs of molten cum into his newest butt boy.

In turn, Denis sent streams of cum all over the lease papers spread out on the desk.

"Shit, Denis, your tight little hole will be seeing a lot of action around here. I hope you can manage with this horny household."

"Between Bruno and me, we should be able to please you and Viktor. I couldn't help noticing that Viktor has quite a package between his legs. I only hope it's not bigger than I can handle."

"If I could learn to take it, so can you. Trust me, once you get used to it, you'll love it as much as I do. You've shown yourself to possess plenty of natural aptitude. Don't worry about the soiled lease. We won't need you to sign it anyway, since no money will be changing hands. You will earn your keep, have no fear of that, my hungry little slut. Now get up, we've been absent for long enough from our friends waiting in the kitchen."

Rejoining Viktor and Bruno in the kitchen, Eric said, "How do you feel about our plans to leave the country so soon, Bruno? Do you think you can handle things while we're away?"

"Since your father died, I've been doing it anyway during all that time, so it should be no problem. I know things are going to become more complicated what with your expanding the business, but I expect to grow with the company, as we've discussed."

"Good, then we'll solidify our plans to make the trip. We'll be going to Washington, DC first to visit an American friend we met in Moscow when serving our respective governments. We expect him to help us to develop a security plan for our new plant in North Carolina and we have a gentlemen's agreement with Denis here who will soon be a frequent visitor to our household." Eric says smiling pointedly at Denis and Bruno.

Chapter 5

When Eric and Viktor were on Autobahn 3 on their way to Regensburg, Germany, Cliff had completed his meeting at the Pentagon and was returning home to Bethesda, MD to his condo apartment.

Home at last and ready to chill, he is about to phone Brad whom he has been anxious to see, thinking about him constantly on the flight back from Russia.

Suddenly the phone rings which he answers, hoping it's Brad.

"Hi, lover, long time no see, where have you been? A girl gets lonely you know! I've missed you. I've — I've missed you a lot."

"Hey, Laurie, how have you been? I just got back from a long — trip — and am kind of wasted. Just about to grab a bite, shower and fall into bed."

"Well, Cliff, you don't have to climb into bed solo, you know. You used to like my backrubs and you know, a little roll in the hay. How about it, want some company?!"

"Gee, Laurie, you caught me kind of flat footed but I — well — I — there's someone else," Cliff blurts out.

"You sure didn't waste any time before moving on. I thought we had something good going!"

"Yes — well — but you know — things change. I'm sorry Laurie, I really am but it's for the best. My work would always have come between us. You need someone who's around more that — you can rely on. That's just not me."

"With not seeing each other for so many months, I just thought you'd miss me, Cliff, but a girl can take a hint. If — you — change your mind, give me a call." They ring off.

"Hell, I really needed that," Cliff mutters.

"Laurie Taylor calls but where the fuck is Brad fucking Ames. I'm starving here. Fucking asshole!" Unable to reach Brad, he resorts to leaving a message on his answering machine before giving in to exhaustion and going to bed.

He sleeps late, having enjoyed a much needed good night's sleep, and around 10:00 AM, Myra, Jason Stone's secretary, calls to set up an appointment for him to see her boss.

He confirms that he'll be there at 3:30 PM that afternoon.

It seems Jason was anxious to discuss with Cliff how to contain information about his mission from becoming conversational fodder for beltway insiders.

Still no call back from Brad.

He decides to go into the office early to have lunch at the cafeteria with enough time to stop by to see his pal Debbie Berger and catch up on what was happening while he was away.

Poking his head into her office after lunch he said, "So, gorgeous, did ya miss me or is it out of sight out of mind!"

"Right back at you, stud. Oh Cliff you look great, I was so worried! Get over here and give me a hug!"

Hugging her he said, "Missed ya, babe, how're the kids and Marc?"

Pulling away, frowning, she answers, "They're ok. Marc's having a bit of — a case of cabin fever, but we're working on it. Sit down and tell me how you're doing. I'm so glad you're back home. I need a kindred spirit to talk to around this spy nest to keep me sane. Sit down and spill!"

Cliff gives her a much abbreviated version of the report he gave at the Pentagon, leaving out the juicier details but giving her the gist of what transpired.

She was aware from their earlier chat before he left that he was moving into some uncharted waters.

She was also aware that the training that Brad had put him through had taken an unexpected turn.

"Been trying to reach Brad but I've been unable to get through. He knew I was coming home. I thought I'd hear from him right away," Cliff says plaintively.

"What's that expression I'm reading on your face, Debbie? What gives?"

"Ah — , Cliff, we've been good friends for a long time so — I hate to have to be the one to tell you this — but — Brad has been — well — back with Tommy Brandon."

"Whaaat! That bastard, that motherfucker. Here I am risking my life and doing god knows what all — to have that — faithless prick — cheat on me!!! God damn! I'm going to kill the bastard — I swear!"

"Calm down, Cliff, you really don't know what's really happening yet. You need to speak to Brad to straighten things out and not jump to what very well could be erroneous conclusions."

"Erroneous conclusions, my ass, oh to think I fell for him when all he wanted — " Cliff is distraught with his elbows on her desk and his hands laced through his hair.

"God, I'm sorry, Cliff, perhaps I should've kept my mouth shut but I was afraid of your being blindsided and caught unprepared."

"No, you did the right thing — I'd expect you, as my friend, to want to protect me. I'm just surprised at how much — it hurts. Well, I'd better get my act together, I have to go in to see the boss at 3:30."

"And I had to lay this on you now. Good going Debbie, your timing is impeccable. You know, Cliff, if it's any consolation — I wasn't going to admit this to you — but I'm — I'm having marital problems myself. Things are not ok at home. They're for shit!" Debbie said, her voice catching.

"Oh, honey, I'm so sorry. Here I am carrying on when you're going through something like that. What the hell is going on! He's not treating you badly is he? I'll punch his lights out if he ever hurts you!"

"It's — another — woman and would you believe, my very best friend outside of the office. His domestic routine has become — tedious — and he needed a change. So, voila, my friend Milly slips in to fill the void. That bitch! They met through carpooling the kids to school and well — one thing led — you know the drill."

"Yeah, that sucks, so what are you going to do, short of decking the bitch."

"We've agreed to try therapy and we've had a couple of sessions. It's already clear to me that I wasn't paying attention to what he was experiencing at home, focusing exclusively on my demanding job. So, we need to get creative if all isn't to be lost."

"So what are you going to do? You're not quitting are you! What would I do without you around this crazy place?"

"Actually, I'm going to take a sabbatical for the entire summer. This way I'll run the house and look after the kids while he writes a book that he's been planning. It's not definite but I think he'll move out of the house for the duration, visiting on weekends. We still have — feelings — for each other. It remains to be seen how this will play out. His affair with Milly is over, they both had something to prove but — whatever — it's over. I've forgiven them both for I know I was not blameless in them seeking solace in each other since they weren't getting what they needed from their respective partners. Sorry to burden you with all that, Cliff, but I wanted you to understand that there are some bumps in a relationship so don't give up on Brad before you talk it through with him. You owe yourselves that."

"Thanks, Debbie, you're the best, thinking of me when you've got all this on your mind. I'm going to follow your advice. I know in my heart that you're right. Oh! It's 3:25, time for me to face the music. Jason awaits! So long, babe, talk to you — " Cliff leaves to go by Myra's desk to check in for his appointment.

She has him wait in their seating area while she informs Jason that Cliff has arrived.

Sitting in the waiting area, Cliff reflects on the first meeting he had with Jason Stone which set in motion the series of events that has brought him to this place.

He starts seething with all the suppressed anger he has felt about the way Jason was so callous in using his "assets" without any regard for the sacrifices he expected them to make and for what — his career advancement! It was always only about his career advancement.

Well, he got some of his own back on the plane coming home but maybe it was time for another installment in Jason's continuing education.

"He'll see you now," Myra sing-songs from her desk.

She gets up to open the door to Jason's office to let Cliff in.

Just as the door opens, Cliff can see Jason get up from his desk to come over to the door to greet him.

"Hey, Cliff, come on in!" he says shaking Cliff's hand.

"Good to see you getting back to normal," he says with a bright if not authentic smile.

"Hold all my calls, Myra, I don't want to be disturbed for the rest of the afternoon," Jason said, closing and locking the door.

"Sorry to ask you to come in so soon, Cliff, but I felt compelled to do some damage control before too much information about your mission becomes known," Jason said, heading back to his desk with Cliff following closely behind.

Before Jason could sit back down in his chair, Cliff swung him around, pushing him against the desk.

"As far as I'm concerned, Jason, the damage has already been done. As I explained to you on the plane, you're responsible for turning one of your best field operatives into a virtual whore. Since there wasn't time on the plane to fully debrief you on the specifics of your assignment, I thought we'd make up for that lack now." Cliff slips off Jason's suspenders from each shoulder over his white oxford, button down shirt, decorated with a red bow tie.

"Cliff, please, control yourself. I'm willing to forget what happened on the plane but — Cliff!" Cliff allows Jason's trousers to fall to the floor, pooling around his wing-tipped shoes and black socks, held firmly in place by his signature garters.

Now the white boxer shorts are yanked down to Jason's knees exposing his boner, which had a mind of its own.

"You loved having your cock sucked on the plane, Jason. You even liked my fingers stuffed up your ass, so cut the bull-shit. You are a sex addict who'll let anyone swing on his dick. Face it, you are a slut!"

Jason is now perched on the edge of his desk with his arms flung out behind him and his hands flat on the desk to keep himself from falling on his back.

"Noooo — ," Jason begins to respond.

But Cliff already has Jason's cock in his mouth slurping the piss-slit and wrapping his lips around the head.

Jason is already toast.

Cliff works his lips down the length of the shaft laving the underside of Jason's stiff prick.

Wanting to make quick work of this phase of Jason's continuing education, Cliff suctions the cock in and out of his mouth, forcing the head against the back of his throat until Jason's prick unleashes ropes of sperm which Cliff swallows to the last drop.

"Ooohhh!" Jason moans.

"You're killing me!"

"No, Jason, that was a reminder of how easy you are, as was evident on the plane. But now, on to broadening your perspective on how a man can be had so he'll forever be in your pocket. It's now a tool of our trade, Jason, which you, of all people, will need to understand so you can exploit it fully which is, after all, what you do."

Cliff pushes Jason onto his desk, flat on his back, which, in turn, raises his legs up, dangling them over the edge of the desk.

Lifting Jason's legs up, Cliff pushes his thighs towards his chest saying: "Grab your legs behind your knees and pull them towards you!" Cliff demands.

"Do it, Jason, or I'll truss you up and leave you naked on the desk for the maintenance people to find. It'll make a nice photo spread in the Washington Post. I'll take the pictures myself!" Jason reluctantly complies.

Using a small tube of lube, which he now always carries with him, Cliff lubes Jason's ass with a probing finger.

Jason's ass has benefited from all the tennis he plays, forming two muscular globes that any top would gladly service.

Jason, ever susceptible, to any form of sensuality, is unable to conceal his obvious pleasure in having his hole toyed with.

In short order, Cliff has three fingers inserted into the now compliant hole.

When his middle finger finally discovers the prostate gland, Jason begins to squirm, loving being finger fucked.

His cock is jumping, slapping against his belly.

Now, grasping Jason's hips, Cliff slides his body over to the edge of the desk so his comely ass cheeks are suspended in the air to maximize their accessibility for plunder.

"You must drive some of your tennis partner's wild in your tight tennis shorts, Jason. Now you'll learn how to accommodate them."

"Cliff, please, I have never ever let anyone — . My coach at Harvard was always after me but I never would let him — ," said Jason panicked.

"You know, Jason, thanks to you, a few men have lost their cherries. Brad had my cherry, in turn I had Viktor Sidorov's cherry and now it seems only fair that you lose your cherry at the hands of the very operative that you sent out to become a male prostitute." Cliff gently slips the head of his cock into the virgin fuck hole, being gentle because he wanted Jason to experience a long, slow fuck that he would carry in his memory forever.

Jason's channel was tight but not unwelcoming.

The velvety smooth walls took Cliff's big cock in to swallow it to the hilt.

Jason, known to be an insatiable pussy hound, seemed to be getting into being just a hole rather than a dominant male.

He knew he was being taken as he had taken so many women, not knowing the pleasure to be had from being on the bottom.

With his dick firmly implanted in the mewling Jason, Cliff bent over on top of him to take command of his mouth, sucking his tongue into his mouth as he had his prick.

All these new sensations were making Jason tremble with lust and longing.

He wanted it now, he wanted Cliff to tear him a new asshole.

Sensing Jason's heightened responses, Cliff pushed himself up on his hands and toes so he could start to seriously bang Jason's pussy.

Plunging in rapidly and hard three or four times, Cliff would let up only to slowly slide in and out of the channel in agonizingly slow thrusts before three or four more hard thrusts to drive Jason higher and higher to a fever pitch of craving.

"Ooohhh — oooo — aaahhh!" Jason moans.

"That feels so incredibly — good — oh Cliff — yes — fuck me — please! Bang me hard, don't stop! Yes — yes — yes like that," Jason said as Cliff power fucks his ass like a jackhammer out of control.

"Eeeooowww!!!" Screams Jason as Cliff's groin is crushed against the suspended ass cheeks to blast an ass splitting load of cum into the conquered asshole.

Jason's cock could not hold back another orgasm, splattering all over his pristine white oxford shirt.

Cliff pulls out of Jason's upturned ass and helps him up to a sitting position.

"Well, Jason, join the club, now your bi-sexual credentials will insure that you'll never have to sleep alone again. And, by the way, you are a hell of a piece of ass. I ought to know, given the experience in the field that you've afforded me," Cliff says with a wicked smile.

"After what happened between us on the plane, I tried to put it out of my mind that I — actually — liked what you did — to me. Now this. I just don't know what to think. You accused me of being a pussy hound which I — have — been guilty of. I guess I've been seeking something which seems always to allude me, trying again and again only to come up dry. What mystifies me is why I wanted you — inside me — so — so much. How can it be!"

"Maybe it's not so complicated, Jason. You are what you are, a very sexual person who, as it happens, has very catholic tastes when it comes to partners. Put simply, you are a bit of a slut. Maybe that describes me too since I've swung both ways. But I'm now situated firmly in the other camp. As for you, who knows, you may just find that passing yourself around is what suits you best."

"You can help me figure this out, Cliff. I want — I want you to come to me here several afternoons a week — until — I can — figure this out. Are you — are you willing — to — help me out here? I can't require you to do this — if you — really don't want to but — well — you owe me — you took my cherry, after all."

"Sure, Jason, but I need you to cut me some slack. What I mean is, I'm going to need some time off to straighten out my personal life which is not in good shape right now."

"That's not going to be a problem, Cliff, I was going to suggest you take some time anyway. You obviously need it after the ordeal you've been through. I am sorry for my part in it. I should have realized that I was asking too much of you, relying on your patriotism to have my way. Clearly, I could have tried harder to come up with a plan to deal with the illegal arms sales without exploiting one of my best operatives. For that I am truly sorry."

"Well ok, Jason, I didn't expect you to admit that to me but I appreciate your saying it. I too am sorry if I was too rough with you — I was just so damn mad!"

"Maybe we can both admit that we took some enjoyment in what's happened between us. I'm not ashamed to say that I did. Well, enough, please go home so you can get some more rest before I see you again on the day after tomorrow at 3:30. My asshole should be recovered by then but I'm sure we can figure out an alternative if I'm so impaired. Good night," Jason said, hugging Cliff close from behind as he turns to leave.

On the way out of the office, Cliff thinks everyone has gone home but passing Debbie's office, she calls out to him: "Oh, Cliff, please come in. I have Brad on the phone." Holding her hand over the receiver, she explains, "He called here to track you down but you weren't available. Since I had him on the line, I felt compelled to admit that I told you about Tommy Brandon being back on the scene." She hands him the phone and leaves the office.

Pausing, Cliff considers hanging up the phone but instead says a curt, "Hello!"

"Cliff I'm sorry I wasn't here to greet you when you got home, I had an emergency with my security business that required me to be out of town on an all-nighter. I only just got back. I was so anxious to see you and worried about how you had come through that lousy assignment."

"Not so concerned that you couldn't warm your bed with Tommy, fucking, Brandon. How did you suppose I'd feel when I found that out!"

"Please, Cliff, I was so stupid. Tommy's wife threw him out again and he just needed a temporary place to stay. I felt I couldn't refuse him, never thinking we'd be — sleeping together again. But I was so furious about your insisting on going on that crazy fucking mission that I — well — I did it — out of anger and spite. I felt that you were willing to toss away what we had to be a hero when we could have stopped them from sending you. There's nothing between Tommy and me except — sex. It's you I love."

"You've — you've hurt me, Brad — very badly. I just don't know — . I need time to — get — past this. I'm really tired and bummed out, I'm going home now. I'll — I'll try to call you — tomorrow." Cliff hangs up and leaves the office to find Debbie waiting down the hall.

"You didn't have to hang around, Debbie."

"What's happened, Cliff, what are you and Brad going to do!" Debbie asks, concerned.

"Well, I really don't know. He said it was only sex with Tommy and that he loves me — sound familiar?"

"Yeah, that's what Marc said to me, the bastard, but I'm over it now and you will be too. Don't give up a good thing over a meaningless indiscretion. I didn't and I don't think you will either."

"Maybe, Debbie, but the hurt is still so — raw — that I just don't know how I'm going to feel — ."

"Go home, sleep on it. You're exhausted and incapable of seeing the situation clearly. Things will look differently tomorrow," Debbie said, wisely.

"Thanks, Debbie, you're a true friend." He hugs her and leaves.

Driving home to Bethesda, Cliff realizes he misses Brad terribly and is sorry he blew him off.

He's tempted to call him back but feels he handled Brad's call badly and didn't want to risk making things any worse.

He parks in the garage under his building and takes the elevator up to the third floor to his apartment.

He never felt lonelier and more desolate in his life.

Opening his front door and closing it behind him while switching on the living room lights, he collides with something.

It's a 6'-3" SEAL instructor! Brad grabs him around the waist, drawing their bodies together while he rains kisses over Cliff's cheeks, eyes, nose and finally his mouth, brooking no argument with the intense assault he mounts with his tongue.

Cliff succumbs instantly, offering no resistance whatsoever.

They hungrily undress each other and wind up nude on the living room carpet in a 69 position.

Cliff is on the bottom with Brad straddling him gorging on his stiff dick, while Cliff is eating Brad's ass out like the starving man he is.

Not wanting Cliff to come too quickly, Brad stops feeding on Cliff's prick to grab his legs behind the knees to lift his beautiful ass up in the air so he can start sucking out his hole.

Tommy's ass was just an appetizer, this is the full course meal.

Brad came prepared with lube and pulling his tongue out of Cliff's ass, he replaced it with three busy fingers.

Cliff's hole wasn't the tight little knot it was when he left for Moscow.

Brad had undeniable evidence of what he knew to be true.

Cliff's pussy had seen plenty of action.

Well it's time for the home team.

Brad pulls Cliff up so his knees now flank his ears and his ass cheeks face the ceiling.

Without any hesitation, Brad plunged his big 10" cock into the upturned hole, ramming deep into the slickened shaft.

"Oooaaahh!" Cliff exclaimed in obvious pleasure.

Brad was fairly certain that Cliff hadn't enjoyed having his ass plowed in this position with any of his various bed-mates across the pond.

He wanted Cliff to remember his homecoming fuck.

Squatting over Cliff's airborne butt, Brad began dropping down hard on Cliff's hole and pulling out slowly to repeat the process, steadily varying the tempo, ravishing Cliff's pussy.

Pleasing our Russian friends had obviously schooled Cliff into knowing just how to treat an invading cock, using his interior ass muscles to caress the probing dick.

Both Cliff and Brad were driven higher and higher to a place of overwhelming ecstasy.

Brad was the first to blow his cork, pile driving Cliff's bung hole until he exploded like a burst of fireworks.

Almost simultaneously, Cliff shot his wad covering his chest with pools of cum.

Reluctant to pull free from Cliff's imprisoning hole, Brad lifted off his lover, allowing Cliff's butt to drop to the carpet.

"Knowing where I've been and what I had to do, I suppose you feel free to treat me like your own whore!" Cliff said dejectedly.

"You know better than that, Cliff, I love you and missed you so much I just couldn't let you push me away without a fight. I'll do anything to make it up to you. I'll be your whore if that's what you want. Treat me like a sex slave. I don't care as long as we're together," Brad says, earnestly.

"Hmmm, that has real possibilities, yes I'd say so, real possibilities," Cliff said, suggestively.

"You fuck, Cliff, putting me on and making me grovel when you already wanted me back. You shit!" he said, wrestling with Cliff and pressing an intense kiss against his smiling mouth.

"It's not like you didn't have it coming, Brad, you faithless dirt ball," Cliff said with mock ire.

"Well I only had Tommy, you were obviously a busy boy when you were entertaining our Russian friends."

"Like I had a choice, I did my duty was all. But you're right, it wasn't all bad."

"Who's the shit now, Cliff? Here I am pining away at home for you, worried every day for your safety, while you're over there enjoying pedaling you ass to the Russians!"

"You taught me how to fake it so I'd be convincing, take some of the responsibility!"

"Don't imagine that you'll ever be able to convince me that you didn't like your butt plugged or having my cock stuffed down your throat or liking to do the same to me."

"No argument, love, you made me yours. You know, Brad we should make a vow to each other right now that despite any extracurricular fooling around that we each may do in the future, that we'll remain the same with each other. No more foolish jealousies that have the potential of driving a wedge between us. We're a committed couple now."

"Those are words I longed for you to say. Yes, we are a couple from now on." Brad says, embracing and kissing Cliff.

"You've knocked me out, babe, time to hit the sack. We have a lot to talk about still but it'll have to wait until tomorrow when I'm sufficiently rehabilitated," Cliff says, getting up and taking Brad by the hand, leading him to the bedroom.

Sitting down at the kitchen table the next morning, they sip coffee and start to talk about their future plans.

"You know, Cliff, you could lease out your condo for now and move into the townhouse with me."

"Oh, I really didn't — think about — the next step, Brad. Maybe it's too soon — .'"

"No it's not, Cliff!! I want us to go to our bed every night and to wake up in our bed in the morning — together. We're a couple now. It's right!"

"Yes, Brad, you're right. I want that too! Jason, and by the way he's another subject for us to discuss, is willing to give me some time off. I'd like to spend the time up at the cabin, maybe the whole summer."

"Strangely enough, that dovetails with some other ideas I had percolating in my head which I wasn't going to discuss with you until you had a chance to return to normal. My business has been taking off and it will be necessary for me to devote myself to it full time, remaining just a consultant to Homeland Security. The business has developed to the point that I can't manage it alone anymore. I will need a partner who can give me some part-time help at first. I thought that person could be you, Cliff, assuming you're willing to negotiate a different arrangement with Homeland Security. By that I mean, working part-time for them, more in a consulting capacity and part-time for us in our private security consulting business."

"It's true that I am weary of being sent to so many trouble spots around the world, risking my life time and again. My job is really for younger men who are fearless enough to ignore all the risks."

"A lot of work can be done on computers in our home office, even out of the cabin when we want to be up there for extended periods of time. However, we do need to keep a strong presence in Washington, requiring us to have a manager in an office we'd keep there, supported by a small staff. I did have someone in mind to fill that spot — if you would be — agreeable."

"Who is it, Brad — no — don't tell me — let me guess — Tommy Brandon. Am I right?!"

"He's really the right guy for the job. Like you, he's worn down from the rigors of being a Navy pilot, flying ever more complicated planes and wants out. He's personable, sharp, and willing to learn. He'd be an asset for us to have keeping the DC office humming when we're on the road or working in our home office. He wouldn't mind being a sandwich between us either. I asked him."

"What a piece of work you are, Brad. There are laws, you know, about sexual harassment of one's employees. You want to get us sued?!"

"We're the ones who would likely be harassed given Tommy's cravings to have his ass filled with SEAL cock. Believe me, once you've had a piece, you'll want more. He loves his wife and they're staying together despite their lousy sex life. So, he likes a no strings relationship outside his marriage and right now, that's us."

"Brad, I really need a change now. As I said earlier, I plan to take the summer off from doing my Homeland Security job. How could this work with your plans for expanding the private security business."

"Cliff, this could be an ideal opportunity for me to put in place the plans I outlined for you. We could spend the summer together in the cabin where I could show you the ropes and bring you up to speed quickly. At the same time I could install Tommy into an office that would be our DC presence, allowing us to be out of the office as much as we like. Tommy could spend several nights a week at the townhouse, providing him with lodging close to the new office and us with a lodger who can look after things for us."

"Sounds like a plan, Brad, I like it. I'll have to convince Jason that this new arrangement, concerning my continued employment, would be beneficial to him. He's bound to realize that I am ideally suited to give his agents a heads-up about what to expect in the field. He won't be blind to the fact that my help will likely assist his operatives and therefore reflect well on him. Brad, I need to explain something about my relationship with Jason." He explains what happened on the plane and the subsequent incident in Jason's office.

"Wow, Cliff, who would have imagined that stuffed shirt being such a sex addict. Since we've made a commitment to each other, this liaison you're having with Jason will be a good test of our resolve not to let outside — dalliances — undermine what we have together. So, do what you must. I'm cool with it."

"I'm going into the office tomorrow for my next session with Jason. Afterwards, I'll run the subject by him of my wish to stay on under different circumstances. By the way, Brad, it occurred to me that since Debbie Berger is going to be taking a sabbatical, allowing her to remain home for the summer, she might be up for some consulting work. She's very knowledgeable about cyber security and could help us develop that facet of the business."

"Great idea, talk to her about it tomorrow. I'll speak to Tommy today to see if he's serious about joining us. We're going to have to make the offer sufficient, such that he'll be able to support himself and the wife. With so much new business coming in, that shouldn't be a problem. Growing so fast is the real problem but with our new team, I think we'll be up to it."

The next day, Cliff goes into the office early again so he'd have some time with Debbie before going in to see Jason again.

"Hey, Debbie, it's me again, got a few minutes to spare, I've a proposition to run by you."

"It's been years since I've had a proposition so sure, shoot — as it were."

"Sorry to disappoint you, love, but this is strictly business," Cliff said, grinning.

"Drat and I thought things we're looking up for an old married lady."

"This is better, believe me. While you're on sabbatical this summer, could you spare some time to be a security consultant in Brad's business?"

"Hell, yeah, I could. Money is tight in our household with my husband's income being so sporadic and unreliable. There is the mortgage, etc., etc."

Cliff explains the plans that he and Brad have for moving in together, eliminating the need for Cliff's condo apartment and living in the country cabin for the summer.

Also, he relates how Tommy will, most likely, come into the business running the DC office.

"You know, Cliff, I have an idea that might be mutually beneficial. Do you think it would be possible to work out a barter arrangement where I could do consulting work for you in exchange for letting my husband Marc live in your townhouse for the summer."

"That sounds like something that would be agreeable to Brad but there's one possible hitch. He'd have to share the townhouse with Tommy who'd be using it maybe three nights a week. Marc would have it all to himself otherwise."

"The townhouse does have three bedrooms so I don't see that there'd be a problem. Tommy would only be there at night on his three days, leaving Marc free to work on his book during the day," Debbie points out.

"Let me run this by Brad but I'd better get going, time to see Jason. Will call you tomorrow. Bye."

"Arriving at Myra's desk, she said, "Good afternoon, Cliff, Jason said to go right in, he's expecting you. I'm leaving for the day, good night," she sing-songs.

"Good night, Myra, see you again the day after tomorrow."

Knocking on Jason's door, he goes right on in, closing and locking the door behind him.

"Afternoon, boss, don't get up, I'll come over to you." Cliff proceeds to go behind Jason's desk where he turns Jason's swivel chair to face him.

"Uh, good afternoon, Cliff, what are you — ?"

"Relax, boss, this won't be a talking session, at least not for now." Cliff unzips his fly and pulls out his stiffening cock.

"You need to know your way around one of these. Once you get your mouth around this big sucker, you'll be able to handle most anything."

Jason stares at Cliff's big dick, now sticking out proudly from his opened fly.

He looks stricken.

"What am I supposed to do with that!?"

"Come on, Jason, don't be up tight, remember the servicing I gave you on the plane. It felt good didn't it? Well sucking on it is good too." Cliff presses the big cock-head to Jason's lips, which instinctively open to accept the big head.

Quickly getting into the spirit of the thing, Jason lavs and sucks and tongues the big tool, looking up to see the effect on Cliff's face.

Jason is enjoying the power to turn this big SEAL stud on, enjoying the intimacy with Cliff's most private member.

Jason reaches inside to extract Cliff's balls from his pants so he can feast on both the meat and the potatoes of a prime stud.

"Jason, are you sure you haven't done this before because you mouth is doing a superior job for a mere novice."

"You taste good, Cliff, I like your prick and I want to stuff all of it in my mouth if it will fit." Gagging with the effort, Jason continues until he's sucking cock like a pro.

Cliff is rising up to the brink.

"J — Jason, I'm going to come in your mouth. Swallow the whole load down after I jam my dick to the back of your throat. Keep your lips tight on my prick so you won't lose any of that tasty spunk. Jaaasssooonnn," screams Cliff as he grasps the back of Jason's perfectly groomed head to slam his cock fully into the welcoming mouth to unload a choking stream of cum in three great spurts.

Jason doesn't disappoint, swallowing Cliff's cock and tonguing the underside to coax out the last drop of cum juice.

There can be no doubt, Jason is going to be a prime cocksucker.

"Oh, Jason, you were — fantastic!!!"

Recovered and now sitting at the desk opposite each other, Jason said, "When you arrived this afternoon, you seemed to allude to something else you had on your mind. What is it?" Jason asks.

"It's about me taking time off. I'd really like to take the whole summer off to regroup and see where things stand. In fact, I have an idea I'd like to float by you which would be a change in my status around here. You see, Jason I think my time for being effective in field operations has come to an end. It's a job for younger men who don't know enough about the danger in our craft to be afraid which would reduce their effectiveness. But I could still be used to advantage, I think, as a consultant, training the new crop of agents."

"You've been very effective acting as my personal consultant, Cliff, and I'm not anxious to give you up so soon when we've only just begun to tap the possibilities. You've become indispensable to me."

"Well, I have an idea about that, boss. There's no need for you to go without now that you have a new area of interest to explore. As you know, I like to work out down in our basement exercise facility here. Clarence Sharkey is my personal trainer and being an ex-army drill sergeant, he's a tough son of a bitch with whom I have a personal relationship. So he'll get the best out of you. I plan on speaking to him about setting up a routine for you to follow which would finish up with a special after-hours — 'massage'," Cliff said, staring at Jason to assess his reaction.

"With your permission, I plan on approaching him with this idea."

"Umm, I do recall that we have someone heading up our exercise facility. I've meant to go down there to check it out. Is he that 6'-1" tall, black man that looks like a cover model for Men's Health magazine?"

"The very same guy, Jason. His wife runs our cafeteria and spends too much time sampling the menu. She's blown up to about 200 lbs., killing any possibility of hanky-panky at home so the guy is pretty frustrated. We don't have any secrets from one and another so he told me about the young sailors who come in to use his facility who will occasionally drop their pants and bend over for him, 'The Shark', as he's called, but he's not getting much. You could change all that and trim up a bit at the same time. A two fer!"

"What makes you think he'd want a 46 year old white guy who has a reputation as a skirt chaser?"

"The Shark and I like to shoot the shit after he puts me through my work-out. He's mentioned, more than once, that he'd like to put a smile on the boss's face. He's caught sight of you leaving the office in your tennis shorts and was literally licking his lips. He wants you."

"Umm, Cliff, interesting. Look, talk to Clarence and let me know. Maybe then I can see my way clear to work out this new arrangement with you, going forward and allow you your summer off." Cliff departs.

Cliff goes by Brad's townhouse where he's virtually moved in.

After explaining the barter arrangement that Debbie proposed, Brad quickly agrees that it's a great idea and will save the business the expense of paying Debbie for her services, at least initially.

"Jason seems prepared to give me the summer off if I can get Clarence Sharkey to take him on as a — 'personal trainer' — two or three afternoons per week with a — deep — massage — session after hours. A couple of times after my workouts with Clarence, we were kind of letting our hair down, acknowledging that we each had a — taste — for guys, as well as women. He let it drop that Jason turned him on. Go figure when it comes to individual taste. I'm pretty sure Clarence will go for this. I'll go by to see him tomorrow so I'll have an answer for Jason the following day."

"Great Cliff and I made our offer to Tommy. He was really excited about the prospect and was anxious to tell his wife, Mary. He has no problem sharing our townhouse with Marc Berger this summer. In fact, he thought he might be able to work out an arrangement with Marc concerning the cooking and cleaning duties. Tommy likes to do the maintenance chores and we know Marc is a good cook. So bingo!"

The afternoon arrives for Cliff's scheduled afternoon appointment with Jason Stone.

"So, Myra, is the boss letting you go home early again today?"

"Indeed he is. It's my husband's birthday and I need to do some shopping so I'm just leaving. Go on in, he's anxious to see you. Good night!" Myra hurries off.

Briefly knocking, Cliff goes on into Jason's office, closing and locking the door.

"Don't get up, boss, I'll come to you," Cliff says, moving quickly towards Jason.

"So are you up for your next demonstration of your key operative's experience with our friends in Moscow? Your education is almost complete!" Spinning Jason's executive swivel chair around, he pushes it against the desk, startling Jason into paying rapt attention.

Leaning over his boss while resting his hands on the arms of the chair, Cliff kisses Jason and explores his mouth with his tongue.

Jason's pants are immediately tented around his crotch.

"Man, Jason, you're always raring to go." Unbuckling Jason's belt and unzipping his trousers, Cliff yanks them down along with the white boxer shorts.

Moving to his knees, Cliff slips off the wingtip shoes and tosses Jason's trousers and boxers aside.

Pushing Jason's knees far apart, Cliff starts making love to Jason's raging rod and fondling his nuts.

Jason's already moving to a peak.

"Relax, buddy, you're in for a special treat!"

Standing up, Cliff proceeds to strip off everything but his black T-shirt.

Jason's google eyed at the strip show.

Having come prepared, Cliff slips a condom over Jason's stiff dick and uses the tube of lube he brought to lubricate his asshole, finishing by lubing Jason's sheathed dick.

Turning around so his back is to Jason, he says: "Take a good look at a choice piece of SEAL buns, if I do say so myself, for you're about to get a sample."

Cliff reaches back to position his hands on the arms of the chair so as to be able to lower his butt cheeks down to the towering prick.

"Ok, Jason, take hold of your dick and aim it at my asshole because you are about to go for a ride, babe." Jason's dick presses against Cliff's hole which has enough mileage on it that it instantly opens, accommodating easy entry.

Cliff's newly acquired talent is apparent as he effortlessly drops his can down to be solidly planted on Jason's groin.

"Oh my god, Cliff, oh my god, that is just — so — so — fantastic! You feel so fucking good, shit!"

"It's only going to get better, hold on, boss, because you are going to be taken to the moon." Cliff moves his love mounds up and then down, up and then down, in a slow cadence.

"Grab hold of those ass cheeks, Jason, and adjust the tempo to suit your taste." Jason clamps his hands on to Cliff's bun feast in a bruising grip.

"Ohhhooohhh!!! Cliff, Cliff, your pussy — is the best — I ever — haddd! It's too, too fucking great. Ah, ah, ooo!!!"

"Plow that pussy, boss man, take your fill. Your dick feels good plowing my hole. Yeah, yeah, stick it to me!"

Jason's back keeps arching as he jams his prick into Cliff's descending ass to skewer the silken shaftway, driving in his cock to the hilt.

"Cliff, Cliff, oh, oh, I'm going to come," as with one last pounding thrust, he plows Cliff's butt hole which is sucking in his exploding prick.

"Aaagggrrr!!!" Jason screams in convulsions of lust.

Jason's body stops spasming and he sucks in breath trying to clear his head.

He knows he's just experienced a life altering event.

Hoisting himself up and off Jason's still rock-hard dick, Cliff gets dressed, observing his wasted boss with some amusement.

"I'd say you really know what it means to be pussy whipped, Jason. So what do you say? Do you like taking it up the ass or plowing ass or both? Or is it too soon to tell?"

Catching his breath, Jason said, "When you fucked me on my desk — there was nothing to compare with that — but this came close. Given a choice, I'd prefer to be on my back with a big dick banging my ass. Servicing women for so many years has given me a taste for being on the receiving end. It feels good to be desired by a man who wants to enter me and enjoy getting his rocks off, screwing my ass."

"Well, now that you mention that, boss, I think you'll be pleased to know that Clarence, 'The Shark', is anxious for you to take up with him. He'll put you through some mild toning exercises before giving you an after-hours, 'deep massage' treatment very much like the one I gave you when you were on your back on top of this desk with your pretty legs in the air. Do we have a deal, I get the summer off before returning to work as a consultant?"

"Done, Cliff, I can't deny you now, you've gone beyond the call of duty still again. I'm grateful to you and will be sorry to see you leave us for so long but I'll take heart that you'll return to us in the fall."

"Thanks, boss, you won't regret it, I leave you in good hands with 'The Shark'. Jason pulls his clothes back on before giving Cliff a close embrace.

"Night, Jason, be sure to rest up before your first session with Clarence, you'll need your stamina to keep up with him," Cliff says with an evil smile.

Chapter 6

Cliff and Brad are in the process of moving to the country for the summer.

Tommy has already moved his stuff in so that he can spend several nights a week in the townhouse and be near the new office Brad has just finished signing a lease on.

The three of them are home on a Monday evening expecting Marc Berger to come by with his things so he will be able to occupy one of the guest bedrooms.

At the ring of the bell, Brad goes to the door to let Marc in.

"Hey, Marc, come on in, we've been expecting you." Marc is about 5'-9" tall, has black hair, a stocky, muscular build, beautiful gray eyes, animating a dark, sensuous Semitic countenance.

Having been a police detective, he walks with a bit of a confident swagger that creates a nice masculine rhythm to his gait that sets off a perfect, high round ass.

"Hi ya — you must be the Brad that Debbie has told me so much about.

"Nice to meet you," he said, firmly shaking Brad's outstretched hand.

"Hope she wasn't too tough on me. I'm not all that bad, you know."

"Honestly, she thinks you're the best thing that ever happened to Cliff. You've got her in your pocket."

"That's good to hear, Marc. Come meet the boys!" Cliff and Tommy enter the living room.

"This guy you've already met, my very own Cliff and this here is Tommy Brandon, once an ace fighter pilot and now a key guy in our security business." Marc shakes both their hands.

"Hey, Cliff, great to see you again. Nice to meet you, Tommy, guess we're going to be roomies this summer."

"Great to meet you too, Marc. We need to huddle later to go over some ideas I have about our cohabiting. Let me give you a hand bringing your stuff in from your car so we can sit down together and have a chat." Judging by the look of that first rate ass, babe, you're going to need some tender loving care, Tommy reflects.

"You guys go ahead and do your thing. Cliff and I need to continue packing up stuff to take to the country," Brad said.

"See you in a bit when we can have a beer together."

After unloading Marc's minivan, Tommy and Marc wind up in the den to chill out and have a get acquainted meeting.

"Glad to get that over with," Marc said.

"Yeah," Tommy said.

"Moving's a bitch. I ought to know, my wife's thrown me out enough times."

"You might have heard that I've been in the doghouse with my wife too," Marc answers.

"We're working things out."

"Yeah, us too, we're still trying to figure it out, but eventually — "

"Did Debbie happen to mention to you what I suggested to Brad and Cliff about us sharing responsibilities in running this house?"

"She sure did, sounds perfect to me.

I hate doing chores.

You know, Tommy, I'd like to run something else by you concerning the book I'm planning to work on this summer."

"Sure, Marc, let it rip. What can I help you with?"

"Ah, well — it concerns the subject matter of the book. It's — well — sort of a — combination of — love story, thriller and gay erotica."

"Gay erotica, you've got to be kidding, man!" How can you as a married, straight guy have any clue about — that."

"That's where you, Brad and Cliff come in as well as others in your circle of — 'acquaintances'. You see, I'd want to interview you to get ideas for my book. Debbie has told me a little about stuff Cliff is involved in at work and I know you guys have an interesting — 'arrangement'."

"This is true, Marc, but I wouldn't talk to you unless Brad was ok with it and I have no idea how he'd feel about opening up — private matters — with you especially since you'd be going public with it."

"The book would be written in such a way as to protect their privacy. Their story is really interesting, it should be told. It really crosses genres, making it appealing, potentially, to a wider audience."

"You've sold me, Marc, but Brad and Cliff may be a tougher sell. They shun the limelight, doing what they do, and may not like opening themselves up to scrutiny. Plus, you being a heterosexual, probably carry baggage that would prevent you from having any empathy with gay or bisexual men. You just haven't been there."

"Take you for example, Tommy, you lead a mostly heterosexual life but you manage in a gay context, why couldn't I?"

"Not to state the obvious, Marc, but you don't know your way around sucking cock or taking it up the ass, not to put too fine a point on it. I swing both ways and am considered a pretty hot fuck. Gay, straight, who cares. I'm a guy who likes sex. Unfortunately, I've chosen a wife who is content to do without it, so I stray — "

"So have I, Tommy, strayed that is? My wife is not very interested in sex either. She has a demanding career and takes it home with her. All the fun has gone out of our marriage. So I — diddled — her best friend. Dumb move!"

"God, yeah. So that's why you're here? She wanted you gone?"

"Not exactly, we think we have a shot at salvaging things if I get out from under the household drudgeries and can be on my own for the summer to write this book."

"Brad and Cliff are going to join us for a beer. Talk it over with them and if they buy it, I'll be happy to work with you too."

Coming into the den with some beers, Brad announces, "Couple more days of sorting through some shit and we should be ready to load up the SUV and leave for the country so you love birds can be alone."

"Funny you should mention that, Brad, because Marc here has something rather personal to ask you and Cliff about."

"Spit it out, babe!" Cliff answers.

"For my pal Debbie, nothing is too much to ask."

Marc explains the subject of his book and the need to interview all of them for background material, including all the gory details involved in their various sexploits.

"Are you sure you're not biting off more than you can chew, Marc. Maybe you should stick to writing a pure thriller or love story but to mix in gay erotica? I don't think so. You don't have the — background."

"With interviewing you guys, I hope to fill in that void. I'm a quick study and open to new ideas."

"Well, look, Marc, why don't you start with Tommy here, if he's willing. Once we see how that goes, we can visit the subject again to see how to proceed from there," Brad suggests.

They finish their beers and Marc goes home.

"So what do you think, Brad," Cliff asks.

"Is this really a dumb idea?"

"Actually, I think it's a really good idea, with one proviso," Brad answers.

"And what would that be?" Cliff asks.

"Our Tommy here would have to pave the way by introducing Marc to the pleasures of gay sex. If the book is to be successful, he's going to have to pay his dues with some — 'field work'. It's the least we can do for our friend Debbie to insure the success of her husband's book."

"Christ, Brad, I don't know. I don't want Debbie pissed at me. Marc's already bummed her out by slipping it to her best friend. Now this!"

"It'll be different for her if it's with another man. She may very well not care. So go see her and ask her. She's in a different place with Marc right now. Could be she'll like the idea of Marc's having to dance to a different tune."

"Jason was supposed to have had his first session with Clarence by now so I wanted to go by the office anyway to find out how it went. While

I'm there, I'll try to broach the subject with Debbie. If she has a problem with it, then forget it, all bets are off."

———————————————

Cliff can just see the underpinnings of their summer plans going crumbling to the ground.

If Jason and Clarence don't hit it off, if Debbie has a shit fit, if Marc balks at taking the book idea further, everything could well go south, starting with the deal he thought he had with Jason.

He so wants that three month summer respite from the familiar.

Phoning ahead, he was able to get a few minutes with Jason before going by to see Debbie.

"Hi ya, Myra, the boss said to come ahead for a brief sit down."

"Go ahead, Cliff, his next appointment isn't until 30 minutes from now, go on in." Knocking, Cliff moves into the room, kicking the door closed behind him.

"So, boss, how did it go with Clarence?" Cliff says, anxiously.

"Well, Cliff, let me give you a blow by blow — so to speak. I'd never seen Clarence before, I mean, up close. He really is rather magnificent and for such a big man, so graceful. Those big brown eyes captivated me at once and then there was that sensuous mouth framing very white, perfect teeth. The body should be captured by an artist in a bronze sculpture. The shoulders of an Olympian, washboard abs, a perfect round and high butt and legs — legs for days. What a specimen!"

"He was more than accommodating to me, showing me around, giving me an initial work-out routine and finally taking me into the shower stalls where we showered opposite each other. We both were sporting hard-ons but managed to finish up and wrap towels around ourselves so we could move on to the massage room. He got me up on the padded table on my stomach and proceeded to give me the best deep tissue massage I ever had. I was in heaven."

"Did you still have your towel on, Jason, or — ?"

"Well actually, he said that he'd take the massage further with me because I was so — 'active' — and removed my towel to massage my butt cheeks. My cock was straining under me and I had to squirm to free it to rest up against my belly."

"Yes, I know his specialty is deep tissue massage. It's addictive once you've felt his hands on you, especially on your tender butt."

"That's an understatement. My tits were tingling in concert with my anus, not to mention my straining dick. He could have done anything he wanted with me and knew it. Before I knew it, he was up on the table with me, on his knees between my legs which he parted. Having seen that huge black dick in the shower, I was frightened for a moment and then remembered your advice about just relaxing and enjoying it."

"Hope you took my advice, Jason. Clarence has been hot for your ass ever since he laid eyes on you in those clinging tennis shorts you like to wear on your way out to a match."

"You know I did, Cliff, I was ready, thanks to you. He put his beautiful hands with the long graceful fingers on my ass, parted my butt cheeks, darted his tongue into my quivering hole and proceeded to eat my asshole raw. I was so — into it, pushing my butt up so he could jam his beautiful face deep into my crack."

"Just to let him know what an easy mark you are, Jason, good move. A top likes an enthusiastic bottom."

"Eventually, he pulled his tongue out of my wasted hole and proceeded to lube it up with probing fingers. Oh, yeah, I was his and he was going to take me. He lay down on top of me, rubbing his prick up and down my crack and then placed his head next to mine, facing me when he darted his tongue in my mouth to lick and suck on my tongue."

"You're killing me here, Jason, what did he do next?!" Cliff asks, imagining the whole scene.

"Out of the corner of my eye, I could see him raise up his big black marble ass before his cock found my asshole and plunged in half way. It was already feeling exquisite and then he pushed in all the way. I could feel the coarse black hair surrounding his dick filling my crack. I was nailed."

"Oh, god, Jason, you took that big black prick so easily. You did me proud, man, wow!"

"Needless to say, I wanted it — badly. Lying there with him on top of me with his dick firmly planted in me, he whispered in my ear with his hands on top of mine, possessing me. He said that you were in to see him on my behalf and you got up on that table just like Clarence had me. You gave him your ass, he said, because you wanted to insure that he would service me. He said he didn't admit to you that there was no problem. But he wanted to fuck you too, in the bargain, so he took you. He said that SEAL ass is tops, man, and that I had a loyal operative in you who would do anything for his boss."

"Damn, he wasn't supposed to tell you that I let him screw me. Well, I'll tell you a story out of school too then. He was more than willing to return the favor. He gladly got on his back with his legs in the air and let me hump that big black ass until I was nearly unconscious with delirium. I nearly burst the condom in his can."

"Good for you, Cliff, maybe I'll get a piece of that black ass too. As far as him telling me that he had you, why not, Cliff. He was paying you a compliment after all and I'm flattered you went to bat for me. I'm impressed how you've learned to use your pussy to get whatever you want. I know that for a fact, having had you. Now I'm ready to give you what you want, letting you have the summer off as you requested." Jason said, grinning.

"Thanks, boss, that's awesome news. I'm really glad you and Clarence hit it off. Now I can leave for the summer with a clear conscience."

"By the time you get back in the fall, I'll be ready for you again, resuming our afternoon visits."

"We'll see, boss, you may find that Clarence is more than enough for you. By the fall, he should have customized the ring in your asshole to fit his big black dick too perfectly for you to want to be dicked by anyone else."

"Go on then, Cliff. My next appointment's due, call in once in a while. I'd like to hear from you. We needn't be out of touch."

"Will do, Jason, and thanks." Cliff leaves and bids Myra good night.

Now for another piece in the puzzle, seeing how Debbie takes the news about Marc doing some — 'field work' — for his book.

Knocking on Debbie's office door, he looks in to find her at her computer.

"Come in, boyfriend, what's up. In to see Jason again? You two are so — tight!" She said with a gleam in her eyes.

"Yeah, well, he's a detail man and never can get enough — "

"Guess I know what you mean. So what can I do for my favorite agent?"

"This is going to be a little — dicey — Deb. You may not like what I'm going to tell you."

"With my marriage on the rocks and my husband ready to move out and our finances in the toilet, what is there that's going to trouble me? I'm actually feeling a little giddy or maybe — hysterical."

"Well, this is really a related subject to all of that. You see, with the kind of book Marc is writing, we, in our household, think that he's taking on too much and isn't likely to be successful unless we — well — give him — a hand."

"Uh, give him a hand, what the hell does that mean!"

"What it sounds like, Debbie. If he wants the book to work as gay erotica as well as a thriller and a love story, he's got to get — more — 'involved' — with the subject matter."

"Meaning what exactly, Cliff. He has to become a drag queen or something?!"

"No, nothing like that but, well, we think he has to have a fling with Tommy to get his feet wet, so to speak."

"Aha — ha — ha!!! Surely you're not serious! We're separating because he fucked my best girlfriend. Do you think cock is going to do it for him?!"

"Maybe not but Tommy's willing to see where it goes, if you're not opposed to it."

"Opposed to it, why should I be opposed to it? It was one thing with my best girlfriend but with guys — . Hmm, I kind of like the idea. Give him a little insight into the other end of the stick, if you know what I mean. Hell, I'm interested in him pulling his weight and earning a little money for a change, instead of me being the prime bread winner. So no, I don't have a problem but does he?"

"Tommy thinks he can bring him around. After all, Tommy lives a more or less straight life with his wife. So who better to help Marc understand both sides? I just didn't want you to feel betrayed by my doing something like this behind your back."

"You're a good friend, Cliff, I appreciate your coming to me first. Let's just see what happens, keep me posted. Marc and I are entering a new phase in our marriage. This will just be another piece of the change."

"Ok, Deb, as long as you're cool with it, I'll give Tommy the green light. We'll keep you apprised of developments. I'd better get going back to the commune. Night, Deb." He kisses her on the cheek and leaves.

Eric Holtz tracks Cliff down through a contact in the German Embassy in Washington to find out where he lives.

He becomes aware that Cliff has moved in with the SEAL instructor who trained him for his mission to Moscow.

While he and Viktor visit Washington to meet with German government officials regarding the automotive parts plant they plan to build in Fletcher, North Carolina, they hope to renew contact with Cliff whom they grew to respect and trust during their ordeal fleeing Russia.

"Hello, Cliff, is that you? This is Eric Holtz calling from my home in Germany."

"Eric, hello! It's good to hear your voice and to know that you are safely home in Germany. How are you and how is Viktor?!" Cliff says excitedly.

"We are, in fact, doing exceptionally well and are planning a trip to Washington, DC which is why I'm calling."

"That's good news. I hope you'll have some time to spend with an old friend. I'd love to see you and share stories."

"We expect to be in the States for several weeks. You see, we're planning on building an automotive parts plant in North Carolina but first must endure some meetings with German officials in Washington to sign documents, letters of intent, etc.

This would afford us an opportunity to get together with you."

"Terrific and you could meet Brad, my partner, too. We just moved in together here in DC."

"By partner you mean lover, Cliff? I thought you were a temporary convert to the pleasures of male companionship. What happened?"

"Brad happened. He was the one who — 'trained' — me for my mission to Moscow. He did his job too well. Now he's stuck with me. We're very happy."

"Viktor and I too have become a happy couple, in no small part, thanks to you. We'll be meeting this time under such changed circumstances. Two married couples steeped in domesticity. How boring we've all become!"

"Knowing you guys for the short time that I did, I very much doubt that you've become boring. As for Brad and me, I'll let you judge for yourselves. So when are you arriving? What's your itinerary?"

"Actually, we're arriving next week after wading through all the red tape that was required. Opening a factory in another country does present some problems. But we seem to have it in hand. We'll be staying at the Ritz Carlton."

"Nice choice. We'd like to have you out to our townhouse for dinner. Why don't you call us after you arrive so we can work out a time to get together that works into your schedule?"

"We'd very much like to do that. Expect our call. We very much look forward to meeting your Brad. Goodbye for now, speak to you next week." They ring off.

Cliff leaves the living room to find Brad.

"Brad, where the hell are you?" Cliff calls out.

"I'm in the den, babe, what's happening?" Brad asks, looking up from the newspaper.

Cliff on entering the den answers, "You'll never guess who that was on the phone!"

"Ok, I'll bite, who the fuck was it? Did we win the lottery or something?"

"You remember my telling you about my experiences in the Moscow interrogation facility at the hands of their chief interrogator and his assistant?"

"Yeah, I remember. They really put you through your paces. Let's see, it was — Viktor — and that German guy — Eric was it?"

"You've got it, babe, Viktor Sidorov and Eric Holtz. They're coming to Washington next week to meet with German government officials regarding opening an automotive parts plant in Fletcher, North Carolina."

"So why did they call us. To renew old acquaintances or something?"

"Don't be obtuse, Brad, why the hell else do you think they'd call!"

"So what are we gonna do, bake them a cake or some shit like that?"

"Close, babe, you know you're perceptive don't you. A royal pain in the butt, but perceptive. I've invited them to dinner here for some time next week, depending on their schedule."

"What did they do while they had you over there, brainwash you when they weren't fucking you?"

"You know you can really be a crude, motherfucker. That was a shitty, fucking thing to say to me!"

"Sorry, love, I was just enjoying pulling your chain. It's cool with me if you want to invite the sadistic bastards over."

"Hopefully, you'll have had a chance to work on your charm before they get here. They happen to be great guys once you get to know them."

"If you say so, sweet cheeks. So who's going to cook for Christ's sake?"

"Since Marc will have moved in by then, I hope to coerce him into doing it with a lot of help from the rest of this talented household. You'll be in charge of clean-up, befitting your limited uses."

"So, you all moved in now, Marc? Got everything you need up in your room?" Cliff asks, sipping coffee at the kitchen table.

"Yep, everything is A-ok. I'm really psyched to be here. I hope I'll get to interview you and Brad before you leave for the country."

"That's entirely possible, Marc, but work with Tommy for now and we'll take it from there."

"We're planning on working out together in your basement gym, allowing us time to become better acquainted before getting into the interview process."

"Good idea. Exercise helps you to cut through all the bullshit and take each other's measure."

"Brad and I will hang around a little longer than expected because we're expecting a pair of guests I met in Russia while on assignment."

"Oh! I'd really like to meet them! They might add some interesting color to my book."

"No doubt they would. That segues nicely into asking whether you'd like to cook dinner the night we have them over. This way you can spend more time with them."

"No problem, I'd really like to see you all together since you're all a piece of the story. Maybe I could follow up with interviews at a later date. Maybe set up appointments — ?!"

"Could be but Tommy is still the first step. Let me know how that goes first."

Tommy comes into the kitchen saying, "Guess what, Mary's decided to spend a couple of weeks with her parents. They love to see the grandkid. So I can be here full time for a while."

"Marc is hot to trot to get going on his book so this will give him more access to you, Tommy."

"Since my wife needed our car, I took my Harley. Do you mind if I keep it at the back of your garage?"

"Sure, Tommy, answers Brad, our garage is deep enough for two cars and your motorcycle. Feel free."

Tommy and Marc start doing morning workouts together in the townhouse's basement workout room when Tommy gets an idea.

"You know, Marc, when I was packing up to move in here, I came across my wrestling singlets that I used when I was at the Naval Academy. Not knowing what I was going to do with them, I tossed them into my suitcase. So I was wondering, did you ever do any wrestling in college?"

"Yeah, I was on our wrestling team but I wasn't really very good."

"Well how about you and me having a go at it. It would help to break the monotony of our daily routine."

"Umm, sounds like a good idea to me but I'm a bit rusty. Haven't done any matches since I graduated."

"We don't have to get real competitive with it. It would just be a fun way to exercise. We're about the same size so you should fit into one of my singlets. We could start tomorrow, see how it goes."

"Ok, let's do it, I'm game," Marc agrees.

Arriving in the locker area of the exercise room the next morning, Tommy finds Marc there ready to change clothes.

Tommy tosses him a black single piece wrestling outfit. "Try this on Marc, looks like it should fit you perfectly."

Marc strips and slips into the singlet. It fits him like a second skin, leaving nothing to the imagination.

"Feels good," he said. "Like I have nothing on."

"Yeah, it looks tailor made," answers Tommy.

"And mine still fits me just fine too. So let's get out there and hit the mat." Christ, with the way you look in that singlet, I'm going to have trouble hiding my stiff dick, Tommy thinks.

They mix it up a bit and although they are pretty evenly matched, Tommy has a bit of an edge, given that he's generally more active than Marc.

The wrestling becomes part of their morning workout and it's apparent that the intimate moves required in pinning one another begin to move into erotic territory.

The skin tight singlets they wear do nothing to hide the fact that they both get highly aroused.

They shower afterwards in the oversized shower designed for two people to use with double showerheads, etc.

Cliff's old living room furniture was relocated down here to form a break area where they like to flop after their showers, lounging in their towels.

Tommy is not working full time at the office yet, still waiting for furniture and equipment to be delivered.

Brad and Cliff are out most of the day, calling on both new and prospective clients to move the business forward.

"Don't you miss your wife, Tommy, when she's away for so long?"

"Yes and no, we live pretty independent lives. She used to complain a lot when I was away on missions but she really likes her privacy, if the truth were known. As for myself, I enjoy her when I'm with her but I have my own life too. So we manage to muddle along. How about you?"

"It's the same thing with us but the roles are reversed. She's a career woman and I'm a stay-at-home dad. It's just that it gets damn lonely. That's how I stupidly jumped at the first opportunity and balled Debbie's best friend which turned out to be a bit of a bust."

"Judging by the bulge in your singlet when we're wrestling, you seem to be pretty horny. What do you do about it, go upstairs afterwards and jerk off in your room?" Tommy inquires.

"Sometimes, you'd think I was back in college where that was my only outlet. Marriage was supposed to change all that."

"Maybe you need to take a different tack as I did which has worked out fine for me, thanks to Brad."

Tommy gets up from where he is sitting and moves over to Marc who is slouched in a black leather sofa.

"You won't need this," he said as he removes Marc's towel.

Marc looks stricken and curious at the same time.

"Now stretch your arms out along the back of the sofa, Marc, and move your feet up to the front edge of the seat cushion. Do it!" Marc hesitates but complies, his dick begins its ascent.

"You know you're horny and I know you're horny so let's see what we can do about it." Tommy goes down on his knees while flipping away his towel, so that they are both buck-naked.

"Let me get acquainted with what you've been hiding, not so successfully, in your singlet." Marc's dick is now fully erect and jumping.

Tommy grasps both Marc's ankles and begins to tease the head of his cock with his tongue.

Moving lower, he begins sampling Marc's ample nuts.

Marc is already moaning, so unaccustomed to this kind of servicing.

"Um, how about a taste of your dick, Marc. Would you like me to suck it into my mouth?"

"Oh please, Tommy, please suck my dick, I need it so bad!"

Tommy sucks in the head, licking the sensitive underside before proceeding to suck his way down slowly to Marc's pubic hair.

"Oh my god, Tommy, I can't believe what you're doing to me!"

"Relax and enjoy it, Marc, you need this. Don't be resistant, just go with what you're feeling." Tommy makes love to Marc's cock, long ignored by anyone who could have serviced it.

Tommy runs his hands along the insides of Marc's thighs, releasing one hand to fondle his balls while continuing the slow suctioning of Marc's prick.

Marc throws his head back, moaning.

"Tommy, Tommy, I'm, I'm close, so close!"

Reaching up to pinch Marc's sensitive tits, Tommy starts to piston up and down on Marc's engorged prick, bringing Marc to the precipice.

"Awwwgggrrr," shouts Marc as his dick, shoved to the back of Tommy's throat, erupts ejaculating waves of cum sloshing down Tommy's throat.

Tommy feasts on the spasming prick, sucking out every last drop.

Marc's feet fall to the floor as he all but passes out, inhaling great gobs of air to catch his breath.

"Maybe, Marc, it was worth it to wait so long to get your rocks off like that. But on reflection, regular servicing might be less injurious to your health. Cat got your tongue, babe?"

"Don't joke, don't joke, Tommy. That was just too awesome. Come here and give me a hug!"

Now lying down on the sofa facing each other, they kiss.

Tommy explores the inside of Marc's mouth and sucks on the tongue of the ex-policeman while his middle finger of his free hand begins an exploration of Marc's asshole.

Marc's still high from the mind blowing orgasm he experienced, made no protest.

He seems prepared for anything, floating on this plane of sexual awareness.

Tommy reaches under the sofa cushion to retrieve the tube of lube he stashed there as well as a condom.

After slipping on the condom, he lubes his finger to be able to penetrate into Marc's virgin hole.

"Uh, oh, ooo," Marc exclaims, as his deflowering commences.

Marc, sated from his intense blowjob, is remarkably calm.

After his initial surprise at being entered, he begins to enjoy the sensations he is experiencing from Tommy's practiced finger.

Soon Tommy's single finger is joined with a second, opening Marc's tight knot to a more accommodating diameter.

Finally, with a third finger worked into the stretched hole, Tommy begins spiraling the three, opening Marc's hole up for Tommy's pulsating dick.

"Ok, babe, show time," Tommy announces.

Getting up, Tommy folds the discarded towels up into a pillow sized square, placing it on the sofa for Marc to lie on.

Rolling Marc over on his stomach, Tommy enjoys the view of his quarry's raised butt.

Getting up on the sofa on his knees between Marc's legs, Tommy spreads Marc's legs to the maximum that space allows, revealing the twitching pink pucker.

"Tommy, I'm a little — afraid," Marc said, tremulously.

"Your dick looks so — big — can I — take it?!"

"You've been well prepared, Marc. We're going to be a perfect fit. Just relax and enjoy the feel of my penetrating dick and the pleasure you'll be giving me. Once you've given me your pussy, you'll have a hold on me that will empower you to get whatever you want in return." Grasping both of Marc's firm butt cheeks, Tommy spreads open the crack, which aids the widening of the hole.

Slipping his cock-head through the unexplored gateway, Tommy presses forward in slow motion, easing deep into the chasm.

"Oh, Tommy, yes that feels so fantastic. I wanted you to be the one to fuck me first and take my cherry. Please take me the way Brad takes you. I want to know how it feels to take a real fucking by someone who wants me totally. Don't be gentle just because I'm a virgin, take what you want. Fuck me, fuck me good!!!"

"It was my intention to slip it to you slowly and gently, Marc, but I'll do as you say because I've wanted to bang your pretty little butt ever since we met upstairs in this house. You'll have no doubt in your mind how much I've wanted you when I get finished with you."

"Talk is cheap, Tommy. Show me! Show me how bad you really want it. I can take anything you want to dish out."

Lying flat on top of Mark now, Tommy raises up his butt to begin the assault on Marc's ass, penetrating deep with every swing, while darting his tongue into Marc's upward facing ear.

Then entwining a hand through Marc's luxuriant hair, he yanks his head back and to the side to begin assaulting his open mouth with his busy tongue.

Both Tommy and Marc are aroused to the peak of excitement.

Tommy moves his hands flat on the sofa cushion just to either side of Marc's tits to give himself maximum leverage.

"Ok, Marc, you wanted it, so take the consequences, baby." Thwack, thwack, thwack — thwack, thwack, thwack are the sounds reverberating off the mirrored walls multiplying the sound of Marc's butt being pounded by Tommy's groin.

Tommy is power fucking Marc's virgin love channel, unmercifully, holding nothing back and screwing the silken shaftway until his frenzy culminates in a last upward swing of his hips flattening the upturned buns with a final deafening smack.

"AAAAgggrrr!!!" Tommy hollers as his exploding cock sends powerful streams of cum into the Marc's bung hole.

Closely following Tommy's denouement, Marc's complicity in his downfall is evident when against all odds, he explodes again, having a second shattering orgasm.

Clearly, this boy has potential that Tommy will exploit.

"You fucked me, Tommy, you really fucked me!" Marc's deflowering is at last complete.

"You bet and now your ass is going to be fair game around here from now on. You are going to be up for grabs because there can be no doubt that you love cock wherever anyone wants to stick it. Isn't that right, slut?"

"Yes and don't pull out yet, you feel too good. You know, all of you were right about my needing a wider understanding if I was to write the book I've been planning. Now I know what you meant."

"If I stay plugged in your pussy for much longer, lover, I'm going to fuck you silly again."

"I'm not in a hurry to go anyplace, Tommy, show me what you can do. As I said, talk is cheap."

Tommy made good on his threat and banged Marc hard again.

When Marc still hadn't had enough, he plowed him a third time before they came up for air and broke for lunch.

Coming upstairs to the kitchen, they find that Brad and Cliff had returned home to have lunch.

"So, boys, how goes it," asks Brad.

"From the howling and carrying on we heard wafting up from the basement, it seems you two have become an item."

"You could say that, Brad. Marc here has proven that a significant challenge that he faced in writing his book has been lifted, like his pretty little ass."

"Glad to hear it Tommy, we knew you could be relied upon to do the dirty deed."

"Well guys, now that that little obstacle is out of the way, how about submitting to some interviews?" Marks asks cheerily.

"No problem, but first Cliff and I will want some evidence that you indeed are no virgin when it comes to pleasing men. So tonight, after dinner, we'll expect you and Tommy boy to join us in the king bed. Believe that you'll be put through your paces. Maybe take a nap this afternoon because you won't be getting much sleep tonight."

"Marc has no problem sharing the duties of the reigning house bottom, do you Marc? You'll be saving wear and tear on my tired tush."

"Looking forward to expanding my range. Tommy's ok but being topped by SEALS is more in my league," Marc said in an effort to provoke Tommy.

"You cheeky little bastard, a first experience and now you're the arbiter of judgment on the subject? Get real!"

"I love it that you're so easy to rile up, Tommy. It's great fun now that you've had me to poke fun at your performance. Cut me some slack, I'm having fun!"

"We'll see what's what tonight, baby cakes, when it comes to pleasing your man. You take Brad since he has the biggest dick and I'll take Cliff which I've been looking forward to, since he's my rival with Brad."

"You two whores settle it between you two. Cliff and I are cool with whichever of your butts we wind up with."

The evening arrives when Eric and Viktor come to dinner.

Apertifs and finger food is served in the living room before the meal.

Marc outdoes himself beginning the meal with a salade nicoise and progressing to a truly epicurean salmon cassoulet and ending with a homemade amaretto cheesecake.

Plenty of a good Pouilly Fuisse flowed with the meal.

There was lively conversation around the table exploring international relations, politics and sports.

After the meal, they settled down in the den to sip glasses of a good port.

The subject came around to the reason Eric and Viktor have come to the US, which is to open an automotive parts plant in North Carolina.

They explain how they intend to receive the components necessary for assembly in the US by containers from Germany coming into The Port of Charleston.

They have already been in contact with the South Carolina State Ports Authority (SCSPA) in making arrangements.

A builder has been retained to build the building from plans drawn by German architects.

The building is about to go into the ground.

The parts assembled at their plant will go by train to be delivered to their main client, the Mercedes-Benz factory located in Tuscaloosa, Alabama.

Brad seizes the opportunity to broach the subject of what security measures they have undertaken to protect their plant, its products, and employees.

Eric admits that it is an open question needing immediate resolution and something next on their agenda to address.

They were aware that Brad had started a business dealing with security needs.

Brad and Cliff launch into an abbreviated version of the presentation they've been giving to prospective clients, inviting them to come to their office for a complete multimedia presentation, which Tommy would be happy to put on for them.

Eric and Viktor are genuinely interested in retaining their services.

They set up a date to see the presentation.

Marc then introduces the subject of his book.

After a brief synopsis of the overall plot, he asks Eric and Viktor if they'd be willing to be interviewed.

Reluctant at first, they agree so long as their names are not used which could cause them problems with their government and former associates.

Cliff explains that they are about to leave for their mountain cabin for the summer and would like Eric and Viktor to spend some time there with them.

Eric said they'd be delighted because they were due for some down time after all the hurdles they have been required to jump in order to move things forward with their business.

Viktor and Cliff, it's decided, would leave first in the rented car while Eric finished up in Washington signing documents at the German Embassy and Brad finished getting the new office organized.

Brad would drive Eric to the cabin in a few days.

Eric and Viktor hug and kiss their hosts and return to their hotel.

In a couple of days Cliff and Viktor leave for the cabin in Beckley, West Virginia leaving Brad and Eric behind.

It's decided that Tommy will show the presentation at the new office to Eric who will be the one to make the decision on hiring a firm to work out their security requirements.

Tommy really knocks Eric's socks off with the professional multimedia presentation.

Oddly enough, the fact that Brad and Cliff brought Debbie Berger in to cover cyber security became the deciding factor.

This was something Eric was very keen on.

Spending so much time with Tommy, Eric began to get turned on to this former Navy pilot who was so hot.

He and Viktor had been so busy doing business that there had been no time for them to enjoy sex.

Tommy, not slow on the uptake, decides to invite the handsome and sexy Eric home to share a meal with him and Marc.

Brad was out for the evening.

Tommy suggests that Eric catch a cab back to the townhouse because Tommy came on his Harley.

Intrigued with riding with Tommy, Eric indicates a preference for Tommy's mode of transportation and climbs on the back of the big Harley to be driven through the streets of Washington.

Fortunately, Tommy packs a spare helmet and off they go.

Eric likes the feel of the hunky American and enjoys having his arms wrapped around his midsection in order to stay firmly planted on the bike.

Glancing down, Eric is turned on by the sight of Tommy's comely butt pooling on the seat in front of him.

Eric, deprived of enjoying his lover's favors for too long is turned on.

His business suit is now tight up against Tommy's leather jacket and he's drinking in the intoxicating scent of the man he's hugging to himself.

His dick rises up straining to be contained in his trousers.

Tommy can feel Eric's arousal pressed against his crack.

"Enjoying the ride, Eric?"

"Can't you tell, Tommy, we're practically having sex. You are a turn-on, no wonder Brad was a bad boy while Cliff was away. You obviously took advantage, possessing an ass that begs for attention."

"We're just coming up to the townhouse's garage. Hold on while I use the remote to get the door to roll up." They ride through to the rear of the deep garage.

Stopping and turning off the engine as the door descends, Tommy activates the kickstand.

"We don't need to go in yet, Eric. We'll give Marc a few more minutes up in his room to work on his book."

"Good idea, Tommy, I've never done it on a motorcycle. I really need to get into your beautiful ass. That motorcycle ride damn near killed me, being so close to you when you still had all your clothes on. Take them off. I need to see you naked!"

Tommy does a slow, erotic strip tease while Eric sheds the trappings required for business.

Tommy finishes stripping and leans against the Harley with his arms folded and his feet spread apart.

His dick is sticking straight ahead.

Eric stares at it.

"Go ahead Eric, get down on your knees and service me if you expect to get some American pussy." Needing no further incentive, Eric falls to his knees and starts slurping on the stiff cock.

"Yeah, Eric, wrap that pretty German mouth around that dick and suck me. You've been too busy to get any lately, huh, well show me how hungry you are."

Eric doesn't hold back as he demonstrates to Tommy that he is a voracious cocksucker, feeding on Tommy's prick as if his life depended on it.

Tommy, no cock-tease, gives up the fight as he unleashes a mighty load of spunk juice down the throat of the German whose head is frantically bobbing to enjoy every last squirt.

"What a divine little slut you are, Tommy. Now get your fanny back up on your bike and lean forward on the handlebars. For your insouciance in forcing me to my knees, you will pay a price." Eric straddles the front wheel facing Tommy.

Being tall, Eric's dick is positioned just right for Tommy's hungry mouth to reach.

"Ok, butt boy, here's a little appetizer before I plug your hole." Tommy sucks in Eric's prick and ravishes it almost to the point of Eric's coming.

"No, no you insatiable little whore, it's your ass I'll have!" Eric swings his leg over the front wheel and moves to stand next to the bike, grabbing a condom and a packet of lube from his suit jacket.

Eric lathers up his fingers to lubricate Tommy's hole.

"Brad has done a commendable job in opening up your portal to pleasure, Tommy. I could almost stick it to you using only the precum leaking out of my piss slit. But no, I like fingering your hole and finding your joy spot to insure that you'll be overwhelmed with need in receiving my cock, revealing what a cock-whore you are."

"Enough talk, Eric, show me what you can do. Think you can compare to SEAL cock? I think not, fucker." Tommy said in an obvious effort to taunt Eric.

"You Americans do indeed have fresh mouths. Well you're about to be brought down, my arrogant young friend, to show the respect due to your betters." Climbing on the bike behind Tommy, Eric grabs the proffered puffs of ass cheeks and jams his dick home to be buried to the hilt in Tommy's captured ass.

"No slow preliminaries for you my sexy little tart."

"Not bad for an opener, pal, but do you know how to take a hard ride worthy of your competition?" Tommy's really pushing Eric's buttons for maximum effect.

Releasing Tommy's freshly bruised ass cheeks, Eric reaches around to grab his dick with one hand as he digs the nails of his other hand into Tommy's tit.

Tommy, pinned to the big leather seat, must remain stationary while an inflamed Eric begins a frenzied plowing of Tommy's steaming hole, unerringly hitting Tommy's joy spot with perfect accuracy, driving Tommy to acknowledge Eric's domination of him.

"Yes, Eric, you own it, you have conquered my ass, give it to me, give it all to me!" The battering continues unabated until Eric reaches the pinnacle and power slams jets of semen into his chastened butt boy.

"Tommy, Tommy, you're so beautiful, so fucking beautiful," Eric said in a low whisper.

Slowly pulling out of Tommy's ass, Eric gets off the bike, helping a savaged Tommy to his feet.

Eric leans against Tommy grasping his hard butt cheeks and kisses him passionately, Tommy wraps his arms around Eric's neck and returns the kiss with interest.

"Tommy you are such a divine fuck. It's no wonder you're in such demand."

Having the availability of some visiting European gentlemen inspired me to extend our brand of American hospitality to you and hopefully later to Viktor, that stud you're traveling with."

"You noticed! Well you're likely to get your chance at the cabin when I tell Viktor what a lusty little piece you are. I think a sandwich would be nice with different participants taking the middle position. Game?"

"Count on it Eric. You and Viktor will have to take a rest cure after we Americans up at the cabin have had our fill. Well, we'd better go inside before Marc wonders what's become of us."

Chapter 7

Traveling along the country roads in West Virginia, Cliff and Viktor engage in a conversation covering past events they shared in Russia.

Glancing over at his companion, Cliff can see evidence of Viktor's arousal in the tent his cock is making in his crotch.

Cliff surmises that Viktor is probably very horny, knowing how little down time he and Eric had to get in on while they were in Washington.

Finally arriving at the foot of the long driveway to the log cabin, they drive up to the garage as Cliff activates the automatic door enabling them to drive into the garage.

"Leave everything in the truck, Viktor. The caretaker will take everything inside for us."

Viktor swings out of the SUV first, heading for the door into the house.

Getting out of the SUV after him, Cliff quickly slips up behind, pressing himself against him and wrapping his arms around his midsection as he cups his crotch, still half hard.

"I think we need to take care of this now, Viktor. Eric wouldn't want you to go without for so long." Viktor can feel Cliff's stiffening cock pressing against his crack.

Parked next to the SUV is Brad's vintage red Corvette.

Yanking a picnic blanket off a wall-hung shelf, Cliff tosses it over the hood of the Corvette.

Half lifting Viktor, Cliff moves him over to the Corvette and slams him face down on the blanket.

"Unbuckle your belt, Viktor, and unzip you jeans!"

"What's come over you, Cliff, surely you are not going to rape me before I've even been received into your home?!" said Viktor with an enigmatic smirk.

"In spades, babe, don't pretend you don't want it. I've been fantasizing about getting reacquainted with your magnificent butt ever since we had you over for dinner. I'm not waiting any longer." As he unfastens his jeans as requested, Cliff removes Viktor's shoes and then his jeans and undershorts.

Stripping off his own clothes, Cliff falls between Viktor's legs, flipping up his shirt tails to reveal the incredible ass mounds.

Memory didn't disappoint, Viktor's ass was unrivaled in Cliff's experience.

Licking his way up the inside of Viktor's thighs, Cliff lavs the sides of Viktor's crack, causing Viktor to lift his buns for more.

Cliff sucks in one of Viktor's low hanging balls before getting his mouth around both and barely managing to stuff them in his mouth.

Cliff's nose was nudging Viktor's musky asshole as he fed on the tasty nut-sac.

Soft moans escaped Viktor's mouth.

Having finished feasting on Viktor's balls, Cliff released them to move up to the hole, now opening in welcome for a sampling by Cliff's busy tongue.

Turning his hands inward, Cliff jams his fingers deep into Viktor's crack to spread the hard cheeks wide-open so he can plunder his target, the succulent hole.

Frantic slurping followed by deep tongue penetration ensued, enjoyed by both as evidenced by Viktor raising his ass high to permit full access.

"God yes, Cliff, my hole was hungry for your attention. Do me, eat me out, I want to feel your face stuffed in my crack."

"My dick is what you really need, Viktor. You'll take it now! Show me what a needy bottom you've become, allowing Eric to take you at will."

"You were my first, Cliff, it will always be special when you take me. Now you needn't be gentle or cautious. Pound my fuck cavern now like you wanted to then, my hole can take it. Screw me like only a first lover can. Fill my pussy with your big beautiful American dick and fill me with great wads of your thick cum."

In great slamming arcs, Cliff worked his hips to smack his groin against the great mounds of Viktor's butt cheeks, smacking the raised globes while his cock skewered the fuck cavern in a punishing pummeling, culminating in Viktor's feeling a gushing torrent of cum filling him and splattering down the insides of his legs.

"No one, Cliff, no one has ever taken me like that." Viktor whispers in awe.

"Ok, Viktor, you need to be shown my appreciation for a fuck I'll never forget. Turnover, babe, I want to ride that big Russian prick that I had to take while in your prison, but now can admit how much I really liked it." After lubing his ass, he slides Viktor down on the hood of the Corvette, pulling on the blanket to move him.

Viktor's feet are now planted on the car's bumper, raising his knees up.

Cliff turns with his back to Viktor, stepping back and up onto the bumper, he grasps Viktor's knees to stabilize himself as he lowers his butt to the towering prick.

Viktor positions his cock at the descending hole as the head pops in to begin the climb to the heights.

Cupping Cliff's floating buns, Viktor applies pressure in concert with Cliff's movements to achieve a mutually stimulating timing.

Each movement up and down gives each of them excruciating pleasure, building and building to an unimaginable peak when Viktor grabs Cliffs hips and jams his cheeks down, forcing them to land hard onto his groin and causing his engorged prick to erupt into waves of explosive orgasms gushing into Cliff's chasm.

Cliff, feeling his shaftway being filled with oceans of hot cum from Viktor's rapidly firing cock, is pushed to another pinnacle of pleasure, sending a geyser of cum from his dick across the garage floor.

"Viktor, your prick is a force of nature, that was all that I remember and then some. Wow!!!"

"That was wild, Cliff, you blew me away. You realize we forgot to use protection. What could we have been thinking!"

"We were horny and cock crazed, I guess. Lucky none of us are what could be described as promiscuous even though we're not exactly monogamous."

"Circumstances conspired against us to make us mindlessly craven sex addicts. We'll be calmer now that we've sated ourselves in each other," Viktor declares.

"Hope you're right, Viktor, but I wouldn't count on it. We will have to monitor ourselves more carefully because you never cease to turn me on."

Brad and Eric pack up Eric's rental car in preparation to leave for the mountain cabin and join Cliff and Viktor who had gone ahead of them, days earlier.

They say their goodbyes to Tommy and Marc but will expect to see them soon when they too will come to the cabin but only for the weekend.

It is decided that Brad will do the driving since he's so familiar with the roads they must take to get to the cabin.

The scenery along the Blue Ridge Parkway is intermittent such as clusters of trees along the roadside permit.

"Isn't there a look-out point where we can stop to see the view, Brad?" Eric asks.

"Most of the look-out points are filled with RVs and families. I know of a spot that few people know about. We have to get off this road onto a logging trail where we can park and access a concealed path to a look-out point."

"That sounds like a perfect vantage point from which to enjoy an unobstructed view, free of tourists," Eric responds.

Soon Brad turns off on the logging trail and after a short ride pulls into a slot between some trees.

"Here we are, Eric, you're going to love the view from here." Brad leads Eric to the hidden path, totally concealed by low-lying scrub.

They pass along the serpentine trail through the dense forest before arriving at small clearing where the view is suddenly vast and stunning.

"Oh, wow," exclaims Eric.

"This is a perfect spot to view the whole valley, it's marvelous!"

Coming up behind Eric, Brad wraps his arms around him, kissing him on the side of his neck saying: "And so are you, Eric, and a credit to your former associates in the East German Stasi."

"Um, Brad, you feel so good against me. Since we've been in your country, Viktor and I haven't had the time or inclination to — "

"Get your rocks off? Well, I have just the medicine for you. You should be able to feel it now pressing against your lovely crack," Brad said as he pushes harder against Eric for emphasis.

"When we met at your townhouse, I knew it was only a matter of time before I would spread my legs to take your big cock up my ass. You've chosen a perfect place to have your way with me."

"And I'd hoped that you wouldn't need special persuasion because I want you bad enough to take what I want whether you were willing or not."

"You can't be too aggressive for my taste, Brad. I like to be stud fucked by a dominant top. You know I haven't had any lately so I'm in extreme heat."

"Let's get those clothes off you then, Eric, except for your T-shirt which you'll need to protect your back for what I have in mind." Soon they are both naked except for the T-shirt Eric still wears.

"Come, Eric, over to this birch tree in the middle of the clearing."

Brad follows to the side and rear of Eric with his moistened middle finger tracing a path up Eric's crack into his hole.

"I can tell Viktor gets plenty of this!"

"He won't mind sharing my special favors with you, Brad, as long as you show your utmost appreciation, meaning enjoy taking a no prisoners fuck."

"Ok, Eric, remember that you asked for it because I'm not going to treat you gently. Now lean back against the birch tree and by springing up, you'll be able to grasp that low branch above your head, which will allow you to raise your legs up at the same time. Do it!"

As Eric raises his legs, Brad squats and moves his shoulders under Eric's thighs so as to support his weight.

I have your weight on my shoulders, Eric, so let go of the branch and wrap your arms back around the tree and clasp your hands together." Eric's cock is now bouncing against Brad's face.

Brad captures the cock-head and sucks it into his mouth, darting his tongue into the piss slit.

Eric is already softly moaning.

"Christ, Brad, you're killing me. Oh yeah, please, suck my dick. I want to fuck your gorgeous face." Brad swallows the whole shaft, working his cheeks and his tongue to maximum effect.

"Christ yes, eat me, eat my meat!" Brad commences an eating frenzy, sucking, gently biting, kissing and licking the jumping dick.

"Brad, oh Brad. I'm going to lose it."

Brad ends the cock tease to swallow Eric's prick to the back of his throat in time to feed on the convulsing cock's spewing load.

"Aaahhh, aaahhh, aaahhh," shouts Eric as his voice echoes tenfold in the valley.

Brad laps the last few drops from Eric's dick, as he gently eases him down lower on the tree which rides up his T-shirt, exposing his tits.

Brad sucks, then nibbles on each tit causing Eric to remain at the peak of excitement, moaning.

Inserting three fingers into his cum drenched mouth, Brad then removes his fingers to insert them into Eric's twitching hole.

"Your hole is about to be breached by 10" of SEAL cock, my Stasi friend." Removing his fingers from Eric's ass, Brad uses his freed hands to grasp Eric behind the knees to raise and spread his legs.

Brad eases his dick into the pinioned German to begin the attack.

"Ummooouuu," croons Eric as his silken shaftway is breached, exquisitely.

"Yes, yes, yes sodomize me, sodomize meeee!!!" Brad intensifies the darting, penetrating assault, driving them both up to an incredible height.

A fierce barrage of cum from Brad's rapidly firing cock, bursts the condom and pours molten cum deep into Eric's gorge.

Screaming in unison, Eric joins Brad in pumping out an orgasm, which for him is a second time when he imagined he had nothing left.

Their combined scream echoes far and wide in the verdant valley below.

"My god, Brad, you — broke the condom, your cum is pouring out of my ass!"

"You drove me to it! Your ass was beyond anything I imagined. Viktor is a very lucky man."

"As is your Cliff too, Brad. What a fucking stud you are! Put me down before I want it again." Standing, they embrace with Eric putting his head on Brad's chest and with their arms around each other.

"You better wipe that shit eating grin off your face before we arrive at your house or we'll be pummeled by our significant others."

They get themselves dressed and get back on the road, arriving a couple hours later to be reunited with their spouses, somewhat less for wear.

"Hey you guys, glad you're finally here!" said Cliff as he welcomes them into the house.

"Hector Rios, our caretaker, has volunteered to make dinner, so we're in for a treat."

The evening began in the living room with everyone drinking from bottles of Cabernet Sauvignon.

Hector made a nice ceviche wrapped in tortillas to act as the appetizer.

He served a native dish of Costa Rica or "Comida Tipica" as they say in his country, called "Arroz Con Polo".

A tossed salad rounded out the menu.

Hector was on his own because his significant other was out of town, which prompted Cliff to invite him to join them for the meal he offered to prepare.

Up until then, Hector provided the usual services of a caretaker for Brad, now Cliff and Brad, for the last four years, mostly when Brad was not around.

Previously, they had no occasion to mix socially.

Brad was under the impression that Hector lived with a girlfriend at his ranch on the neighboring property.

"Is it true that you have horses on your ranch, Hector," Eric inquires.

"In Germany, we keep a few horses in our stable of the Holsteiner breed."

"Yes, Eric, we have Palominos and Mustangs at our ranch and a Morgen that my partner rides in rodeos. We also board horses for people in the area."

"Really, Hector, what a rough and tumble sport. Is your partner from Costa Rica too?"

"No, he's from Montana originally. His name is Cole, Cole Strong. He rides in rodeos in North Carolina, mostly."

"And all this time I thought you lived on your ranch with a girlfriend," said Brad.

"That makes two of us, Brad, I thought you lived here with your wife."

"Well, I did, but she passed away shortly after I bought this cabin."

"Sorry, I never knew that. I just thought you liked to come up here alone or with — 'friends'." The innuendo wasn't lost on Brad.

"Well now our secrets are out, we both have boyfriends and I'm sure glad of it.

In fact, here we all are in this room, in committed relationships!"

"By the way, Hector, you are a treasure that Brad and Cliff should take advantage of. That 'Arroz Con Polo' was spectacular." Viktor compliments.

"What do you have up your sleeve for dessert?"

"It's called 'Tres Leches'. Hope you'll like it."

"Judging by your main course, I'm going to love it. I hope Cole appreciates your skills," Viktor said. "Well he prefers my skills in the bedroom to those I have in the kitchen," Hector jokingly responds.

"It's just too bad he's away on the rodeo circuit so much that he doesn't often get to enjoy it."

"Really, Brad and Cliff, what kind of neighbors are you to leave your beautiful Spanish friend to live a life in solitary confinement when you could extend a hand in friendship," Eric declares.

"We've heard how you treat your factotum, Bruno Jahn, of your household in Regensburg, Eric. Hector comes from a good Catholic family in San Jose. He's hardly a candidate for boy toy in this household, are you Hector?" Brad inquires.

"Well, actually, Brad, I'd be lying if I said the thought hadn't crossed my mind. It's not like you and Cliff are not — studs. And well, your guests here, Eric and Viktor, wow, what hotties!"

"Jesus, Hector, how many glasses of wine have you had?!" Brad asks.

"Do you want this group of horny fucks to take advantage of you? What would Cole think if you were passed around at a neighbor's home!?"

"Hell, he'd be pissed only because he wasn't here to participate. What do you suppose he does when he's away on the rodeo circuit? He's so fucked out 'bunking' with his cowboy friends that when he comes home I can't touch him for days."

"Let's go into the den to have our dessert and coffee before we see what develops from there," Cliff posits with an air of suggestion.

"Good idea, let's do it," said Brad, getting up from the dining table.

Everyone adjourns to the den.

The dessert was served and was as delicious as the main course, as could have been predicted.

Everyone sat around drinking coffee laced with ample amounts of Kahlua.

Spirits were indeed high.

"You know, Hector, you have the most beautiful olive skin, beautiful black hair, and gorgeous brown eyes. Is that typical in your country?" Eric asks.

"It is true of many of us of Spanish descent. We trace our family back to Spain, generations ago."

"Being small in stature, what 5'-8," you pack a lot of muscle into a small package," Viktor observes.

"Working on the ranch and here on this spread, gives me a total work-out, believe me. This is no gym body."

"But to give credit where it's due, Hector, your body is choice," Cliff observes.

"You guys, you guys, you're circling! I think you want to get into my pants, knowing I'm an easy mark because my lover is away."

"Would you strip and let us share your favors, if we asked you nicely," Viktor inquires.

"In a minute, babe, everyone is welcome to have a sample. I like to think there's enough here for everyone," Hector brags, smiling at everyone in turn.

Hector is seated, legs wide apart, in the corner of the floating L shaped sectional sofa with the two couples flanking him.

"How about you, Eric? You were big with the compliments to my eyes, hair, skin, etc., what about my chorizo or sausage to you." he said, grabbing his crotch suggestively.

Eric gets up from the sofa to stand between Hector's outstretched legs.

"Ok, my quequito (little cupcake), let's see if you really have something to brag about." Eric bends over to undo the fancy silver belt buckle.

"Nice belt buckle and in German silver too. A gift from your lover, no doubt.

Does he suppose this is a chastity belt?"

"He might be a little whacked from being thrown from horses so often but he's not delusional," Hector answers.

"Good, so off come the boots and then these tight jeans. You knew when you poured your cute little ass into these that one of us was going to poke your sweet hole and sample you meat." Eric strips Hector from the waist down.

"That denim shirt with the pearl snaps becomes you, I hate to have to take it off." Hector is left wearing only his tight wife beater, tank top undershirt.

Eric falls to his knees and slides his hands under Hector's buns, blowing on Hector's cock, now at full mast.

"Very respectable I see, my Spanish friend, let's see if it tastes as good as it looks!" Eric runs his tongue on the underside of Hector's prick, laving circles around the big head and entering the piss slit.

"Um, yum, a prime piece of Spanish sausage."

"Quit playing around and start sucking, after all there's a line forming behind you!" Hector said, as he laces his hands behind his head.

"Eat me, I took you for an expert cocksucker, so show me what you can do!"

Eric's hands, cradling Hector's butt, clenches the cheeks and raises him up slightly as he goes down on the fat 7" dick.

Eric routinely pork's down on Viktor's huge cock so this dick is far more manageable but provides plenty of good eating.

With Eric's mouth creating a hot hole for his prick to be lodged in, Hector arches his back and begins to fuck Eric's face while he holds on to the back of his head.

"Oooaaahhh," Hector moans, as he forces Eric's head towards him and jams his cock deep into Eric's mouth.

"Fuck, your mouth is so fucking good, oh you're going to take my load!" As he slams Eric's nose into his groin, Hector arches his back a last time with help from Eric's hands, pushing him up so he could ram his dick in deep, releasing jets of cum down Eric's throat.

"That was better than an after dinner drink, Hector, but now you owe me for pinch hitting for your absent lover." Brad tosses Eric a condom.

Rising up and slipping on the condom, he lubes his dick with cum from his mouth.

Now clutching Hector's ankles, he hauls his legs up into a vertical position while simultaneously poking his cock into the expectant hole and jamming it home.

Hector whimpers at the brutal invasion but his well-used hole can take it.

"So go ahead, motherfucker, bang me good, you wanted it so bad. Don't you think I'm ridden hard by my dickhead cowboy lover?!"

"You Spanish slut, you'll know you've been ridden hard when I get finished!" Eric said.

Still clutching Hector's ankles, Eric pushes his legs to the back cushions while falling on top of him, his dick planted deep into the smaller man.

Pushing off on his knees for leverage, Eric begins the battering plunder of Hector's pussy.

"Take that and that and that, you little tart. I own your pussy and will take everything that is mine!" Eric's cock kisses Hector's prostate, converting the provocateur into a fawning sycophant.

"Oh, Eric, you make me feel so special, like you really, really want me. Yes please, fuck me. I want to give myself to you!" Uttering a deep guttural cry, Eric blasts a load of spunk into a mewling Hector.

"You are one hot piece of ass, Hector that was so good. Who is next to sample the wares?"

"Since we want to defer to our guests, Eric, then Viktor should be next," Brad announces.

After Eric gets up off of Hector and stands aside.

Brad pulls Hector to his feet and maneuvers around behind him.

"Strip, Viktor, and come here. Eric has been kind enough to prime our little Spanish treat so that you can be next to service his hungry hole." Nude, Viktor moves over to stand before Hector, his big dick is already extended to its full formidable length.

Brad reaches under Hector's armpits and lifts him off the floor.

"Raise those sexy legs up Hector. Viktor, help Hector to raise his legs high so you can have at that asshole now stretched open for your big dick." Hector begins to reconsider his braggadocio when he sees the cock that he's about to be impaled on.

Viktor, seeing the fear in Hector's eyes, said, "Relax, Hector, I would never hurt you but I'm going to have you so help me out. Relax, you know you can take it and once we stretch your pussy just a little, you're going to love it." True to his word, Viktor eases in with a little lube provided by Cliff.

Hector is tightly sandwiched between Brad behind him and Viktor in front, now fully planted into the crammed hole.

"Wow, Hector, your hole is so tight and so wonderful. Just relax now, while I begin to slide my dick in and out, so very slowly until you get used to it."

"Jesus, Viktor, I really didn't believe you when you said it would feel good but it does. Will I ever like a smaller dick again? God, I want to be your favorite whore. Go for it, Viktor, I'm ready now to take a screwing!"

"Hector, Hector, you hot fuck! Yes, I'm going to give it to you now." Viktor's massive buns, functioning like a counterbalance, propels his immense dick deep into Hector's pussy with every forceful thrust.

Hector felt like he was being split open but loved every minute of it.

"Oh my god, Hector, your pussy is sucking my cock, I'm going to — ! Ooohhhooohhh," screams Viktor, as his prick unloads volleys of steaming cum into his new best friend.

Just before lowering Hector's legs and pulling out his spent prick, Viktor kisses Hector.

"Good show, Hector, said Brad, now It's time you turn your talents to the masters of this house. Get back on the sofa! This time on your knees, facing to the back." Hector, still dazed from the last screwing, obeys as if in a trance.

Cliff, standing behind the sofa, drops his pants displaying his turgid shaft.

Brad, standing behind Hector, drops his pants to display his big boner.

Hector braces himself by grasping the back of the sofa and sucks in Cliff's dick, excited to be getting some cock to suck.

The sight of Hector's tight round, bubble butt inflames desire in Brad as he stuffs his sheathed prick into the hole, ravaged by Viktor.

Eric and Viktor decide to complete the tableau by slipping on condoms, lubing up, and entering their hosts.

Viktor plunges his dick deep into Brad as Eric does the same to Cliff.

"Our visit wouldn't be complete, Brad, if I didn't get to fuck your butch ass that Cliff obviously gets to enjoy regularly. And my lover never got to plug your lover either so now we're arriving at almost parity. You'll need to spread your legs for Eric and Eric will have to spread his for Cliff. Then we'll feel like honored guests."

Like exotic dancers, Viktor works his hips plowing Brad as Brad swivels his hips plowing Hector.

Brad is really enjoying being filled with Viktor's immense tool, causing him to bang Hector's raised cheeks all the harder.

Loving it, Hector's head bobs furiously as he works Cliff's cock.

Cliff and Eric, picking up on the gyrations they see their lovers displaying, do the same so that now Hector is being fucked hard front and back, to his great delight.

Brad reaches back to pull Viktor's head over his shoulder so he can enjoy plundering his mouth as he receives Viktor's big dick up his ass.

Both hosts receive shattering orgasms up their asses from each of their guests which plunges them over the edge to give up copious loads into Hector's rectum and slurping mouth.

There is a collective sigh as everyone is so wonderfully sated.

"You and Cliff, Brad, are the most divine hosts we've ever had," Viktor said with wonder.

"No one will ever top that! And your Hector makes a most delectable house whore!"

A short time later, everyone, in a post coital haze, goes up to bed except Hector who will stay in the maid's room off the kitchen because he said he'll get up first to make pancakes for everyone.

Soon the household sleeps soundly.

The mood is light the next morning around the breakfast table.

"Your pancakes really hit the spot this morning, Hector, and I'm sure I can speak for everyone at this table in saying that we have you to thank for a glorious night's sleep," Brad said, flexing his eyebrows.

"Here here, Viktor agrees, I second that and only hope that we can persuade Hector to make us — dinner — again. I especially like the after dinner entertainment. Such a talented household, I take my hat off to you!"

"It's not your hat we enjoyed seeing you take off, Viktor," Cliff said.

"You and Eric are no slouches when it comes to talent, shaking your booty with the best of them. We'll look forward to our next session when you can strut your stuff for us again."

"Well I, for one, enjoy outdoor sports too. How about it, Hector? May we come over to your place to get a load of your horses and maybe get to ride out on your trails?" Eric asks.

"Sure, none of the people who board their horses with us will be around today, so this afternoon would be a good time for you to visit," Hector said.

"Why don't you and Viktor go," Cliff suggests to Eric.

"Brad has errands to do to prepare this place for our extended stay and I must touch base with the office to make sure Tommy has everything under control. We'll see you back here tonight."

"Sounds like a plan. We'll come over to you late morning, Hector. We'll pick up a picnic lunch that we could eat out on the trail somewhere of your choosing," Eric said.

"Perfect, Eric, I'll leave the menu up to you. I'm not a fussy eater, just bring plenty of beer." Cliff goes to the study just as the phone rings there.

"Hello!" he answers on the third ring.

"Oh, Cliff, I'm so glad I caught you!" Debbie said breathlessly. "Something's come up that could be a problem for you. I need to see you right away. This isn't something to talk about over the phone even though I'm calling on a throw-away phone. Can you meet me at lunch time?"

"You have me worried, Debbie, why all the mystery? Is there some kind of danger?"

"Not exactly, Cliff, but I really can't talk on the phone. When can you get back here?"

"If I leave shortly, I could meet you say, at 1:30. Where do you want to meet?"

"Our little hide-away when we don't want to run into people from the office. I'll be there at 1:30, don't phone me, just be there!" She hangs up.

"What in the hell is going on!" Cliff mutters.

He decides to take Eric and Viktor's rental car so Brad will have the use of the big SUV for all the shopping he must do.

He goes to tell Brad he's leaving and Eric and Viktor that he needs to use their car.

"You'll be returning today, won't you, Cliff? Tommy and Marc are arriving this afternoon and staying for a long weekend. What's so urgent that you have to drive all the way back to Washington?" Brad asks.

"Don't know but Debbie wouldn't ask if it wasn't important. I'll just have to wait and see until I meet with her. I'll call you later when I know something."

Eric and Viktor give permission for Cliff to use their car and ask Brad to take them to pick up picnic lunches before dropping them off at Hector's place.

"See you later, guys, have fun," Cliff said to Eric and Viktor.

"Go easy on Hector, he's not used to so much — 'company'." Cliff leaves for Washington.

Driving back to Washington, Cliff keeps noticing a car in the rear view mirror that seems to be following him at a distance.

When he gets into the densely populated Washington area, he decides he'll take some evasive action on the off chance that it's not paranoia and someone really is following him.

Parking near the out-of-the-way café that he and Debbie enjoy having lunch in when time permits, he double checks to make sure that car isn't still in evidence.

When the coast appears to be clear, he enters the restaurant, designed in the Country French style in blues and whites.

He finds Debbie there already, seated in a booth at the rear.

"Hey, Debbie, great to see you!" He leans over to give her a peck on the cheek before sliding into the blue vinyl upholstered booth opposite her.

"Sorry for the cloak and dagger routine but I was anxious to talk to you without anyone knowing about it. Both our jobs could be at stake or worse but let's not go there."

"Now you're scaring me, Debbie, what gives?!"

"Well, I've acquired some information that I shouldn't be privy to. It seems that there are two gentlemen from Regensburg, Germany visiting the Capitol, in advance of their building an automotive parts factory in North Carolina, that have come under suspicion. They'll soon be brought in for questioning. I believe you know these men, Cliff." They are interrupted by the waitress to take their order.

They order their usual, anxious to catch each other up.

"Yes, Debbie, I certainly do. What in the world are they suspected of doing? There must be some mistake!"

"Word has come down from our agents in Moscow that these two men, who do run a legitimate business, are permitting their business to be used as a front for the shipment of bomb-making materials into the US."

"What! That's just not possible! They would never be involved in anything like that. Who here has been told such nonsense? How did you find this out?"

"Well I have a — confession — to make, Cliff. I have been engaged in an — inappropriate — relationship with a — colleague — at work. I overheard a conversation he was having about the two in question. Then I connected the dots and realized these were the guys that helped you escape from Russia. In speaking on the phone to Marc at your townhouse, I learned that they were going to be your guests up at the cabin. It was then that I became concerned that your association with them could be viewed negatively by people in Homeland Security."

"Debbie, I'm sorry but I must ask you who it is that you're having an affair with for I must know who has been infected with these lies."

"Cliff — I really don't — very well — it's Jason Stone," Debbie says with her eyes cast downwards.

"My god, Debbie, this can't be happening! I just can't believe it! You were so upset with Marc for doing the same thing with your best girlfriend and all along — !"

"Yes, I'm a hypocrite. I acknowledge that but please let's not get off the subject of what's important now. You could be in serious trouble!"

"All right then, how was Jason informed about this conspiracy. Did someone come to see him?"

"No, it was a phone call I was able to overhear. You see Jason has a hidden space next door to his office where he can hide out when he wants to escape. It's an interior office converted to a — well — study/bedroom. My private data collection library is adjacent with a concealed connecting door. That's how we manage our — assignations. After office hours last night, we were in there doing our thing when the phone rang in his office. He threw a robe on and went out to answer it. That was the call from our special agent in charge of our Moscow office. From the conversation, I gathered what I just told you. It wasn't until I spoke with Marc at your townhouse later that night that I put two and two together, realizing you were harboring suspected terrorists."

"So you agonized over whether to telephone me or not."

"Just so. I thought I might be jeopardizing my job which is so vital to my family, particularly with Marc's income being nonexistent until he publishes another book. But your well-being means a lot to me too so I decided I had to take the risk of having the leak of this information being traced back to me."

"Debbie, I'm really sorry that you find yourself in this position but I thank you for giving me a heads-up on this. It may prove vital in my ability to get to the bottom of these spurious charges so as to exonerate Eric and Viktor, whom I consider to be close friends."

"It may be necessary for you to get them out of your cabin before they're apprehended there and taken into custody. That would be disastrous for you!"

"When I leave you, I'll drive straight back so Brad and I can find a way to hide them out while we try to investigate this." They finish their salads quickly and depart.

Outside, Debbie says, "Don't phone me, Cliff, at the office or at home. If you need to reach me, call my new throw-away phone. Sorry but I feel that we must avoid contact until this is resolved."

"No problem, Debbie, I understand and don't want you compromised. I'll call you only if it's absolutely necessary or if the problem, by some miracle, goes away." They kiss goodbye.

On the road again, Cliff has the nagging feeling that he's being followed again, but how? He was sure he lost whatever tail he had earlier.

But he has learned not to discount his instincts, they are often correct.

He decides to lay a trap for any would be shadow.

Pulling off the two lane road he normally uses, he turns off onto a little used dirt road that had once been the main road.

He finds the perfect spot to pull over to park his car in plain sight and abandons it to take up a position behind a nearby rock formation and wait.

A short time later, a sedan cruises by his car and pulls off the road up ahead, the driver trying to conceal the car in a thicket of bushes.

A man gets out and with some stealth, approaches Cliff's abandoned car.

He looks around trying to figure out where the occupant went.

Unsuccessful at that, he conceals himself behind some trees, affording a view of Cliff's car and waits.

Cliff decides he needs to capture this guy in order to find out who the hell he is and what his interest is in following him.

Using his SEAL training, Cliff manages to get around behind the man and steal up on him, delivering a blow to the side of the neck that knocks him cold.

Dragging him to his car, he uses each of their belts to secure his arms and legs before gagging him and lifting him up into the trunk.

When he makes it home, he took out his Smith and Wesson pistol, which he had taken with him, before he opened the trunk.

The man had regained consciousness and managed to undo his inadequate restraints, thinking he'd get the jump on Cliff.

Seeing the gun, the man pleaded with Cliff not to shoot.

"Get out of the trunk, you little bastard. You have some explaining to do and I'd better like what I hear or your ass is mine!" The man gets out with his hands up.

Holding the gun on the man, Cliff unlocks the door into the house and calls out, "Brad! Brad, come here!"

"What is it, Cliff?!" Brad said when he comes in answer to the urgent call.

"What's going on?! Who's this?!"

"Never mind that now, just come tie his hands behind his back so we can take him into the house and down to the basement." Brad does it and they push the man into the house and force him down into the basement.

Now with the man tied to a chair, Cliff begins to question him.

"Who the fuck are you and why were you following me?!" There was no response.

"What's going on, Cliff? You're saying this motherfucker was following you? Since when?"

"Since I left this morning I think. I noticed what I thought was someone following me and took precautions to lose him, only for him to show up again later."

"Hmm, that sounds suspicious. Let me go upstairs and check out the car you were driving." Brad goes upstairs only to return a short time later with the little black GPS device in his hand.

"This was attached under the rear of the car."

"He must have been following Eric and Viktor in their rented car, only to find that you were driving it," Brad surmises.

"That's got to be it, Brad, which only goes to support something I heard at lunch but more about that later. Let's search him for identification and any other clues we can find on him."

"Shit, he's clean except for his international driver's license which I can tell is fake, but a good fake. It gives his name as Alain Damont with an address in Paris," Brad said.

"So what is your interest in following our guests?" Cliff asks the man.

No response.

"Ok, we can do this the easy way or we can take you apart, the choice is yours," Brad said.

Again no response.

"Ok, Brad! Let's strip him and tie him to the bench press, face down." They strip and drag the man to the bench covered in black leather and secure his arms and legs to the iron legs of the bench.

"Well, my friend, we have a nice collection of riding crops down here that we seldom use when riding our horses but that we will use on your pretty little ass." Still no response.

"Stand back, Cliff! This little fucker asked for it, now he's going to get it!" Piercing the air, the first whir from the riding crop could be heard landing across the man's buttocks.

"AAAhhh!" he cried out in pain.

Again the whir and again, until the sound continued unabated when the man pleaded for Brad to stop.

"I don't know — anything — I was just — told to — follow the two men in the car and report back — by cell phone!"

"Don't lie to us, asshole, you know more than you're admitting. Don't take us to be fools!" The man falls into silence.

"The whirring begins again, this time on his back and legs as well as his ass.

"Please, please stop!!"

"Well, tell us what we want to know and then we'll stop!"

"I told you, I don't know anything!"

"What's your real name and who are you spying for?!" Still no answer.

"Ok, maybe you need a different kind of persuasion! My buddy here has a very big dick and he is going to stuff it up your ass," Cliff said.

"Gotta do what we gotta do, Brad.

Untie him, I want him lashed to the bench on his back with his arms tied to the bar of the big weight above the bench."

"Ok, good, now lets each take an ankle and tie them next to his wrists."

"Are you getting the picture, my silent friend, you are about to be screwed by a former SEAL with a very big dick who's seriously pissed off! Nothing to say, huh, well maybe you'd like him to tear you a new asshole! Is that it?"

"Oh no, not that! I can't tell you anything! This will gain you nothing!"

"Maybe, maybe not, but you know we kind of like the idea of taking turns poking your pussy. When we get tired of banging you, we'll invite our guests that you were following to have a go at you too. You're in for a real good time."

Brad strips and jerks on his cock to get it up to its full thick 10" length.

Cliff slips a condom on his lover's dick and proceeds to lube their captive's hole.

"I didn't — think — you were serious!" the man said.

"I can't tell you what you want to know!"

The man, flat on his back with his ass suspended in the air with his hands and feet secured over his head, is poised to take a punishing screwing from an angry Brad.

"You following my lover around doesn't set well with me, fucker, you're going to tell us what we want to know or else!" No response right away until — .

"All right, all right, don't do it! I'll tell you what I know for all the good it'll do you. The two men Holtz and Sidorov are known to be building an automotive parts plant in North Carolina. What I was charged to do was following them and record their movements so that all details would be known about their activities in getting the parts plant built in the US."

"Who are you working for? Why do they care about the parts plant? How do you contact them?" Cliff asks.

"Who they are and why they seek this information, I don't know. As far as contacting them goes, I speak to my handler at designated times to give him a report."

"When must you place your next call?" Cliff asks.

"In approximately 25 minutes. He's just a voice on the other end of the line. I don't know who he is!"

"Why are you doing this? What's in it for you?" Brad asks.

"There's nothing in it for me! They forced me to do it or they would kill my wife. I had no choice!"

"Where is your wife now?" Cliff asks.

"That's the problem, I don't know. They kidnapped her from our apartment in Stuttgart when I was away. They called me on her cell phone to say they had her and would kill her if I didn't do what they wanted.

They explained what they wanted me to do and said I'd be contacted by my handler. Coming to the US, I proceeded to follow their directions, fearing the consequences if I didn't comply."

"We better start preparing for what you're going to tell your handler when you have to call in a report." Brad unties the man.

"Tell them only that you've followed the two men to the mountains of West Virginia and are attempting to approach the secluded house where they disappeared. I'll want to listen in on the call." Cliff declares.

"Now get dressed!"

The time comes to place the call as Cliff huddles with their captive.

The call is brief and to the point since there's really nothing definitive to report.

After they hang up, Cliff searches his mind to recall where he's heard that voice, for he's certain that he has.

The handler spoke English with a slight foreign accent, which was Cliff's strongest clue as to where he had heard that voice.

Cliff's face contorts with intense concentration when it finally hits him.

He heard the voice in Moscow and on his recent trip, but where?! Then it finally dawns on him.

The voice belongs to Uri Koslov, the double agent he met and worked with in Moscow.

"I knew I recognized that voice. It belongs to Uri Koslov, a double agent I met in Moscow! No one's sure with whom his allegiances lay. He's as slippery as an eel. What his role is in this mess is anyone's guess but I still have some friends in Moscow who may be able to help us. Brad, where is everyone? Since I came home with this problem, I haven't even thought about our guests."

"Well, Eric and Viktor have spent the afternoon with Hector, having a picnic and enjoying riding around Hector's ranch. When Tommy and Marc arrived, they had lunch here and then took off to walk the trails on our property. Either couple could be returning here at any time now."

"Brad, we can't have Eric and Viktor found at our house, It wouldn't look good."

"What do you mean found. Who's looking for them?"

"Actually, agents from Homeland Security. They're suspected of allowing their legitimate business to be a front for terrorists to bring bomb-making material into this country. I learned this from Debbie when I met her for lunch today."

"Oh my god, I didn't know that they were suspects in such a scheme!" the man laments.

Suddenly, they hear footsteps upstairs.

Someone has arrived back.

"I'll go see who it is, Cliff."

"Eric, Viktor, I'm glad you're home. We have a big problem." He explains the situation they find themselves in.

"Come with me to the basement. I want to know if you may have seen this man before who has been following you."

"Descending the stairs, they arrive in the basement and walk over to the man sitting on the bench with his head cast downwards.

"Look at me!" Eric demands.

The man looks up sorrowfully.

"Good god, it's Denis Giraud. What can you be doing here, Denis. Is it possible that you are involved with these terrorists?!"

"Surely you can't think me to be so low, Eric! I've been forced to follow you, not knowing why, but now I know. You have been targeted by terrorists to be an unknowing participant in their plot to smuggle bomb-making material into this country. I was forced to help them because they kidnapped my wife and threatened to kill her if I didn't do everything they asked."

"You're married!! How could you have deceived us like this? How could you betray Bruno? He'll be devastated, you bastard!" Eric rails at Denis.

"I didn't want to do it! What choice did I have when they threatened to murder my wife?!"

"So you insinuated yourself into my household so you could spy on us. You are beneath contempt. How can you be a married man when you obviously enjoyed being passed around amongst us?"

"The marriage was arranged by our parents. Her parents were Muslims at birth, mine are French converts. My wife, Nada, and I were forced to marry by our imam. While we did go through with the ceremony, we never consummated the marriage. To say that we have a loveless marriage is by far an understatement. Someone at our mosque in Lyon, where I come from, must have conspired to help get me my job with Mercedes-Benz so they could eventually use me in their schemes for world domination. When my connection to your automotive parts business became known, they saw their opportunity to exploit the connection."

"You're suggesting that they forced you to marry this girl, knowing all along that they could use her to compel you to do their bidding whenever they wanted to?!" Eric asks, stunned.

"Yes, that's exactly what I'm saying. They knew I'd never consider doing anything like that unless I had no choice."

"Eric, Viktor, I found out earlier today that you are probably going to be apprehended and brought in for questioning," Cliff informs them.

"You must not be taken into custody and be stigmatized. I'm going to need time to sort this out and you mustn't be found here for then I'll be stopped dead in my tracks. Brad, do you know a place where we can hide Eric, Viktor and Denis?"

"It just so happens that I do. The reason I built this house here in the first place was because my wife's parents had a cabin not a mile from here, reachable on paths that connect the properties. We wanted to be near them. As it happens, they died in an auto crash and later she died of cancer. I've kept the cabin and seldom use it, but it will come in handy now."

"Good, Brad, let's clear all traces of Eric and Viktor from the house in case someone comes calling. Eric, after we help you load up your car, the three of you must leave immediately. Brad will come with you to show you the way and he can make his way back on foot. I must make some urgent calls." The four leave and Cliff makes his calls to Moscow.

Not 45 minutes after Eric drove away, a car rolled up the driveway to the cabin.

Cliff could see that it was an unmarked car carrying two agents, probably from Homeland Security.

He prepared himself for what he was going to say.

There was no point in denying that Eric and Viktor had been there.

It would be too easy to check.

At the ring of the bell, Cliff goes to the door.

"Cliff Bradshaw, we're field agents sent by Homeland Security. May we come in?"

"Yes, certainly gentlemen, what can I do for you?" he asks while ushering them into the living room.

The two men are nondescript in their gray suits, white shirts, and rep ties.

"We are looking for Eric Holtz and Viktor Sidorov who are in this country on a temporary visa. Do you know their whereabouts?"

"While those gentlemen had dropped by for a brief visit, they have since left, driving to Fletcher, North Carolina where they are building a factory. Is there a problem?"

"There may be. We need to take them in for questioning. How long ago did they leave?"

"Yesterday, it was right after breakfast."

"You don't happen to know the route they took?"

"No, not really, they have a navigation system in their car, so I imagine they took the most direct route. What's this all about? Have they done something wrong?"

"That's what we want to question them about. There have been accusations of wrong doing but we don't know, as yet, if there's any truth to this intel."

"I'm sorry I haven't been able to help but you should be able to track them down while they are in transit." The agents, while not convinced of Cliff's cooperation, decided that they had no choice but to leave.

"Thank you, Mr. Bradshaw. Please contact us if they should contact you. Here's my card. We'll be going now." Cliff sees them to the door, relieved that they seemed to buy his lies.

After they leave, Tommy and Marc arrive back from their afternoon walk.

"Oh, your property is marvelous, Cliff, so many wonderful paths with great views. The fresh air is intoxicating." Marc said excitedly.

"Glad you like it, Marc. Guys, we're in a bit of a pickle here." He explains the situation.

"It might be best if you stayed with Hector until things calm down. Should the Homeland Security agents return, I don't want you to get involved. I'll phone Hector to make sure he's up for doing this for us. You better plan on extending your stay until we see our way past this crisis."

"No problem here, Cliff. Staying in the country for a few more days is hardly hardship duty." Tommy said.

"Agreed, Marc chimes in. Hector is an interesting character that I may find a way of including in my book. In any case, he'll make for an interesting — interview."

When Cliff phones Hector, he quickly agrees to have Tommy and Marc stay with him. They pack up and drive over. Brad comes through the back door, having secured the three men at the camp. He walked back home.

"So what's the latest?" Brad inquires.

Cliff gives him a rundown of events since he left.

"Wow, we timed that close! Were you able to get in touch with your contacts in Moscow?"

"Yes and I hope they'll come up with some answers soon before this problem spirals out of control."

"This is serious shit. We could all be in real jeopardy depending on how this thing plays out." Brad frets.

"Don't I know it! There's a lot at stake for all of us. The shit could really hit the fan!" Cliff agrees.

Chapter 8

"Gee, Hector, this swimming hole on your property is the perfect place to get away from everything and enjoy escaping from the real world," Marc said animatedly.

Hector, Tommy and Marc drove up a dirt road in Hector's Dodge pickup truck to a high point on the ranch where the swimming hole was to be found in a small clearing.

Getting out of the pickup, they emptied the truck bed of the blankets, beer and el casado (lunch).

The mountain stream feeding into the swimming hole and continuing down the mountain makes for a pleasant gurgling sound which envelopes the clearing.

The sun slanting through the trees dapples the ground with patches of sunlight.

The pine needles covering the open area make a nice cushion for the blankets.

"So who's up for a dip in that beautiful clear water," Tommy said, stripping off his clothes.

"Get real, Tommy, that water is ice cold!" Marc said, wrapping his arms around himself.

"Hector, I think Marc needs a little help with his decision to partake of your healing waters," Tommy said with a mischievous gleam in his eye.

"Fuck, yeah, come on Marc, we want to see your cute little tail descending beneath the depths of this refreshing bath." Hector said, rubbing his hands together.

"My baths are in hot water, babe. There's no way — Get your hands off me you fuckers!" Marc is stripped naked, unable to fend off his attackers, taken over to the edge of the swimming hole, and thrown in.

Quickly popping up from beneath the surface of the water, he lets out a piercing yell. "You bastards!"

Hector and Tommy have peeled off their clothes too and hand in hand, they jump into the water with a great splash, which washes over Marc, still recovering from the initial shock of being dumped into the cold water.

"What dumb fucks!" Marc said smiling.

Tommy pops up behind Marc and Hector takes up a position in front.

"So, Marc, How's your winky?!" Grabbing a handful between Marc's legs, Hector asks.

"A little on the petite side, I'd say." He makes a gesture with his thumb and index finger indicating the small size.

Cupping Marc's butt cheeks, Tommy said, "His buns are still a nice handful." Marc dog paddles away from his molesters.

"You horny shits, go fuck yourselves!"

"There's an idea, Hector," Tommy says while wrapping his legs around Hector's waist.

Hector's prick springs up to poke between Tommy's ass cheeks.

"Tommy, I think your asshole and my cock need to be introduced."

"You got that right, Hector. Hell, I've been waiting for you to make a move ever since we landed on your doorstep. That picnic blanket looks like the perfect opportunity." They swim to shallow water and emerge from the water.

Hector already has the middle finger of his right hand up Tommy's ass.

"Ooo, yeah, Hector, play with my pussy, but what I really want is your dick inside me."

"Get your delectable butt down on the blanket. I want you on your back with your knees beside your ears." Tommy falls on the blanket stretched out on his back.

Hector falls on his knees at Tommy's feet.

"Ok, babe, raise 'em, I want to have at your butt hole." Tommy puts his hands behind his knees to bring them alongside his ears.

Hector dives into Tommy's crack, mounting an intense attack on his hole.

Grasping each butt cheek, Hector's tongue traces a trail along the whole crack with frequent stops at the hole for deep tongue penetration.

"Suck out my hole, Hector! Yeah, feast on my asshole." Hector feeds voraciously as if it were a feast for a king.

"Oh, Tommy, I haven't had me a fly boy before so send me to an earth orbit!" Hector says.

"Slip on a condom from my backpack. You'll find lube in there too. Don't keep me waiting, Hector, I'm ready for a pounding now!"

Hector is now sheathed and Tommy lubed when Hector gets up on his hands and toes to mount Tommy.

With one great shove, Hector's prick is lodged deep into Tommy's airborne ass.

"Shit, Tommy, I knew you were going to feel good!"

"Don't tease me, Hector, screw my pussy. I need it hard and deep. Bang me good!" Hector's cock becomes like a pile driver, furiously driving up and down into the fuck hole, pressing the shaft in deep.

"Oh, oh, Hector, yes, oh yes, I'm going to come!"

"Man, you have company!" Hector answers.

Tommy's prick shoots several streams of cum as Hector pumps Tommy's cavern with his load.

Their deep guttural cries join in chorus as they spend their seed.

As they fall in a heap on the blanket, panting, Marc emerges from the water.

"Thanks for the entertainment, guys, but what about me?!" Marc said, his hands on his hips in mock annoyance.

"You went all virginal on us when we had you in the water. Did our display on the blanket suddenly put you in the mood?" Tommy asks.

"What else, watching a hot fuck like that. Why wouldn't I want to get a little too?!"

"Let's have a little change in venue," Tommy suggests, pulling Hector to his feet and leading him over to the pickup truck.

"Grab a blanket, Marc and throw it into the truck bed." That done, Tommy directs Hector into the truck, "Lie down on the blanket, Hector, turnabout is only fair play."

With Hector on his back in the truck bed, Tommy, standing behind the truck pulls Hector toward him, using the blanket to slide him into position.

"Marc, grab some condoms and lube out of my backpack."

"Raise your legs, Hector," Tommy said, inserting three lubed fingers into his hole.

"Ok, Marc, get up in the truck. I want to look at your pretty little ass as you sit on Hector's face." Marc bounds up into the truck to get into position, straddling Hector's face.

"Let him eat your pussy, Marc. He's starving for ass crack, stuck in this remote mountain retreat."

With Hector's perfect little ass globes right at the edge of the tailgate, Tommy places his knob against the winking hole and stuffs his cock in to his pubes.

"What a fine hot hole you have, Hector. I knew you could be counted on to have a tight, silky smooth pussy."

Hector can be heard slurping on Marc's ass as Tommy gets in a rhythm of servicing Hector's hole, using fast then slow tempos to drive Hector into sensual overdrive.

Tommy is nearing a peak when Hector pleads, "Tommy, pound me, really pound me!" Now drilling Hector's pussy rapid fire, Tommy's dick detonates in Hector's ass, spewing fireballs of cum.

"Marc, back that ass up and sit on Hector's dick. He's about to blow and you'll want your hole to suck in his prick." Marc backs up and with his hole well slickened from Hector's tongue, drops down on the rigid shaft.

"Work your ass, Marc, show Hector a good time. Ride him!"

"Hector's dick is so fine, oh, oh, I could ride him all afternoon!" Marc exclaims.

Not requiring much of a ride, Hector thrusts his hips upwards as Marc's ass is descending and sends a searing blast of cum into the author's bowels.

"Christ, Marc, your ass is sucking my dry. It feels sooo, sooo, good!!" Hector said.

"You're not done yet, Marc!" Tommy instructs.

"Pop Hector's dick out of your ass so you can fuck his face." Lifting off of Hector, Marc moves to position his cock at Hector's mouth while balanced on his hands and toes.

Hector opens his mouth to form a welcoming hole.

Marc slips his dick past Hector's full lips and deep into his mouth.

Hector's tongue dances around the invading cock before vacuum sucking it like the pro he is.

"Hector, oh Hector, shit — I'm — coming!!!" Slamming his prick to the back of Hector's throat, Marc feels a sense of vertigo as he unleashed a dizzying orgasm, washing down Hector's throat.

"Ok, you sluts, it's time for lunch and a couple of beers," Tommy announces.

They move back to the blanket to have lunch, knowing what dessert was going to be.

It must be the mountain air.

———————————————

Meanwhile, back at the ranch, Cole returns home unexpectedly.

He canceled the last rodeo he was entered in because he was homesick and wanted to be with Hector.

Besides, the cowboys on the circuit this year left something to be desired and he wasn't getting much action in the bunk house.

Since Hector wasn't home, he seized the opportunity to shower and spruce himself up in readiness for Hector's return.

Knowing how Hector likes to see him in full cowboy regalia, he put on his leather chaps over his jeans, leather vest over his denim shirt, cowboy boots and black suede hat.

Impatient that Hector still hadn't returned, Cole decides to investigate whether he was over to Brad's place doing caretaker chores.

He moseys on over there to see that there's someone on the back deck.

Moving to the deck, he discovers Brad and Cliff sitting around a picnic table, tossing down some beer.

"Hello!" Cole calls out to announce his arrival.

"Howdy, neighbor, you must be Cole Strong by the look of you," Brad guesses.

"Yep, you nailed me, Brad I take it?"

"You got it, partner, what brings you around to these parts? Let me guess.

You're looking for Hector.

Am I right?" Brad is taken with what is obviously the reigning local hunk.

"Right again, partner, where the hell is the little punk!"

"Actually, he's entertaining a couple of our guests, doing us a favor. So maybe we can return the favor and entertain you in his absence. How about joining us for a beer?" Brad's wheels are already turning as to what to do with this vision of manhood.

"Don't mind if I do, I'm parched." Cole comes to join them at the picnic table up on the deck.

He's 6'-2" with broad shoulders, narrow hips and long legs.

He shakes their hands and flashes a high megawatt smile, lighting up a ruggedly handsome face.

"When I last telephoned Hector, he told me about the entertainment he provided you guys the other night."

"Hope you were ok with it, Cole. What's with all the western duds? I thought you came home from rodeo country." Cliff asks.

"For sure but — well — my little partner likes to see me in this get-up before — you know — "

"We sure as hell do, Cole, sorry your homecoming was such a dud," Brad sympathizes.

"Especially since you weren't around the other night to enjoy our little — party. So drink up, enjoy some beer with us now."

"Hell I know, sorry I missed it. Hector gave it a rave review, the little prick." He drains his beer.

"Now, now, Cole, don't be ticked off at him. I'm afraid we were a bad influence. He's quite a little package you know," Cliff points out.

"Yeah well, it's nice he's spreading it around but his lover is starving for a little right about now."

"No need for that, Cole, a big stud like you needn't go unappreciated," Brad said.

"You know I really like your outfit but it could be improved if you wore only the chaps, boots, and hat."

"Ya think so. Well that's no problem." He strips to reveal a truly spectacular body, hardened from an arduous life on the rodeo circuit.

He puts the chaps back on, then the cowboy boots and finally the black suede cowboy hat.

"Well, cowboy, you are one hunk of a man!!" Brad allows.

"Come set yourself down at the end of our big picnic table and spread your legs wide. I feel like getting a piece of your big dick!"

Cole sits where Brad wants him, throwing his arms back and resting on his hands.

"Come and get it, partner, it's all yours." Brad kneels between the cowboy boots and gobbles down the 8" cock.

Cole throws his head back, gasping.

Brad, hungry for the studly cowboy meat, feeds furiously not neglecting the low hanging ball sac but focusing on servicing the thick shaft.

Cole is toast in record time, giving up a massive load to his cock slave.

"Holy cow, Brad, you bone good, real good!" Cole enthuses.

He stands up to clear his head.

"That was just for openers, stud muffin, now Cliff and I really want to express our feelings for a very desirable neighbor. Cliff, strip and get your ass up on the table where Cole was sitting. Do it now!"

Cliff is now sitting at the end of the picnic table with his ass close to the edge, cock craning high.

"Ok, stud," Brad said to Cole.

"Get up on the table facing my lover and sit down on his big cock." Cole climbs up on the table, the heels of his boots flanking Cliff's hips, and squats down slowly until he is impaled on Cliff's dick.

"How does that feel, big guy?" Brad asks.

"Way good, man, oh yeah. I needed this!"

"With a butt as beautiful as yours, Cole, you really need some extra loving," Brad said.

"So, Cole, hike yourself up! Because my lovers cock is about to have company."

With Cole squatting so that only Cliff's cock-head is still implanted in his ass, Brad presses his dick-head into Cole's hungry hole to join his lover's cock.

Cole's great muscled orbs are now stuffed with two big dicks.

Cole lowers his butt to fill his asshole with two very big stiff dicks.

"Come on buddy, let's see how you ride those broncos in the rodeo. Shake it, baby, move that big ass, suck up our dicks!!!" Brad demands.

Cole, loving the feel of two dicks plugging his hole, rides them like the professional he is, enjoying having his pussy stretched to the limit.

"Whoa, man, Christ yeah, oh man that's what I needed!" He rides Brad's and Cliff's cocks, sucking in the stiff shafts, savoring his defilement.

Jerking his meat, Cole plops down on Cliff's groin to coax out a spewing orgasm as his fuck cavern is ravaged by two exploding dicks.

He lifts up and drops down again to insure that he has drained his invaders dry.

Brad wraps his arms around Cole as Cole turns his head to receive Brad's plundering tongue in his mouth.

"Those cowboys you left behind must be crying in their beer that a prime fuck buddy like you isn't around," Brad said.

"Brad, good buddy, you can be sure that I didn't toss them pussy like this. For you guys, anything, anytime. We're going to be best pals!"

"Glad to hear it, Cole, and you can expect that we'll give as good as we get." Brad answers.

The telephone rings inside and Brad goes in to answer it.

Coming back out to the deck, he tells Cliff the call is for him.

"Hello!" The field agent he'd contacted in Moscow was on the line with good news.

The network of operatives dealing in illegal arms and explosive materials was routed and brought down, exonerating Eric and Viktor of having any involvement with them.

Uri Koslov was apprehended by Russian agents and hasn't been heard from since.

Cliff is ecstatic, knowing what this news will mean to all his friends here and in Washington.

After ringing off with his contact in Moscow, Cliff goes back out on the deck to find Cole dressed and ready to depart.

"Thanks, guys, you're the best but I need to get home now to see what's up with my Hector." They exchange hugs and Cole leaves.

"Brad, it's over!!" Cliff exclaims, joyously.

"The illegal arms network that also was involved in trafficking bomb making materials has been uncovered and Eric and Viktor are cleared of any involvement!" They embrace, relieved that the crisis is at an end.

Again, the phone rings.

Cliff goes back in to get the call to find Debbie on the line.

"Cliff, have you heard what's happened in Moscow?!"

"Why yes, Debbie, I just got off the phone with my contact in Moscow. He told me the covert network dealing in illegal arms was broken, clearing Eric and Viktor!"

"Didn't he go into any further detail, Cliff?"

"No, it was a rather rushed call. He could only give me the bottom line. What's up, Debbie, do you know more of the specifics?!"

"Perhaps a bit more. It seems that when Uri Koslov, a triple agent, felt the net tightening, he panicked and tried to cut his losses. He gave the order to terminate Denis Giraud's Muslim wife so that her kidnapping couldn't be traced back to him. Little did he know, we had a mole in the Russian Mafia who could supply us with the evidence we needed to connect Uri with that organization and his role in her killing. The wife was discovered at the side of a remote road in Stuttgart with her throat cut. Jason is aware that you are probably detaining her husband and wants you to be the one to inform him of her death. It has also become known that Denis was clearly under duress when he agreed to keep tabs on Eric and Viktor while they were in the US. Homeland Security has no interest in him anymore than they do with Eric and Viktor."

"While I'm glad my friends Eric and Viktor are free to pursue their business interests in the US, I'm sorry that Denis has sustained such a personal loss. It will be my sad duty to inform him of this tragedy. It's hard to believe that Uri Koslov was not only a double agent but a triple agent with the Russian Mafia, as well. Thanks for the update, Debbie, you've been a rock throughout this ordeal."

"It's a great relief to me that you didn't manage to irreparably damage your career with your loyalty to your friends Eric and Viktor. And I must say that I'm relieved for myself too that I didn't get drawn into what could have been a vortex to the bottom with my career in the tank. And before I forget to ask, what in hell is happening with my dear husband Marc?"

"As you know, he's been diligently pursuing interviews with everyone here to add fodder for his book. He seems to be progressing nicely but no one has been allowed to get an advanced look at his jottings."

"He and I need to have a serious heart to heart about where we stand with our marriage. Obviously, I haven't been honest with him about my misadventures but I plan to make amends and admit that I too have strayed."

"Please understand, Debbie, that I don't judge you. You're my friend and I'll always support you no matter what. But I'm damn proud of you for facing up to the challenge of dealing with your marital troubles, head on."

"Yeah, well we'll have to see won't we? Glad to know I'll have a shoulder to cry on when everything blows up in my face. Well I'd better get back to work before the boss demotes me to the file room." They ring off.

———————————

Cliff drives to the cabin where Eric, Viktor and Denis are hiding out.

Entering the cabin's living room, he finds Eric and Viktor slumped in chairs flanking the fireplace looking like they just received dire news of a loss in the family.

"Cheer up, guys, I bring you good news! You've been cleared of any culpability in the plot to smuggle arms and explosives into this country. You're free to travel and complete your itinerary!"

Looking up, both men smile and thank Cliff for the good news.

"So why are you two still so glum? You should be hopping around this room. You're home free for Christ's sake!"

"We've got a problem, Cliff. It's Denis. He's holed up in his room and despondent for fear that Bruno will never forgive him for his betrayal. We're seriously worried that he might do something foolish."

"What I didn't mention is that along with the good news, I also have some bad news. Denis's wife was executed in Stuttgart and found with her throat slashed by the side of the road."

"How very sad," Eric said, grimacing.

"This news won't assist us in trying to bring Denis out of his funk. What are we going to do?!"

"You need to arrange to get Bruno here at once!" Cliff said.

"He's the only one to bring Denis around. We can only hope to stabilize him so he won't become truly dangerous to himself. Eric, why don't you get on the phone to Bruno to get the ball rolling with flight arrangements, etc.? Have him catch a connecting flight from Dulles into the Raleigh County Memorial Airport where we can pick him up. Viktor, take me to Denis so I can break the news of the end of your predicament but also the sad news of the demise of his wife."

Viktor and Cliff enter Denis's bedroom to find him sprawled on the bed looking up at the ceiling with a blank expression on his face.

He's unshaven and generally unkempt, obviously distraught.

"Please get up, Denis. Cliff is here to see you with some important news," Viktor said and then leaves the room.

Denis, in a trance-like state, sits up in bed to face Cliff who pulls up a desk chair beside the bed.

"Denis, you'll be happy to know that Eric and Viktor are known to be innocent of all the allegations leveled against them that they were planning on smuggling arms into this country, using their business as a front. They are now free to leave for North Carolina and go about their business. With the good news, there is some bad news I'm afraid. Your wife was — executed and found dead in Stuttgart."

Looking like he'd been shot, Denis bends over with his face buried in his hands and weeps uncontrollably.

Cliff goes to him and wraps him in his arms, letting him weep against his chest.

They remain like that for many minutes until Cliff said, "This is not the outcome you wished for, Denis. You did everything possible to protect her. You mustn't blame yourself for a tragedy that you did everything you could to prevent."

"It's true that the marriage was forced upon me and that I didn't love her but it was no more her fault than mine that we found ourselves in such a terrible situation. As her husband, I wanted to at least protect her from harm and in this I failed too. She didn't deserve this!" he said sobbing.

"Neither one of you deserved the fate that fell upon you. But you must accept that you were victimized too. This wasn't your doing. Eric and Viktor are your friends and are very worried about you. Please don't add to their distress with all they've been through by allowing yourself to fall apart. They need to know that you are going to be ok," Cliff said staring into Denis's stricken eyes.

"Promise me you will sleep tonight putting this as much out of your mind as possible until we can all meet again tomorrow to discuss the future."

"You and Brad have been very kind to all of us, Cliff, so yes I'll do as you say. Thank you for your understanding and support." Cliff gets up and leaves the room.

"So, Cliff, what happened? How is Denis taking the news?" Viktor asks.

"If I read him right, I think we bought ourselves some time until Bruno comes on the scene to do the major repairs. Is Bruno on his way?"

"Yes, we spoke to him, bringing him up to date on developments.

While he was badly shaken to learn of Denis's activities that served to compromise us, he was understanding and has forgiven him.

He'll be on a flight tonight from Munich, arriving at Dulles tomorrow morning and with a connecting flight, he'll reach the airport in Raleigh around lunch time," Eric said.

"Perfect, don't leave Denis alone tomorrow morning, giving him too much time to think. Try to distract him with your travel plans to North Carolina. Get him involved with planning lunch for when Brad and I come over tomorrow, hopefully with Bruno in tow."

"Yes, we can do that. We'll slip a sedative into his supper tonight so he'll sleep through the night," Viktor said.

Cliff, Brad and Bruno arrive at the cabin after picking Bruno up at the airport.

Entering the living room, Bruno is received warmly by Eric and Viktor.

"We're relieved that you've come, Bruno," Eric said.

"Denis is still skittering along the edge, unable to stop beating on himself for his shame in betraying us but most especially you. He still can't imagine that you could ever find it in yourself to forgive him."

"Where is he, Eric, I must go to him!"

"In an effort to distract him, we've busied him in the kitchen helping us to prepare lunch. He has no idea that you'd be joining us."

"Let me bring him into the living room to greet you. I hope the shock will not be too great," Viktor said.

Slightly disheveled from all the lunch preparations, Denis emerges from the kitchen and enters the living room, first seeing Cliff and Brad before realizing there was an additional member of their party.

"What — what are you doing here, Bruno!! I can't imagine why you've come, I can't — I can't even look you in the eye." With this, Denis whirls on his heel and rushes out of the room with Bruno in hot pursuit.

"We can only hope that we haven't made a terrible blunder in bringing Bruno here. Perhaps Denis is just too fragile to pick up the pieces so soon," Eric ponders.

"You saw the way Bruno was looking at Denis, Eric. There can be no doubt of his intentions to take his lover back by whatever means he must," Viktor said with conviction.

"There's no point in our holding lunch for them. Clearly they'll need time to sort through their conflicted feelings. So I'd suggest we sit down to lunch and wait for the outcome," Viktor suggests. "It's a cold lunch so it'll keep for them."

Over lunch Eric tells Cliff and Brad of their intention of leaving the next day to drive to Fletcher, North Carolina where their plant is to be built.

If they leave early, they can be there by lunch time, it being about a four hour drive.

Assuming that Denis is sufficiently recovered to make the trip, they plan to take him and Bruno with them.

They'd like Bruno to see where the plant will be constructed.

Later that afternoon, they plan on putting Denis and Bruno on a flight out of the Asheville Regional Airport that will fly them to Dulles where they can catch a Lufthansa flight to Munich.

"Perhaps this isn't the most opportune time to bring up another matter but given our time constraints, it'll have to do," Eric announces.

"You see, Cliff and Brad, even though we've been here a short time, we've fallen in love with Washington and the Blue Ridge Mountains of West Virginia. Our expanding business is going to require that we make frequent visits to the States and we will want to have our own home or homes to stay in when we're here. To put it right out there, we'd really like to buy your condo in Bethesda, Cliff and your cabin here, Brad. Would you consider selling them to us?"

"Speaking for myself," Cliff answers, "It would be my pleasure. Now that I've moved in with Brad, I no longer need the place."

"Actually, I've been thinking about selling this cabin because I really have no use for it. Since it had been my in-laws cherished home, I felt constrained from selling it too quickly after their deaths and I was worried about who might buy it in terms of what kind of neighbors they'd be. But hell, you guys would be ideal neighbors for us. So yes, I'd be happy to sell you the place." Agreeing on a friendly price proved to be no problem and the deals were struck with a handshake.

The lawyers could handle the paper work.

While lunch proceeded in the dining room, Bruno and Denis had repaired to Denis's bedroom.

Denis, staring out the window with his back to Bruno said, "You shouldn't have come, Bruno. I know you can't stand the sight of me. I don't blame you for hating me. I hate myself for what I've done."

"Don't flatter yourself that you know how I feel for you don't have a clue! Your disgusting bath in recriminations and self-pity is over. I've heard enough of it. Pull yourself together and be the man I've fallen in love with. I don't want this pathetic vestige of yourself. Turn around and come over here, now!"

Turning with an expression of confusion and wonder, Denis said, "You — you love — me? But how could you after — ?"

"Didn't you hear me? I said get over here!" Denis moves to within two feet of Bruno, looking perplexed. Bruno closes the distance between them and wraps Denis in a tight embrace, raining kisses on his forehead, eyes, nose, mouth, and cheeks. "I love you with all my heart, you foolish man."

Kissing Bruno back, Denis said, "Oh, Bruno, I love you too and was consumed with fear that I'd irrevocably broken the bond that we shared."

"Now you know differently. My happiness is now completely dependent on your being happy too. We're a couple now. I'm sorry for the tragedy of you losing your wife. We can only take solace in the fact that you did your best to spare her harm. If you hadn't stood by her as you did, that would have been the only reason I could ever have turned away from you."

"Bruno, love, I hope I can prove myself worthy of you. It's hard to accept my good fortune to have found you when I thought my life was predetermined for me, a life I didn't want. The Muslim religion isn't for me and never was."

Wiping tears from his lover's face, Bruno said, "We mustn't remain in here any longer, everyone expects us to share lunch together. We'll have the rest of our lives to be together."

"What I want to do right now is drop to my knees and take you in my mouth," Denis replies.

"We'll be leaving for Regensburg tomorrow afternoon so there'll be plenty of time to catch up," Bruno answers, cupping Denis's ass cheeks.

Bruno kisses Denis while his tongue explores the interior of his mouth, sucking on his tongue before exiting.

"Come, we'd better go out there before I rip your clothes off and plunder each and every one of your orifices. I'm going to help your forget the awful years you've spent as a Muslim lackey"

Rejoining the lunch guests, it's apparent to everyone that the crisis has lifted and Denis, having made a remarkable improvement, joined the living.

After everyone finished their lunch, Cliff suggests, "You know we're all about to depart in different directions so what say we all gather at our house for a going away dinner, We'll enlist Hector and Cole to help.

Come over for cocktails at 6:00 PM and we'll eat at 8:00.

The dinner, thrown together quickly, consisted of all American fare, barbecued hamburgers and hot dogs, french fries, potato salad and a tossed salad.

The beer and wine flowed and everybody relaxed, knowing that tomorrow everyone would be on their way, back to their lives.

By this time Marc had interviewed almost everyone, but he hadn't had a chance to be with Cole.

After dinner, he and Cole had the cleanup detail while everyone else went back inside to watch a college football game on tape.

"You know, Marc, I'm exhausted. Guess I'm not cut out for domestic chores.

What say you and me go downstairs to the hot tub under the deck? It's a great way to relax. Tonight, with a clear sky, we can see the mountains in the distance with bright stars overhead."

"That'd be perfect, Cole, I was working up to asking you a few questions to provide some more background for my book. While we're soaking, I could do an informal interview. Ok with you?"

"Sure, partner, let's do it." Descending to the hot tub area under the deck, Cole starts undressing, removing his shirt.

Marc, carrying a six-pack of beer, drinks in the sight of Cole's big shoulders, tapered back funneling down to a narrow waist, incredible buns and long, gorgeous legs.

His dick is already half hard.

"Guess there's plenty of room in the tub for two of us."

"Hell, yeah, the tub seats four. Come on, take your clothes off, babe, we're going to have us some fun." Cole watches as Marc strips and reveals his trim body, much more muscular than his loose fitting clothes revealed.

"You're sure a tasty little package for a city boy. My Hector says you, being an ex-cop, are new to man on man action but have picked up a few tricks very fast."

"Oh well, I don't know. Hector maybe exaggerated — you know — I'm just sort of learning, being an old married man."

Cole, now buck naked, gets into the tub getting comfortable in one of the corner seats and sighs with contentment with the water bubbling all around him.

"So what are you waiting for, city boy, I won't bite. Get that cute little butt in here and hand me a beer while you're at it. You're about Hector's size. I like my men on the smaller size." Marc gets into the tub and moves to another corner seat.

"Not over there, babe, park that pretty cop butt on my lap. I can see your cock's practically hard so let's not be pretending to lack interest in what I've got between my legs."

Needing little encouragement, Marc moves towards Cole with beer in hand, turns and settles himself against the big cowboy.

It is very apparent to Marc that Cole's big dick is rapidly rising and filling his entire ass crack.

He's awed and a little afraid that he's entering into something from which there will be no escape.

"Maybe I'm too heavy to be sitting on top of you, Cole. I can move to the other — "

"Not on your life, Marc honey. You and me are just getting acquainted. Can't you feel my big old dick nudging your crack. I want a little piece of that tight little ass you've given everyone else a sample of."

"There's no way I can handle a big cowboy dick like yours, Cole. You'll tear me open. Sure Tommy's been getting it regularly but he's not anywhere near as big as you."

"My Hector's hole was sure tight enough before I stretched his asslips to take me. Now I can plug him using only a little spit. Believe me, you're no different. Ya just gotta trust me. Now stand up and face me! You need a little priming's all."

Turning to face Cole, Marc's prick is immediately suctioned into Cole's mouth, his dick-head poking the back of his throat.

"Unh, unh," Marc exclaims, now smitten with this hunky cowboy.

Reaching in to his discarded jeans, Cole extracts a condom and a packet of lube, having come to the party prepared.

While sucking Marc's cock and deep throating him, Cole works a lubed finger into his hole, playing with Marc's prostate.

"How does that feel, buddy. Are you ready for another finger?" Cole proceeds to insert a second finger before Marc replies.

Marc is moaning, knowing he's toast.

Marc's asshole is much looser than it was only weeks ago, given all the recent attention his new friends have given it.

The third finger goes in remarkably easily, establishing that Marc is ready to please Cole with his submission.

Cole slips on a condom.

Letting Marc's dick pop out of his mouth, Cole said, "Ok, my good buddy, turn back around and sit on my dick, you know you want it." Marc squats down until his hole encounters the fat head of Cole's dick.

Grasping Marc's hips, Cole lowers the creamy smooth ass down on his big Johnson.

"Christ, babe, your tight bung hole is like a velvet glove." Cole's dick is now buried to the hilt inside Marc's bowels.

"You ok, kid? Because I'm ready for you to take a ride." Cole is pinching one of Marc's tits, as he grips his cock with his other hand.

"Yeah, cowboy! I'm all saddled up and ready to join the rodeo." With this, Marc, good to his word, raises and lowers himself on the big dick in a rapid rhythm, driving Cole over the top, feeling Cole's convulsing dick filling the condom in his ass to the limit.

Simultaneously, Marc's cock explodes in Coles's hand, spewing jizz into the gurgling waters.

"Shit, man! Hector was right. You're one hot fuck, author man. You really know how to ride and that's a compliment coming from a cowboy."

Just then they hear someone coming down the stairs from the deck above.

"I wondered where you two disappeared," Tommy said.

"Should have guessed that Marc couldn't keep it in his pants with a big cowboy stud around. You're really racking up the mileage on that ass, Marc. But maybe Cole would like to poke a hole with a little more talent to offer. What do you say, stud? Can you keep that dick stiff long enough for me to take a ride around the ring?"

"Come on ahead, Tommy boy! I've been itching to sample you too. You were next on my list." Marc dismounts while Tommy lubes up his ass.

Marc climbs up to stand at the edge of the tub flanking Cole and lowers himself so he can fuck Coles's face, holding steady by gripping Cole's hair.

Cole sucks him in furiously, bobbing his head enjoying every angle.

Floating to the entwined pair, Tommy runs his legs up Cole's chest until Cole embraces him and maneuvers him over his cock when with one powerful thrust, Cole jams his dick up Tommy's ass, grinding his pubes into Tommy's crack.

Cole proceeds to long dick Tommy's ass while continuing to feed on Marc's engorged phallus.

Crying out, Marc gives up his load, his dick pulsing out his come, filling Cole's mouth most of which he swallows while the remainder drips out of the corners of his mouth.

Almost in unison, Cole pounds his pelvis into Tommy's upended ass cheeks, flooding his intestines with blasts of hot come.

Finally, Tommy bucks his hips up to send a geyser of come above the surface of the water, splattering Marc's hovering ass.

Resting in the corners of the hot tub afterwards, they each take stock.

"You make quite a tag team, boys. Wish you would be around when I'm on the rodeo circuit."

"Hector is a lucky man," Tommy said.

"He gets to ride that big schlong all the time."

"I'll say, Marc chimes in, that was a hell of a ride. Sign me up for a return engagement next time we visit Brad and Cliff."

"Hector and I will be glad to take care of you boys whenever you're around. Well I'm going to leave you love birds to your own devices and find out what Hector is up to. He better not be entertaining the troops again when he hasn't taken care of the man he came with."

Slipping on his boots and leaving the rest of his clothes where they lay, Cole went upstairs to the deck to find Bruno and Denis sitting huddled together on a bench, looking out at the stars.

Moving on into the house, Cole found his way to the den where the party goers had gone.

Entering the room, he encountered another specialty of the house, a tableau involving, this time, two couples.

On one side of the sectional L-sofa, Viktor, facing Cole, was suspended above a seated Brad, riding his cock, legs splayed wide while pumping his cock.

Similarly, on the other wing of the sofa, Eric rode Cliff's cock while pulling on his stiff dick.

"Whoa, guys, this is where all the action is. I'm gonna have me some cock!" Falling to his knees in front of Viktor and Brad, Cole grips one of Viktor's muscular thighs with one hand and cups his balls with the other while working his lips around Viktor's cockhead. In record time, Cole felt Viktor's dick jump as he deep throated him causing Viktor to give up hurtling jets of semen, pouring down Cole's throat.

Getting up and licking his lips, Cole said, "Glad you saved a little for me, babe." Turning to Eric and Cliff, Cole again falls to his knees to service Eric, cramming his mouth with Eric's stiff prick.

While Cliff had Eric's asshole stuffed to capacity, Cole slurped on Eric's shaft steadily, taking him over the edge.

With a guttural moan, Eric's body convulsed producing a gargantuan orgasm almost choking Cole before he swallowed it all down.

"Wow, you foreigners are sure a horny bunch!" Cole observes with glee.

"Glad you're going to be part-time neighbors because I could do with more of that." Now, in a renewed state of frenzy, Viktor and Eric ride their host's cocks in perfect synchronized movement, impaling themselves forcefully to the root of Brad and Cliff's dicks, filling their fuck caverns.

Sitting and squirming on their hosts engorged pricks, Viktor and Eric feel their assholes being flooded with wetness for the third time tonight.

Their hosts can't get enough, knowing their guests are leaving in the morning.

Enjoying the end of the show, Cole leaves in search of Hector.

Hearing activity in the kitchen, he goes in to find Hector putting a final load into the dishwasher.

"Whatchadoin' in here all alone, guy! Thought you'd be entertaining the troops again."

"They've been doing well enough entertaining each other and this mess was not something anyone would want to face the morning after." Hector answers.

"Looks like you're about finished now, babe. How about some after dinner entertainment. This here cowboy would like to toss his main man a little fuck. You up for it?"

"You know I like to pork your ass as much as anyone else, big guy. Walking around like that with only your boots on was bound to net you someone willing to stick it to you. But I'm glad it's going to be me." Hector pushes Cole down on top of the sturdy pine breakfast table, grabbing his Frye boots and raising his legs high.

Cole spits on his hand and then rubs Hector's cock to slicken it for easier entrance.

Spitting on his other hand, Cole inserts his slickened fingers into his hole in preparation for Hector's sensitive crown, now displaying a pearl drop of precut.

"Oh, yeah, my Spanish stallion, show your lover what his main man can do when he's horny for ass action." Hector pushes his shoulders against the back of Cole's thighs, freeing his hands to roughly pinch Cole's tits, producing baritone grunts from his prone lover.

Hector begins pistoning Cole's lush ass while kissing him with a bruising ferocity.

Cole's grunts turn to trembling howls as his Spanish stud power slams his hole with a pounding intensity.

"Yes, Hector, don't stop, give me all you've got. I want you so bad! Screw me hard and deep, babe, show me how much you love me!!!"

Squealing at the top of his lungs for the whole county to hear, Hector fires hot milk into his lover's ass, flooding his intestines.

Cole, in turn, growls as his load pulses out of his long dick, showering his lover's abs.

"Oh Christ, honey, no one fucks the shit out of me like you do!"

"That's because you're mine, asshole, and don't you ever forget it no matter what cowboy you spread your legs for. You will always come home to me; the one who you know loves you, even though you are a big slut."

"Thems are harsh words, Hector, for someone who just tossed you a major fuck," Cole protests with a sly smile on his face. "If I behaved like a choir boy, you'd have no use for me. Admit it, you like the fact that I'm a cock whore."

"Sometimes maybe but mostly when it's me that you're getting it on with. You're lucky I haven't locked you in the barn, lashed to a post so I could have my way with you at will and share you with no man." Hector said with some heat.

"Umm, babe, that sounds like a plan. Would you whup my ass too and force me to do depraved sexual acts?!" Cole said in excited anticipation. "Get up off that table, slut, I've got to clean this place up before I drag you home where I intend to spend the night with my cock buried in your ass."

"You mean motherfucker! What are we waiting for!?" Cole said, lasciviously.

They slip out the back door, pick up Cole's clothes, and return home.

Bruno and Denis stroll back to their cabin, hand in hand, on the path lit by the moonlight.

Tommy and Marc have returned to their room where they are doing an extended session in the 69 position.

Cliff and Brad take Viktor and Eric up to the master bedroom where they'll spend the next couple of hours on their backs with their legs over Viktor and Eric's shoulders, alternately, while receiving a deep plowing from each.

This needed to be done before Brad and Cliff would allow their guests to drag themselves home, their lust sated.

It was agreed in advance that everyone would return to Brad and Cliff's place for a going away breakfast.

Waking up to a picture perfect day, everyone was remarkably energetic the next morning, probably due to all the sex they enjoyed the night before.

Marc announced that his book was virtually complete except for a final rewrite.

He planned to submit it to his publisher in a couple of weeks.

They all agree that they will attend a book signing cocktail party at a bookstore in Dupont Circle sometime in the fall, assuming the book gets the nod from Marc's editor at his publishing house.

Chapter 9

    Cliff reports back to work the following Monday to review with Jason Stone the status of his continued employment with Homeland Security.

    "Good to have you back among us, Cliff. You were sorely missed. I've had the summer to reflect on how we could continue to work together going forward. You have been of great service to your country and I don't want to lose you. Obviously, you're gainfully employed in the private security business that you and Brad have developed so successfully. But I don't want us to be deprived of the expertise you've gained in the many special operations you've handled for us so very well."

    "What I'd like you to seriously consider is to become head of a special office in charge of top secret covert missions. We anticipate that you can manage your new job with devoting only two days a week to it. You'd be supported, of course, with a fine staff of say four people who can handle the day-to-day running of this office. This approach would free you up to continue to work with your partner Brad on your own private business transactions."

"As for our personal — shall I say — affair, you were correct in suggesting that Clarence Sharkey could serve me well in exploring — what shall I call it — alternate interpersonal relationships. I've been enjoying his massages, as well as his black ass, regularly this summer. Debbie's told me that she's informed you of our own — special circumstances. In a perfect world, perhaps these clandestine couplings would be unnecessary but for now, everyone involved seems to be comfortable with the new status quo. I hope you will be too."

"No problem from this quarter, Jason. I'm just glad that everyone is managing the new normal. Hopefully Debbie and Marc have reached an accommodation as well."

"Surprisingly enough, Debbie's situation works for Marc because he and Tommy are now joined at the hip and other parts, not to put too fine a point on it. Both Debbie and Marc, as well as Tommy and Mary, are content to maintain their marriages, while allowing their spouses to have relationships outside their marriages. You may not be aware of it but Tommy's wife Mary is pregnant with their second child. Somehow they managed their conjugal duties sufficiently for this to happen."

"This is all good news, Jason, and yes my new assignment, as you've described it, works well for me. While I never imagined liking what amounts to a desk job, I'm obviously ready for it, given what's going on in the rest of my life."

"Well then it's settled, Cliff, and I'll say again how sorry I am for my part in causing you such anguish in your last assignment. With the way things have worked out for all involved, maybe I can feel assured that the end results turned out to be good."

"Definitely, Jason, with the bad came so much good. When I said how happy I was to find Brad, I meant it with all that's in me. We bring each other joy." They hug each other and Cliff leaves for home.

Arriving home, Cliff gives Brad the rundown on what transpired in his meeting with Jason.

Brad is delighted that all the pieces are beginning to fit into place in their lives.

They hug and kiss each other, appreciating how well things are working out for them.

"You know, Cliff, Tommy has approached me with a proposition I think we ought to consider. He would like to continue using one of our guest bedrooms, say on weekends. Actually it would be his and Marc's bedroom where they could spend weekends together. They both feel this arrangement will save their marriages and protect their children. We'd often be at the cabin anyway. For the privilege, they'd run the house for us, alleviating us of any of the usual chores, freeing us up to devote more time in developing our business. They'd also be available for a roll in the hay, whenever we're so inclined."

"If their wives are ok with it, why shouldn't we go for it? It seems to be a win win situation. You won't have to give up the obvious pleasures you get from sampling Tommy's favors and I'm anxious to explore the possibilities with Marc, assuming that Debbie has signed off on this arrangement."

"Cool, Cliff, but you know what, it's you that I really want despite the diversions we've allowed ourselves. When push comes to shove, these dalliances are just that. The time will come soon enough when our raging hormones simmer down so that we might well be content with a monogamous relationship. Apropos that, I want us to go upstairs now because I have a real yen to service my lover."

Cliff gets to their bedroom first and starts removing his business attire, suit, shirt and tie, etc., leaving on solely his boxer shorts.

Brad stops him from removing those, getting down on his knees in front of Cliff and removing his dick through his fly to proceed to give him a long, slow blowjob.

Running his hands up under the shorts to knead Cliff's high round buns, Brad works his lovers cock up to its full throbbing 9".

Cliff with his hands grasping Brad's buzz cut, moans, moving to a high plateau of sensual pleasure.

No one works his cock like Brad.

Brad gets to his feet and strips off his jeans and T-shirt and drops his jockeys to the floor, flipping them and his socks aside.

Jabbing his fingers into the waistband of Cliff's boxer shorts, he slips them down and off, revealing his lover's boner that he had worked to its most tumescent state of arousal.

Now Cliff drops to his knees and proceeds to demonstrate, still again, that he has no peer when it comes to pleasuring his lover's dick.

Mouthing the plumb like crown and fondling Brad's big balls, Cliff sucks his way down the 10" shaft swallowing his lover's boner.

Working the inside of his cheeks and tongue on the big prick, torturing Brad with pleasure, he frees up his middle finger on his right hand and sticks it into his mouth to wet it with saliva before slipping it up Brad's asshole.

Unerringly finding Brad's joy spot, Cliff sends him to an even higher plane of pleasure.

Reaching his peak, Brad's balls tighten, signaling the advent of a massive orgasm that erupts from his rock hard cock, exploding volleys of cum saturating Cliff's mouth before it rushes down his throat in molten flows.

Brad reluctantly slides his cock out of Cliff's mouth, turns around, and moves over to the side of their king bed.

Reaching into the night table, he removes a jar of lube and proceeds to grease up his asshole.

Accomplishing that, he gets up on the side of the bed on his knees and rests his head on his forearms, raising his beautiful SEAL ass for his lover to thoroughly plunder.

"Ok, babe, take me. I want you inside me so bad. Take it slow. I want to enjoy your dick, servicing my asshole. Love me, babe, love me long and slow until neither one of us can stand the slow torture anymore. Then fuck me full out like only the one I love can do."

Cliff, already trembling with excitement, tries to ratchet down his need to take his pleasure quickly and complies with Brad's wish to be fucked with slow deliberation, establishing his complete domination over his willing body.

Brad is high with the exquisite pleasure derived from Cliff's prick's relentless, slow plunging in and out of his fuck cavern, driving him to unexplored heights of sustained pleasure.

It's almost beyond endurance for both of them to bank their fires while their senses are driven to unimaginable pinnacles of sensuality.

"Oh, Brad honey, I can't wait any longer!" Clawing Brad's great butt mounds, Cliff begins the intense rutting dance, raising his hips high to power slam his lover's ass cheeks, flattening the mounds with a seemingly endless sound of thwack, thwack, thwack until he's unable to contain himself any longer.

"Brad, oh Brad honey, oh yes!" Cliff, with one last buck of his hips, almost lifts Brad off the mattress as his cock drives deep into his lover's hole, rocketing round after round of cum, jetting deep into Brad's bowels.

They fall to the bed together in a heap, spent from an intensity they never experienced before.

"Christ, Cliff honey, you — you've made me your bottom. I can't get enough of your cock up my ass. You're top man in our relationship now."

"That's good, Brad, because I'm not nearly done with you yet. Spread your legs wide, sweetheart, 'cause I need to slowly plow you some more until I can fill you up again with my seed."

In what seemed to be no time at all, Cliff fulfilled his promise and filled his lover up again with great streams of spewing cum. They fall asleep this way only to awake a short time later, still molded together, until Brad's ass was again filled with copious amounts of his lover's hot cum.

"My god, Brad, if we keep this up we'll kill each other inside of a week!"

"Oh but what a way to go, lover, you can really fuck me now so as to make me but putty in your hands. I feel so needy and vulnerable, like all bottoms must feel. It's great but a little frightening."

"You need to trust me, Brad, because we're not separate entities anymore. I love you and you love me. We're in it for the long haul now, no question about it. I'll always be there for you. I may be the dominant top but you get to get into my ass whenever you get a yen to plow me."

"I'm always going to be there for you too, anything you need, anything you want." When Cliff pulls out of Brad's ass, they lie facing each other to embrace.

Wrapped in each other's arms, they rain kisses over each other's faces and plunder each other's mouths.

Sitting in his new office in Homeland Security, Cliff picks up the phone on the second ring, eager to face whatever challenges his new job poses.

"Cliff Bradshaw," he announces to his caller in a take-charge voice. "Cliff, it's Debbie! Can I come by your office now? I have something to tell you!" she said, obviously excited with some news.

"Sure, Debbie, I'm still floundering around my new office trying to figure out how everything works. You could probably give me some tips."

"You've got it, babe. Be right over!" Swinging into his office and closing the door behind her, Debbie said, "Marc's editor loved his new book and they're going to publish it right away in the on-line version first! This means the world to Marc and to me too! Oh I'm so excited. This comes at such a critical time when Marc really needed positive reinforcement that he had the requisite talent to be a writer."

"That's exciting news, Debbie. I'm so pleased for you both. So when will it hit the bookstores?!"

"By mid-October the initial printing will be available at bookstores. Now we can have the book-signing party that we promised everyone. I can't wait!"

"Have you read the book yourself, Debbie, or is it too gay specific for you?"

"Yes I have read it and enjoyed it very much. As you know, I like a lot of women, enjoy love stories. Marc's book combines a love story with a mystery and gay erotica. The genres mix nicely to produce a book that can be enjoyed on several levels. The love story part appeals to me most but I surprised myself by enjoying the sex scenes too. We women usually prefer that the featured couple or couples are more monogamous but hey, the sex between so many hotties also worked for me. The mystery part to the story was icing on the cake."

"Your liking it portends well for the possibility of women reading it. As we know, men, even gay men, are pigs so there's little doubt that they'd like it. Marc should hand out condoms to those buying his book at the book-signing cocktail party, just to be politically correct."

"Oops! Almost forgot to mention the most important thing I came in here to tell you. We're having the book-signing party in our favorite bookstore in Dupont Circle on Saturday, October 15th at 6:00 PM. You and Brad must be there! You were so instrumental in insuring that Marc could pull off a story like this."

"There's no way we'd miss it, Debbie. When do I get to read the book or must I wait until its printed for the general public?"

"You can read my advance copy after Tommy returns it to me. You may recognize yourself in there but Marc was at pains to obscure the characters real identities so don't worry that someone could identify you."

"Great! I'll look forward to reading it. The party is coming at the perfect time because Eric and Viktor will be coming to Washington for a couple of weeks in October, allowing them to attend. As an added bonus, they're bringing Bruno and Denis."

"The whole gang is going to be reunited! Marc will be thrilled because he loves you guys. Time to return to the salt mines, see you for lunch — 12:30?" Cliff smiles and nods as she whirls back out of his office.

Eric and Viktor are ensconced in the condo in Bethesda that they bought from Cliff.

Bruno and Denis are there as well.

Viktor and Eric are planning to slip in a trip to their West Virginia cabin before the book-signing party.

They've sent over two horses from their stable in Regensburg.

Hector and Cole will board the horses for them.

Eric will take a side trip to Fletcher, North Carolina to view the new parts plant that is just being completed.

Viktor will remain at the cabin to see to the horses, accustoming them to their new home.

"Goodbye, Bruno and Denis! We'll see you at the end of the week when we return for the book-signing party. Bruno, you'll meet with Cliff to review some of the new security features being installed at the plant. We all need to get a handle on these new technologies. And Denis, don't let your meetings with the Mercedes-Benz reps from Tuscaloosa prevent you from attending the book-signing party. They don't need to drag you around Washington on Saturday too," Eric admonished.

"No, I should be able to give them the boot by Friday. After all they have wives and kids to go home to back in Alabama." Eric and Viktor leave for the mountains of West Virginia.

Many hours later, they arrive at the cabin to find Hector, whom they've hired to be their caretaker too, stocking their refrigerator with all the food items that they e-mailed him that they'd need for the week.

"Hey, Hector, how's our resident Spanish stallion and his hunky cowboy doing?!" Viktor said, grabbing Hector in a bear hug.

Eric joins them for a group hug.

"Doin' great, guys. Welcome to the ranch! Sorry you'll only be staying for such a short time!"

"We hope you and Cole will return to Washington with us so you too can join the festivities at the book-signing party. You'll bunk with us at our condo of course."

"Wouldn't miss it! Cliff and Brad said they'd drive us back because they'll be spending a couple weeks at their cabin."

"So where's Cole? I thought he may like to go riding with me tomorrow morning." Viktor said.

"He's in the barn feeding those hungry beasts. I'll tell him you'll be over in the morning say 9:30 AM?"

"Perfect, Eric will have left for our factory by then and I can get busy getting our Holsteiner horses happy with their new mountain home."

The next morning, Viktor sees Eric off and leaves to meet Cole at the stables.

Hector will be spending the day at Brad and Cliff's place, getting it ready for their arrival on Sunday.

"There you are Cole, bent over a feed bucket showing off your best feature." Viktor said leering at Cole.

"Howdy, Vik, you got a feature or two yourself well worth lookin' at."

"What might they be, Cole? You can level with me. Being a foreigner, it's hard to tell what you locals like in a man."

"Whatever I like, you can be sure you've got it, Vik, in spades. You know you've got a fine pair of horse flesh here in these Holsteiners. What say we take a ride up to the swimmin' hole, but American style? I'm talkin' bareback, Vik, but not just the horses. I want to see your naked backside bouncing along on the back of that powerful beast. You'll like the feel of it, I guarantee it. So strip! I'll lend you a pair of my boots but that's all you're gonna need. In fact that's all I'll be wearin' too."

Now mounted up on the Holsteiners, the two men canter from the barn to the trail that leads up to the swimming hole.

With Viktor in the lead, they get into a comfortable canter, moving up the trail through great stands of oak trees.

Cole can't take his eyes off of Viktor's magnificent ass mounds, lifting then settling on the horse's back, driving his cock to full attention.

Viktor's broad shoulders, which narrow to a small waist, seem to emphasize the fullness of his buns.

It's a bubble butt that needs to be serviced at every opportunity.

Cole plans to get to it as soon as they reach the swimming hole.

"Just keep bearin' to your right when the trail forks, Vik. We'll be there in about 15 minutes. Hope the trail in not too hard on your backside."

"No, it feels good to be skin to skin with my horse. I think he likes it too."

"Yeah, you're right. Why wouldn't he. I know I would," Cole said with conviction.

"Maybe you'd enjoy a sniff of my crack when we stop at the end of the trail, Cole. You can always be counted on to be a horny bastard."

"Well I'm gonna want me more than a sniff but a sniff will make for a good place to start. Being a cowboy, I like the smell a horse leaves on a man. It makes my cock throb."

"Riding bareback with my ass hanging out has made me horny, Cole. I'm ready for a little servicing from the hired hand. Do you think you can do as you're told and mount me?"

"If calling me the hired hand makes you think I'm going to give you an angry fucking, you're dead right, Vik. You'll be schooled in who's the real boss around here, fucker!"

Arriving at the clearing, Cole dismounts and said, "Stay mounted up, Vik. You're ride ain't over yet." Cole ties up both their horses to an oak tree at the edge of the clearing.

The sun is dancing on the gurgling waters, sending ripples of light on the horses and their riders.

Vaulting himself up on the back of Viktor's horse, Cole's body slams up against Viktor's, his big cock sandwiched between their bodies.

Wrapping his arms around Viktor, Cole's hands move to fondle Viktors balls beneath his raised shaft, while using the other hand to feel up each of Viktor's tits in turn.

Viktor signals his approval by pushing his ass back against Cole's prick.

"You like that big cowboy dick, Vik, because you're about to have it shoved up your beautiful butt."

"What are you waiting on, Cole. Can't you get that big thing up enough to do the job?!"

"You offered me a sniff first and that's what I'm hankerin' for, Vik baby. Raise that pretty fanny off the horse's back and rest your chest against his mane." Viktor places his massive arms around the horse's neck and assumes the position demanded of him.

Sliding back on the horse's rump, Cole grabs fistfulls of Viktor's ass-cheeks.

Diving into Viktors crack, placing the tip if his nose against the pink pucker, Cole inhales the man/horse aroma.

Not content with merely a sniff, Cole laps Viktor's crack before his tongue pokes through the sphincter to lav Viktor's succulent pussy.

Viktor's guttural moans are building to high-pitched cries.

"You taste good, Vik honey, are you ready for the main event because I really want to stuff your hole with the biggest cock these parts have to offer."

"Do it, Cole! I don't expect a rodeo jock to be gentle. Don't disappoint me."

Viktor's hole has been well lubed with Cole's saliva and Cole had the foresight to roll a condom down on his prick before setting out.

Viktor, a virgin for so long, no longer has a vice-like hole.

Eric, Bruno, Denis as well as Cliff and Brad, among others, have pummeled his asslips so they are accommodating to all comers.

He prefers a big dick and will be well served by Cole's great cock.

Cole places his big stiff boner to the quivering hole and bucks his hips to force the passage of his long dick deep into Viktor's asshole, grinding to a halt when his groin slams into the perfect orbs.

Cole's big ripe nuts, filled with hot cream, fill Viktor's crack.

"That ok for you, babe, you like it so far?" Cole inquires.

"Oh, man, you know it! Show the boss who's really the boss of him. Ride me!!!"

Steadying himself by grasping Viktor's meaty shoulders, Cole begins poking his boss's hole with a punishing rhythm, bucking his hips to increase the force of each thrust, plowing Viktor unmercifully.

Cole's hips serve to both thrust his prick forward and also to gyrate his cock in a punishing spiral in the fuck cavern.

Every inch of Viktor's colon is stretched by the invading cock-head, reducing Viktor to a needy receptacle for Cole's lust.

Pulling out his cock completely, Cole repeatedly bucks his hips forcing his shaft into the ravaged channel, fucking the mewling Viktor fast and deep.

Smashing his pelvis into Viktor's upturned ass a final time, Cole flattens the great orbs into long ovals of pulsating flesh as he unleashes wild blasts of searing cum.

"Oh shit yeah, man, your ass is mine!" Cole exclaims.

"Wow, Cole, you really know how to show the boss a good time. I guess I have to thank the cowboys on the rodeo circuit for creating a first rate top like you."

"They like to get into my ass too, boss. What do ya say? Do you want to take a cowboy?"

"What do you think, Cole? Bend over that fallen tree so I can show my appreciation by giving as good as I got." Cole throws a blanket over the tree and gets into position, handing Viktor a condom and a packet of lube he had concealed in his boot.

Slipping the condom on and using the packet of lube to prepare Cole's asshole, Viktor quickly mounts Cole and fucks him flat out with the vigor born out of just receiving a dynamite fuck himself.

Cole, used to quick fucks on the fly when he's on the road with the rodeo, loves to be taken without the preliminaries.

They get up and throw the blanket down on a bed of pine needles to take a brief nap before awakening to give each other a lengthy blowjob in the 69 position.

A short time later, they ride on back home.

Eric is expected to return late when they all plan to have a late supper together at Hector's table, enjoying more of his Spanish cuisine.

They will spend the remainder of the week enjoying getting into each other's pants before they pile into the rented car and return to Bethesda on Friday so as to be available to attend the book-signing on Saturday.

Meanwhile, Cliff is home in the townhouse working in their home office on some cyber security issues for Eric and Viktor's plant in North Carolina.

Debbie identified the critical issues that needed to be addressed.

Like so many other industries, the auto parts businesses have to concern themselves with many security concerns including piracy of intellectual property, as vague a concept as that is.

Just as Cliff is putting the finishing touches on a report he's prepared for Eric and Viktor, which they expect to review upon their return from West Virginia, the bell to the ground level of the townhouse, where the office is located, rings.

Getting up and opening the door, Bruno Jahn appears before him, a vision in a clinging Lacoste shirt, khaki pants and penny loafers.

"If I didn't know better, Bruno, I'd swear you were a graduate student at Georgetown University. You've got the preppy look down, kid. On you it looks good!"

"Thanks, Cliff, hope you don't mind my dropping over unannounced. Denis dropped me off on his way to meet Tommy and Marc at the bookstore to help in making arrangements for the book-signing affair. I spoke to Brad at your Washington office. He told me you'd be home working on a report today. Perhaps I can be of some assistance to you."

"As it happens I'm just finishing my report and was planning on doing a three mile run to work some of the kinks out. These reports can be draining. How about joining me? You might enjoy getting the lay of the land around here."

"Hell yeah, I'd love to. I've missed doing my daily runs since I've been in Washington. But I haven't got my running gear with me."

"We've got stuff that will fit you, no problem. Just let me close down my computer and we'll be good to go." Leaving the office, Cliff escorts Bruno to another part of the ground level where the home gym is and through to the small locker room.

Opening up a locker full of extra running gear, Cliff tosses Bruno a T-shirt, running shorts, socks and running sneakers.

"Try these on for size, Bruno. If these don't fit, there's plenty more here for you to try on." Bruno strips and carefully puts his street clothes in an available locker.

Cliff has undressed and is slipping on his shorts while viewing Bruno's spectacular physique, honed by a life of skiing and all manner of outdoor sports. Cliff tries to bring the instant rush of seeing Bruno's perfect body under control. Bruno pulls a T-shirt over his head, trying it on for size.

Turning around to face Cliff, Bruno asks, "Is it a bit tight do you think, Cliff?"

Trying to keep his eyes off of Bruno's amazing cock, Cliff said, "Well if you want to get through the neighborhood unmolested, you'd better try on something less revealing."

"You're shitting me I know, Cliff, but maybe something larger would be more comfortable to run in." Bruno turns back to the locker to take off the T-shirt and try on another.

Cliff is again presented with the broad, muscled shoulders, long curving back, ripe bun mounds, and sensuous long legs.

Cliff is struck with a wave of dizziness and drops to the long bench serving the locker room.

Seemingly unaware of the effect he's having on Cliff, Bruno selects two or three pairs of shorts that he slips on and off over his sculpted ass cheeks before finalizing on a pair that does nothing to conceal the lushness of his butt.

The sneakers selected fit perfectly.

"Guess I'm all set at long last, Cliff. Sorry to make you wait on me."

"We're not under any time pressure today, Bruno. We can enjoy a leisurely run in Cherry Hill Park." They leave, running through local streets to gain access to the park.

Running behind Bruno proves to be torture for Cliff who can't seem to look at anything else except Bruno's bouncing buns.

"Must be getting out of shape on this trip. I'm already winded," Bruno admits, yelling over his shoulder to Cliff.

"There's a couple of private spots in these campgrounds that we can plop down to rest a spell. It's starting to cloud up. We're in for a shower. Let me run ahead of you and I'll show you the way through the trees." They arrive at a small clearing that has a tiny empty shack in the middle of it, just as the raindrops start to come down.

"Better take shelter in that old abandoned shack before we get drenched by a cloud burst."

They don't quite make it to the door of the shack before the skies open up to produce a drenching rain, soaking them.

The interior of the cabin was empty except for a bedroll, open in the middle of the room, and a two-seat wicker sofa.

Overhead the rain can be heard pounding on the tin roof.

Obviously, the interloper who's been secretly using the shack was elsewhere.

"That was a break, Cliff, your knowing about this shack so we have a dry place to wait out the storm."

"Unfortunately, we got wet before we had a chance to duck inside.

Our friend, the squatter, has strung up a clothes line in the corner where we can hang our wet things out to dry."

"Good idea, looks like we're going to be here awhile. This storm looks pretty intense. I didn't even see it coming," Bruno said.

Removing his clothes, Bruno reaches up to hang his T-shirt, shorts, and socks on the line.

Also stripping, Cliff hangs his items on the line next to Bruno's.

It is no longer possible for Cliff to hide his now very stiff dick.

But now he has company because Bruno is also sporting a major hard-on.

"Wow, kid, I was embarrassed earlier when you were changing into running clothes that I was getting so turned on, but I see that I'm not alone in that."

"You can be pretty dense sometimes, Cliff. Why did you suppose I went through so many unnecessary costume changes if not to turn you on. I thought I was a dismal failure until now. Ever since I met you when summoned to come from Regensburg to West Virginia, I knew I'd have to be fucked by you. That's why I came by your house, to seduce you."

"Looking like you do, Bruno, you can have pretty much anyone you want. I haven't come on to you for fear that you had an understanding with Eric and Viktor that precluded your straying too far from their company."

"We have a very fluid relationship which doesn't in any way restrain me from doing as I choose. I couldn't imagine returning to

Germany without having had your cock up my ass. Repeatedly, if you don't get fatigued easily."

"You're used to having Viktor's big cock servicing your ass. I may not be able to satisfy you with my more modest equipment."

"Viktor tells me you have a solid 9" prick. Certainly it's nothing to be ashamed of and I want it now. Sit down in the wicker sofa and spread your gorgeous legs for me, Cliff. It's feeding time at these campgrounds and I'm up for some choice American meat." Cliff now in position, Bruno licks his lips viewing Cliff's dick craning out of his pubic hair, starving for attention.

Dropping to his knees, Bruno grasps the shaft at its root with both hands, forming a ring around Cliff's cock and balls.

Cliff's jizz-heavy sac is now lovingly suckled by Bruno's lapping tongue.

Bringing Cliff close to the edge.

Bruno stops momentarily before proceeding to suck on the big cock-head, poking his tongue into the piss slit.

Throwing his head back, Cliff moans with the pleasure this cock-hungry preppy is giving him.

Not content with the extent of his cock-tease, Bruno now swallows the thick shaft to the back of his throat, using the sensitive insides of his cheeks to torture Cliff's prick further.

Bruno can feel the veins pulsing in Cliff's dick, signaling his readiness to spend his seed.

Bruno allows Cliff's cock to pop out of his mouth, preventing Cliff's release.

Getting to his feet, Bruno moves over to the bedroll.

He finds the condom packet he tossed there that he had concealed in his running shorts and throws it to Cliff.

You'll need to put one of those on, Cliff.

Also concealed in his shorts was a small tube of lube that he now uses to grease his passage.

Lying on his back, Bruno raises his legs, grasping his calves, to spread them wide.

Bruno's hole is open which he's now able to do easily, given the frequent plowing he receives from his employers.

Moving between Bruno's legs, Cliff drops to his knees and leans forward to place his hands flanking Bruno's bulging pecs and then stretches out, balancing his weight on his hands and toes.

Aiming his dick for the welcoming hole, Cliff invades Bruno's fuck cavern and stuffs it to capacity.

Bruno, now a talented bottom, clenches down on the big dick with his powerful ass muscles, working it like a seasoned whore.

Stud-slamming his prone butt boy, Cliff builds to a steady rhythm, relentlessly sodomizing his hot willing hole.

Bruno emits a keening wail, beside himself with primal pleasure.

Reaching the summit of rapture, Cliff's body convulses, hurtling cum into Bruno's insatiable hole.

Joining Cliff at the summit, Bruno's cock erupts into a showering orgasm.

Cliff mounts Bruno twice more before sating himself on Bruno's pussy.

Cliff leans down to kiss Bruno's full, cock-swollen lips as Bruno purrs like a satisfied cat.

"You've turned out to be a rather delightful slut, Bruno. It's no wonder Eric and Bruno like having you around so much."

"Umm yes, I like to please my men. I'm glad to include you and Brad in the circle of men who can expect my favors. You were all I'd hoped for in feeling very well fucked. Wow!!!"

"You're welcome, sweet thing. Now we'd better get dressed and get back. The rain seems to have stopped. There are initials on this bedroll that we fucked on. Let's see 'JS'. I wonder what that stands for. Probably something common like Jim Smith. Well no matter, thank you Jim whatever-your-name is!"

Chapter 10

The bookstore where the book-signing party is to take place is just above Dupont Circle.

It's located in a small, charming, white stucco building with French blue trim.

The large picture window in front is shaded with an oversized blue and white stripped awning.

Featured in the window display is Marc's new book.

The owner of the bookstore, Kurt Black maintains an apartment above the store.

Marc and Tommy have been busy all afternoon setting up the large main room of the bookstore with folding tables for hors d'oeuvres, wine and liquor, etc. as well as a center table stacked with copies of Marc Berger's books, fresh from the printers.

Kurt, a big bear of a man with chiseled features, jet black hair, graying at the sides has a great body kept fit with daily weight lifting exercises.

A former history teacher at the American University in Washington, he's now content being out of academia, running his own bookstore.

He's been a strong supporter of previous books Marc has written and has been enthusiastic about his latest effort now featured in his store window.

Shortly after Denis arrived to offer a hand in making preparations for the party, Kurt commandeered him to assist with coordinating with the caterers and suppliers to insure that all the finger food, wine and champagne, soft drinks and wait staff were arriving as ordered and on schedule.

Leaving the main room to Marc and Tommy to deal with, Kurt took Denis back to his office at the rear of the store.

Kurt's office also served as the rare book room and was lined with floor to ceiling mahogany shelving which had a brass-rolling ladder to provide access to the uppermost shelves.

Kurt's English antique partner's desk floated in the middle of the room with Kurt sitting on one side and Denis on the other, manning the phones.

"Hell, that was a lot of calls to make," Denis said.

"But I think we have everything under control, don't you think?"

"Without a doubt, Denis. You've been a great help. Your English is excellent by the way. Where did you go to school?"

"The American University of Paris, majoring in International Business Administration," Denis answered.

"But I enjoyed taking courses in the History Department too. It's exciting to see that you have so many fine, rare history books in this room." Denis glances around at all the impressive bound books.

Taking a break after making marathon phone calls, Kurt and Denis slouch back in their chairs, hands clasped behind their heads.

Kurt stared at the beautiful Frenchman, intrigued with his luxurious curly black hair, dark complexion and piercing blue eyes.

Denis, equally taken with Kurt, is drawn to this large man with the handsome, contemplative visage and courtly manners.

Their feet touch under the desk and an electrical charge appears to pass between them.

Kurt, who lost his lover to a brain aneurysm three years ago, has not been with anyone for some time.

Kurt's face reddens with the realization that he is turned on by this young Frenchman.

"What is it, Kurt, you — you've become so red in the face. Did I do something inappropriate?"

"Hardly, Denis, it's — it's just that I want you. I haven't wanted anyone for a very long time."

"Marc told me about your losing your lover. It's understandable why that has made you so withdrawn. Maybe a visitor to your fair city could affect a change so that you'd become open to new possibilities."

"That — that would be very nice indeed, Denis, especially if you're the one willing to provide this service." Kurt said expectantly.

Standing up, Denis begins slowly removing his clothes, gauging Kurt's reactions with each article of clothing he drops on the desk.

"Do you like what you see, Kurt? Please don't hold back, talk to me. Say something — inappropriate — perhaps even dirty."

"There's not an orifice in your entire body that I don't want to experience with my tongue before poking it with my prick. Will that do or should I explore the ways I want to fuck you up the ass until I collapse from exhaustion." Kurt said, meaning it.

"That conveys to me what I needed to know, Kurt. You are a bit naughty for a dignified former history professor. But I like it. I like you. Do you have a big prick? Big works for me the best." Denis said with a sly smile on his face.

Moving to the rolling ladder, Denis, now buck naked, hops on, stretching a leg out to propel the ladder towards the seated Kurt.

Having gauged his speed correctly, Denis winds up posed on the ladder right opposite where Kurt is seated.

Poking out his high, round ass, he said, "Well, Kurt, what do you say. Can you manage to do a little rimming? My asshole is just twitching for some tongue action. And, Kurt you're way overdressed for your part in this. I want to see what those barbells have done to sculpt your body. Those clothes you academics wear don't hint at much." Denis undresses Kurt with his searching eyes.

"Glad to oblige, Denis. I don't work out expecting no one ever to see the results." Kurt strips off his shirt, revealing a torso qualifying him to play King Leonidas in a Spartan epic war movie.

"So, Denis, do I live up to your expectations?"

Denis's jaw drops as he stares transfixed at the vision that one expects to see only in a Hollywood movie.

"Does — does the rest of you — look like that?!"

Dropping his trousers and undershorts, Kurt shows Denis the full monty.

Any doubts Denis had about Kurt's attributes were stunningly allayed.

Kurt's cock was now displaying its full size, easily in the 10" range.

Viktor is the only man Denis knows similarly endowed.

He's learned to take Viktor.

He knows he can take Kurt with the greatest pleasure.

"Kurt, not to overstate the obvious but — I think I'm in love."

"You're one fine butt boy, Denis. I'm going to take advantage of your too brief visit to enjoy what you are so generously offering me. Climb up the ladder a couple of rungs until that pretty butt is at the height of my face." Denis climbs up as requested.

Parting Denis's perfect cheeks with his big hands, Kurt pokes the index fingers of both hands into Denis's hole, stretching it open to facilitate his tongue's deep penetration.

Truly a connoisseur of rim jobs, Kurt eats out Denis's asshole with a ravenous appetite born of long abstinence.

Murmuring endearments, Denis said, "Kurt, please, I need you to take me. I'm aching to feel your prick servicing my asshole."

Then turn around, Denis so you can drop down a rung while you reach up to the rung over your head to hold on.

Denis is now posed, looking like a sacrifice to King Leonidas which he surely is.

Kurt reaches into the top drawer of his desk to find a condom and a tube of lube left over from the days his lover used to work in the shop.

Rolling on the condom, he then lubes up an index finger and reaches between Denis's legs to lube his anus.

Denis is obviously used to being well fucked, requiring little preparation.

With his great, powerful arms, Kurt clamps his hands behind Denis's knees raising his legs high and wide.

His prick is now grazing Denis's quivering asslips.

"How do you want it, Denis? Fast and furious or slow and gentle?"

"You know what I want, what I need, Kurt. Don't fucking play with me, screw me. Show me how doing without for so long has made you crave to plow me like a paid hustler."

With that endorsement, Kurt felt free to give expression to his craven need to rut like a dominant buck.

Uttering a great baritone roar, Kurt jammed his huge tool deep into the sacrificial Frenchman, ramming and cramming him with his throbbing big cock.

"Uhhoooh, yes, oooh, harder, faster, deeper!" cried Denis.

The ladder barely remains on its track as Kurt batters Denis's ass cheeks.

Pulling out completely and driving back into the yawning hole, Kurt reaches nirvana, releasing torrents of steaming cum into Denis.

Overwhelmed with the intensity of his mind numbing screwing, Denis's prick explodes, sending jets of semen over Kurt's magnificent torso, washing down his abs in rivulets.

"My, god, Kurt that was truly awesome!"

"Thank you, Denis. You can't know what this means to me to finally emerge from a deep, dark place." Kurt helps Denis down as they collect their clothes, heading to the bathroom to take a shower before joining Marc and Tommy in the front of the store.

"There you are guys! Is everything all set with the caterers?" Marc asks.

"Everything is A-ok, Marc. Relax it's all coming together. No worries. The first guests should be here in about an hour and a half. The caterers are due shortly. You've got the store looking great! Wow, linen tablecloths, and floral centerpieces. The place never looked better. Thanks for the loan of Denis. He made my day!" Kurt risks a lascivious glance at Denis who flushes slightly, eyes cast downward.

Cliff arrives first, with Bruno and Debbie.

Since Marc came out ahead of Debbie, Cliff picked her up so she could later return home with Marc.

Shortly afterwards, Brad arrived with Jason Stone and Clarence Sharkey following close behind.

The party was getting started.

Soon Eric and Viktor arrived with Hector and Cole.

Everyone was in a festive mood after the champagne was served by four studly waiters, wearing skintight black pants and open, white silk shirts.

Surely they must moonlight working for the Chippendale's, dancing for the ladies.

The hors d'oeuvres were splendid and in danger of running out.

Looking around the room at the collection of couples who constitute the core of his good friends, Cliff reflects on the events leading up to this gathering, beginning with meeting with Jason Stone.

Who could have imagined that upon meeting Brad Ames at a subsequent meeting that they would wind up together as a couple whose love for each other would endure through many trials.

Then there is Jason Stone standing next to his lover, Clarence Sharkey, enjoying a close but not exclusive relationship, needing what Debbie can give too.

And next to them is Eric and Viktor who found their love in an inauspicious place, a Russian interrogation facility.

With them are Bruno and Denis whose arranged coupling blossomed into a love match.

A truly odd couple can be found in the liaison between Marc and Tommy who, while maintaining their marriages, have found an enduring love, sustained by weekends spent together.

Of course, a fine example of a love match is Hector and Cole.

Who would have imagined that they would choose each other? There they stand, arm in arm, happy in their own skin.

With Marc stands Debbie, a stalwart of their marriage, loving her man enough to share him with Tommy.

The sex is wild with Jason, allowing her to give expression to her needs as a woman.

Yes, I am fortunate, Cliff reflects, to find myself amongst friends such as these.

Reaching to his lover standing next to him against the floor to ceiling bookcases, Cliff slips his hand across Brad's sumptuous butt, pausing on one bulging cheek to give it a proprietary squeeze.

Whispering into Brad's ear, Cliff said, "We won't be staying too late, babe, I need to get you home."

Returning Cliffs half-lidded, penetrating stare, Brad answers, "Sure, stud, it's a comfort to know I'm still your favorite piece of ass, given all my competition in this room.

And by the way, invite Clarence over to watch the next golf tournament. While Tiger kicks some white ass, we can take turns servicing Clarence's black ass. Man, he's gorgeous. He could easily pass for Michael Jordan. Jason definitely needs help keeping that black bubble butt well serviced. Sign me up!"

"You, my love, are not my favorite piece of ass! You're the man I love and don't you ever forget it! Fooling around is one thing but commitment is another." Cliff professes.

"I hear you, babe, you know you are the only one for me, regardless of my roving eye."

Taking a fork to clink on his champagne flute, Marc called the partygoers to attention.

"Thank you, thank you one and all for coming to this book signing party. This store is filled with all the people who inspired me to write this book. You've been generous with your time and friendship, allowing me to approach writing this book."

"Special thanks must go to Cliff Bradshaw who, as many of you know, is certainly the model for the hero in this book. His dedication to his work has been truly inspirational to me. I'm awed by his commitment to protect this country and its citizens."

"It has been my great good fortune that I am married to a woman who has stuck by me during difficult times and has always been there for me, offering her unwavering support." Marc grabs Debbie in a bear hug and kisses her on the mouth.

"Thanks, honey." He receives a round of applause.

"Now everyone, I'm going to sit at the table stacked with my new book and sign a copy with a personal note for each and every one of you whom I consider dear friends. With that we will officially launch my latest book, 'Crossover Spy', for public consumption at book stores here and across the country!"

"Here here!!!" Everyone intones, lifting their champagne flutes in celebration.

About the Author

After enjoying a successful career in New York City at his chosen field, Buck Roberts turned his attention to what has given him so much pleasure over the years: books. Mysteries & spy novels are among his favorites but the men featured in them seem needlessly constrained by heterosexual sex. In this book, Buck suggests that by broadening their once limited sexual appetites, they can accomplish much more for their country. Buck writes his novels from his home in the Chelsea neighborhood of Manhattan.